lazy /
bored / ᶜ
plicitous / frustrated
/ voyeuristic / obses-
sive / destructive

C000089507

To AMANDA,
A LITTLE LIGHT
HOLIDAY READING WHICH
SHOULDN'T REMIND YOU OF
ANYONE YOU KNOW.....
It's ALL FAKE NEWS!
David
x

lazy / likeable /
bored / amoral / du-
plicitous / frustrated
/ voyeuristic / obses-
sive / destructive

THE
WTCHER

DAVID WHEELER

1
Hoe
2018

To A.

INTRODUCTION

'So much for unconditional love,' thought Richard as he pushed the lawnmower, down the excessively long garden of the excessively expensive house that his wife had pushed him into buying through the simple expedient of implying he might actually be on the receiving end of some sort of sexual activity if agreed to pay the sellers' exorbitant asking price. The much hoped-for revival of his sterile love-life hadn't happened. Not that he was really that surprised. Most of Richard's marriage had involved him in doing things that he didn't really want to do, in the vain hope that Victoria would involve herself in one of his orgasms.

'The French put it so much better,' he pondered,

'Le petite mort. The little death.'

Unfortunately, neither of them knew how a petite mort could lead to something larger...

PART 1

INNOCENCE AND ACCEPTANCE

CHAPTER 1

1979

Their relationship had started well enough. They'd met as teens, next-door neighbours in an affluent street of detached houses in a Thames Valley commuter town not far from Reading. Both innocent in the ways of the world and even more innocent in the joys of the flesh. They'd been casual acquaintances until they found themselves at a mutual friend's party, shortly after turning 18. Richard Marsh, slightly below average height with unkempt hair and at the tail end of the acne years had, for once, put on a clean pair of jeans, even if the T-shirt should have gone in the laundry bin the night before. His permanent smile made him likeable, although he tended to be a loner. Victoria Bristow was also a bit of a loner, although in her case this was more due to her shyness than a desire to be on her own. Just an inch or two shorter than Richard, Victoria was skinny and plain looking, but again, a happy person that others liked to be around.

The party was noisy and alcohol fuelled. Richard and Victoria were both uncomfortable with the way it was building up and Richard offered to walk his neighbour home. It came as much of a surprise to him as it did to her when he then asked her out – "Maybe to the cinema?" – and she accepted.

They'd gone out together two or three times before the first chaste kiss and it took a couple more months of dates and silly presents before she relented enough to allow an occasional hand on her small breasts. But always outside of the frumpy blouse or jumper that she'd be wearing. Hands under the clothes? No, she was too good a girl to allow that! Richard had thought that this was all normal. But that was back in the late 1970s, where copies of *Mayfair* would be surreptitiously shared at his all-boys grammar school, giving the lads an unrealistic view of the female body and bugger all knowledge of relationships.

Richard and Victoria's 'courtship', as he thought of it now, had plodded on. After some months, he'd managed to progress a bit further towards his carnal goal, but it was still a rare day that he'd touch a breast or get a hand under her dress anywhere close to her upper thigh.

She'd steadfastly refused to go anywhere near his trousers. "Sorry Richard," she'd say, "much as I'd like to, I can't before I'm married."

Richard thought himself lucky on the odd occasion that

he discovered what colour her knickers were. Their contents remaining very much a mystery.

While he was trying to learn the practical side of whatever he'd read in whichever soft-porn, soft-focus magazine he'd found in the woods, he was also learning the basic lessons of middle class, middle-income life in the Home Counties.

He wasn't enjoying his last few weeks of 'A' level studies. He'd ended up doing biology, physics and chemistry on the basis that, as his parents had declared, he wasn't bright enough to be a doctor, architect or other worthy professional. So he should look to a career in high-level research or another worthwhile but anonymous field where he could earn a reasonable salary and talk about subjects that no one else around the dinner table would understand (and therefore realise how average he really was).

His parents were wrong. He was easily bright enough to pass 'A' levels. The problem was that the lessons were boring and he couldn't knuckle down to homework or revision.

"Could do better" was the repeating theme of his school reports.

He was no better at sports, being very much a loner who found no interest in team games. His physical activities outside of the bathroom extended to a bit of jogging and cycling. Not so much to turn himself into some perfect specimen of manhood, but more as a way of getting out of the house and being on his own.

At the same time, a real interest in photography started to grow. It has originally been an excuse to buy *Amateur*

Photographer in the sure knowledge that there'd be at least a couple of artistic pictures involving scantily-clad females, but then he'd started to get interested in the technicalities of picture taking and bought his first camera. It was a second-hand Zenit E, Single Lens Reflex with 58mm f2 Helios lens. A cheap but solid piece of kit, the stamp on the back, "Made in the USSR," making it feel even more exotic. Back then, of course, you had to buy a roll of film with 24 or 36 exposures. Then get it developed at the local branch of Boots, or trust it to Royal Mail and some anonymous photo lab advertised in the magazine, before eventually seeing the results a week or so later. He was generally pleased with the way the pictures came out and even got a complimentary comment or two from his family, so he joined the local camera club.

There the interest turned into a passion. Friendly and interesting people of all ages were happy to talk to this otherwise lonely teenager and share their knowledge of the art. There was Joe Brown, an old boy always smiling and permanently smoking, whilst somehow also managing to operate both the zoom lens and shutter release of his 10-year-old Nikon. He somehow produced vivid pictures blown up to sizes that were unimaginable compared to Richard's snaps of blackbirds in the garden. Jane Houghton, a middle aged housewifely sort, with pictures of kids (presumably hers) getting up to all sorts of mischief. Dave Fletcher, a slightly dodgy looking 30-something who was often talking about the models he'd met, but who never seemed to have any photos of them. All in all, it was a world apart from Richard's usually monotonous existence.

At the first meeting, a professional landscape photographer projected vast, immersive vistas of mountain ranges that Richard wanted to experience in real life, nothing like the usually holiday slides that he had to endure when Auntie Gwen got back from her two wet weeks in the Lake District. The next was a demonstration of "AV New Technology". Two slide projectors, beaming solarised and stylised frames onto the screen, with the clunk of the slide changer synchronised to Pink Floyd's *Welcome To The Machine*. Richard was inspired to experiment with abstract colour and became aware of a new style of music, so very different from Dad's choice of Radio 2 at Sunday lunchtime.

And then there were the practical evenings; an opportunity to "learn the craft" as one of the old hands put it, as well as a chance to try out the other members' far superior kit. During the first of these Richard managed to get his camera to capture a close-up image of a drop of water, suspended in mid-air, glistening and monochrome. The sort of picture that filled the pages of every *How to master SLR Photography* book, but a challenge that he'd never risen to before.

The next practical evening came around and his life was never the same again.

Listed as a "Life Session", in his innocence, Richard didn't give it a second thought; it probably meant taking pictures of plants. On arrival, he found Joe (always first there to open up the village hall for the club) chatting with a girl who looked slightly older than Richard's barely 18 years. Medium height with a mass of brown curls perched above a radiant smiling face, and an even more eye-catching cleavage. Another new member of the club Richard hoped. He wasn't the only one to have noticed her figure; Dave Fletcher sidled over and suggested that, "These will be the best pair of tits that you'll see this side of Christmas".

Unable to think of any smart reply, Richard just said, "Sounds good," as he felt his face start to turn red.

Dave didn't seem to notice, being clearly more interested in the backside of the girl as she turned to chat to another of the club members.

"Looks a bit innocent though," Dave suggested, "bet she keeps her knees together."

Richard didn't really understand why this could be worth commenting on, based on his own lack of knowledge of the fairer sex.

A bit more chatting and all became clear when it was announced that Julie was their model for the evening and there would be a session of swimsuit wear before full figure after the tea break.

This was going to be a good evening Richard realised.

The model disappeared off into the ladies loos to get ready, while lights, backdrops and props were being arranged. Usually, Richard would have been engrossed in the technicalities of the set-up; colour balance, minimisation of shadows and all of the other lessons that he wanted to learn. This time though, he was unable to concentrate on any of this, and just wanted the model to come back out so that he could get a better look. After what seemed an age, she reappeared draped in a turquoise silk gown and made her way in front of the lights while the experts (or at least, the ones who professed to know most) spent yet more precious minutes lining up lights and fiddling with reflectors or colour filters.

Eventually, everything was set up to their satisfaction and she slipped off the gown to reveal a tiny blue bikini which seriously emphasised her bountiful curves. Cameras were lined up with a multitude of calls. "Right arm on hip please, love." "Can you lick your lips?" "Look this way." "Can we have a smile please?"

A couple of minutes of this and Richard realised that he was just staring at the girl and, if the others hadn't been so occupied in their own actions, he would have stood out as the inexperienced teenager that he was. Bringing his camera up to eye level, he found himself looking at her through the anonymity of the lens; just another camera pointed in the same direction as the rest. But now he could concentrate on every detail of Julie without being obvious. He let the lens roam over her body, revelling in the detail that a little bit of zoom could make clear. Hazel eyes, the freckles on her cheeks, those moist full lips. Then down to the deep valley between her breasts and the faint outline of nipples through cloth. Richard's shutter clicked away as he did his best to immortalise all of this; a couple of full-length photos and then a zoom-in on the tight bikini for some close-ups.

All too quickly, the lighting was turned off and the mid-evening break came along, usually an enjoyable chat with people who were so different from his distant parents and macho peer group. These were people who he could have a proper conversation with, who didn't exclude him or put him down. This time though, Richard was lost in his own thoughts, already recreating the images that he hoped he'd managed to capture.

Tea and coffee finished, the 25 or so members of the club drifted back to the studio setup as the model reappeared, once again in her silk gown. This time Richard made sure that he had his camera ready. The gown came off and he marvelled at the first naked woman he'd seen. Again he used the camera to anonymously pore over her body, with the shutter recording the detail. Small pink nipples, full breasts and a light bush of pubic hair with a vague vertical cleft, were all preserved on the film.

The model worked her way around the cameras, rewarding each of them with a smile and a pose or two until Richard found himself looking through the viewfinder directly into that smiling face. He felt a surge of adrenalin as she smiled – just for him. "Click" and that smile would be his to relish again and again.

The mood in the room was more serious than it had been during the earlier session. It was quieter too, until Dave asked her to raise her right leg and rest it on a chair. Richard may not have understood Dave's hidden agenda, but the model certainly did.

"You've only booked me for glamour," she purred. "If you want continental it'll be another fiver."

Dave, clearly embarrassed, was subjected to a barrage of tutting and "behave yourself" comments. Apologising loudly, he added that he'd not been trying to do anything untoward, it just seemed a good pose. But the mood was broken and someone suggested a five-minute break to give the model a rest and allow for a change of lighting and set-up.

While most of the group were busy sorting out the equipment, Richard noticed Dave wander over to the model; whether to apologise or try to pick her up he didn't know.

A couple of minutes later, the lights were back on and he got back to lusting after this dream girl through the lens. At the same time, he became aware that Dave was making his way through the male club members, or most of them anyway, chatting briefly to each and moving on as he got a nod or a shake of the head. Dave approached and quietly asked whether Richard would be up for staying on for "something a bit special".

Anything that resulted in more time with this angel of a woman was good for Richard and he replied with, "Yes, what's happening?"

Dave, with a smirk, replied that they'd let the rest of the members go in the usual way under the pretence that the ones staying on would be doing the packing up. "However," he added, "real reason is that Julie's up for something a bit more explicit if we all chip in."

"How much?" Richard asked, being well aware of how little he had compared to the working adults who surrounded him.

"Just what you can. 50p's plenty as there will be enough of us."

"Count me in," Richard found himself saying, while at the same time mentally checking that he had more film (yes), 50p (yes), and a desire to see whatever more there was (definitely).

Half an hour later, a much smaller group of camera enthusiasts remained and the studio area just consisted of lights and a chaise lounge borrowed from the amateur dramatic clubs prop store. Julie reappeared and lay naked on the couch.

"Anything in particular?" she asked to no one in particular.

Dave, with a grin bordering on a full leer, responded with, "Just show us what you've got."

Julie spread her legs wide and in the next half hour Richard learnt more about the female body than he'd ever picked up from any magazine or the biology lessons at school. He used every frame of his film and whilst he had a nagging doubt over how he'd get it developed (let alone how to get it past his parents when it came back in the post), he was on cloud nine, realising that the study of the female form, preferably through a lens, was going to be a major part of his future life.

*

Over the next couple of weeks, the events of that evening caused Richard more than the odd problem.

First, he had to evade questions from his well-meaning parents about why he'd been back late and what the camera club had done that evening. He knew that even taking pictures of a girl in a bikini would be a bridge too far as far as his mother was concerned. So, instead, he said that they had been working on portraiture – a satisfactory answer as far as he could tell.

Next there was Victoria. Again, he knew he couldn't share the details of the evening to her, but in the end she didn't ask any questions about it. She just wittered on about some new

TV police drama that she'd watched. "Shoelace" or something similar, he thought she called it.

Then he had to get the film developed. No way could he take it to the local branch of Boots. Mrs Welch from along the road would look at the pictures and declare them obscene before reporting him to the police and telling everyone that Richard Marsh was a perverted young sex maniac who should be locked away. Instead, it would have to be one of the photo labs that advertised "Confidential Processing" in the classifieds at the back of *Amateur Photographer* magazine.

As soon as he could, Richard put the five precious reels of film (more than he'd sent off in the past), together with a cheque for just about all of his meagre savings, in the postbox and felt a small level of panic that he might never see the end results. He needn't have worried though. A week later a fat envelope postmarked Liverpool arrived on the doormat. His mother spotted it first and deliberately placed it on a table where she could keep an eye on it until Richard came home from the "A" level Analytical Chemistry exam that he'd taken that afternoon. Of course, she wanted him to open the envelope in front of her, but Richard simply said, "Don't worry mum, you'll get to see them, but I just want to weed out the overexposed ones first."

Before mum had a chance to object, Richard sped up the stairs to his room, shut the door and put a bag against it.

Quickly opening the envelope, he found a bright yellow and black Kodak Photographic Paper box and inside it were a stack of prints, about 180 of them, all far better than he'd ever hoped for. Taken under perfect lighting and with a high

11

level of concentration, they were in focus, well-lit and perhaps surprisingly, given the circumstances, free of camera shake meaning that virtually every photo presented a sharp, detailed snapshot of a part or all of the model. The first few were all face shots, safe enough to show to the parents and keep them satisfied that his hobby was wholesome and not likely to lead him astray. Whether he could show them to Victoria though he wasn't so sure. She'd had a go at him in the past for just remarking that a girl had good legs.

The bikini shots were all pretty good, but he skimmed through them rapidly to get to the nudes. 'Fantastic!' was his immediate thought, his heart racing from the excitement. The final few frames in particular, where he'd brazenly zoomed in to get as close as he could between her parted legs, left him flushed, breathing heavily and needing to deal with the effect these pictures were having on him. Self-pleasure, however, would have to wait for a moment as it struck him that these treasures would have to be extremely well hidden. His mum's reaction if she found them wouldn't be good. He'd been in trouble when illicit items had been found in the past, but X-rated photos would definitely trump pennies nicked from her purse. More to the point, she'd take the irreplaceable pics and negatives away and destroy them.

He had a few hiding places, but none that he felt were secure enough. But inspiration came when he read: "Photographic Paper. Open In Total Darkness," on the Kodak box. He placed the treasures back inside, adding a handwritten page on top to emphasise that under no circumstances should anyone open it.

These secrets remained hidden for many years to come, while their edges became well worn from his own frequent handling of them.

*

Over the next couple of years, Richard's life plodded on. His 'A' level results came through; two Ds and an E. Insufficient for university and only a minor letdown really, as he'd got no desire to spend another three years studying, and had only applied because it seemed to be the right thing to do. His parents put on a show of being disappointed whilst being quietly relieved that they wouldn't have the associated costs. Victoria passed her exams (of course) but said that she'd rather stay at home and join her dad's company, ostensibly acting as the good daughter, while her real motive was wanting to avoid risking exposing herself to the outside world.

The only education that Richard was keen to pursue was the practical side of human reproduction. Not for procreation. Purely for recreation. In this ongoing quest, and because it seemed the right thing to do, Richard found himself asking Mr Bristow for his daughter's hand in marriage.

This was met with, "Of course, as long as you never do anything to hurt her." and shortly afterwards, Richard was down on one knee proposing to Victoria. She accepted without hesitation and immediately started planning every detail of what was clearly going to be an expensive and very traditional wedding. Her father, seeing that Richard was unlikely to be able to support his sole child in the style that she was used to, offered his future son-in-law a job in his company's laboratory, whilst at the same time making it plain that a refusal would not go down well.

So Richard started his career at Bristow Pharmaceuticals. He actually enjoyed the work which mainly consisted of carrying out routine quality checks on the medicines they made. The relative freedom of the job, compared to his days at grammar school, brought out the best in him and he started to thrive and prove himself a competent and trustworthy employee, rising from the bottom level in the laboratory through to the assistant lab manager's job in just a couple of years. Of course, marrying the boss's daughter didn't exactly harm his prospects either.

The boss's daughter herself joined the same company as an accounts assistant, diligently applying herself to the detail of the job and studying for accountancy qualifications at Reading College just a few miles away. She passed with flying colours, despite knowing that she didn't really have to put the work in, as no matter what she did, she'd always have a job there while daddy was the boss.

Meanwhile, Richard honed his photographic skills, using a chunk of his earnings to kit himself out with a secondhand Nikon F2A and a selection of lenses and accessories that weighed a ton but enabled him to master not just the basics, but start to win prizes at the camera club quarterly competitions. There were also more models to lust after, and despite the fact that several ended up naked in front of Richard's voyeuristic gaze, none of them had the "something" that the first one, Julie, had, and none of them stayed on for another "continental" session. Despite this minor disappointment, he thoroughly enjoyed growing his collection of photographs of breasts, nipples and nether regions.

He also solved the problem of risking film by sending it to unknown processing labs (and of sensitive photos being then discovered by his mum if she 'accidentally' opened his post), when Camera club Joe took Richard under his wing. This came about after Richard expressed an interest in learning how to develop and print film, and under Joe's tutelage he learnt the basics of opening a film cartridge in total darkness and sliding the unexposed film into the spiral holder that went into the developing tank. With his growing laboratory skills, the chemistry of processing was simple. Dilute the developer to the right strength, get it to temperature, pour it into the developing tank and gently agitate for the time stated in one of the many textbooks on Joe's shelves. Then rapidly pour out the used developer and pour in the stop bath. Get this bit wrong and the film could be lost forever. Then it was just a case of pouring in the fixer solution (made up at the right strength and temperature again) and leaving it to stand for 10 minutes before rinsing the film for another 10 minutes or so. All of this took the best part of an hour before the negatives were hung up to dry (preferably with a bit of rinse aid added to the final wash to prevent drying marks).

Richard would then hang the film up and find himself peering at it – not too close in case of scratching it – and trying to make out whatever details he'd manage to capture. Joe always insisted that negatives should dry overnight before they could be printed. This was an eternity for Richard, knowing that any frame could have just that one detail that his libidinous eyes desired to see.

Printing the negatives gave him even more opportunity to get the exact image that he wanted. The technicalities of printing were more forgiving than developing the negative; get something wrong and you just tried again rather than losing the memory forever. It was also much easier working under the red glow of the darkroom lamp compared to handling the film in total darkness. With Joe's help, Richard was soon adept at getting the negative into the enlarger, focussing the image onto the baseboard whilst deciding which part of the overall picture he wanted to print. He'd then slide a sheet of virgin photographic paper into place, expose it and place it in the chemical tray, watching as the white sheet turned into a proper photograph before his eyes.

Joe was quite happy to leave the eager student alone in his darkroom, but Richard wanted his own set-up so that he could work privately and be uninterrupted whenever it suited him.

The opportunity arose when he and Victoria bought a small two-bed flat with the help of her father. It was within a modern development less than five minutes' walk from work, but the location was a minor plus compared to the major benefit of it having both an en-suite and also a bathroom, meaning a darkroom could be set up in the latter, giving him the ongoing freedom to make the pictures and hide them in the growing stack of yellow and black photo-paper boxes.

Richard moved in straight away, relishing the freedom of no longer being under his parents' control. Victoria apologetically told him that she couldn't follow until they were married as it wouldn't be seemly to do so.

"Even if *we* know that we're sleeping in separate rooms, other people might not believe us," she said apologetically.

Richard didn't mind; it wouldn't be long until they were married, and in the meantime, his burgeoning collection of homemade softcore porn kept him happy.

CHAPTER 2

THE STRANGLERS. "Peaches"

July 1982

The day of the wedding arrived and the two virgins walked down the aisle hand-in-hand. Geoff Bristow had made sure that his daughter had everything that she'd asked for; church, Rolls-Royce and a champagne-laden reception for 80 odd guests at the golf club (although it was clear that the guest list had been picked principally by Lorna, Victoria's mother). Richard's parents, Reginald and Heather, had wanted to give something solid and durable that the newlyweds would keep and which would gather dust over the years. But when Geoff Bristow revealed that he was giving the couple a brand new Austin Mini Metro, Reginald Marsh realised that competing with anything tangible would cost far too much. Instead, he told anyone who would listen that they were giving the couple a luxury honeymoon in the South of France. They neglected to mention that it consisted of 10 days on a bed only rate, at a three-star hotel, several kilometres inland from the Riviera, plus tickets for the Dover – Calais car ferry.

Richard hated every moment of the wedding day. He didn't like being the centre of attention (or rather, the slightly off-centre one as Victoria got most of it) and he felt hot and constrained in a tight suit and new shoes. He'd nothing to say to the endless ranks of elderly and unknown relatives, and soon developed a slight headache from the effects of drinking a couple too many glasses of bubbly when a pint of light & bitter would have been his preference. He ploughed on through, again partly because it was the right thing to do, but more because at the end of the day he would achieve his three-year goal of finally bedding Victoria.

It didn't go quite as he had hoped…

They'd agreed (or, at least, he thought that they'd agreed) that they'd leave the reception that evening at nine o'clock. The plan was to drive a couple of hours to the country hotel that he'd booked in Kent for their first night as Mr & Mrs Marsh, spend the night in extremes of passion, and then drive the next day for the morning ferry from Dover.

Nine o'clock came and went with Victoria engrossed in conversation with anyone and everyone, despite her new husband's best attempts to draw her away. Nearer to ten she told him, "I'm just off to change into my going away outfit. Back in five."

Half an hour later (and an hour and a half after the agreed time), she reappeared in a strikingly elegant, dark brown trouser suit with a crisp white blouse buttoned up to her neck. They did the rounds saying their farewells, receiving leery comments from their workmates and a pointed "take care of her" to Richard from his father-in-law and employer.

Alone at last in the car with Richard driving, they awkwardly chatted about the day, the highlights, the bits that each thought the other had missed. It was after midnight when they drew up to the front of the hotel and the night porter let them in. He spent an age writing their details in the hotel register and then carried their bags up to their room before leaving with a £1 tip that Richard felt obliged to give because it was the right thing to do.

Alone in the room, Richard moved towards Victoria and they embraced with a long deep kiss. They took it in turns to go to the bathroom and he again moved towards her.

"Undress me," she said in a low voice.

Whilst the thought of this was all that he desired, he also felt a little uncomfortable with her so clearly taking control. His shaking fingers seemed to take forever undoing the blouse buttons before she slipped it off and turned around so that he could fumble his way around the catch of the flesh-tone lacy bra that lay underneath. It dropped to the ground and before he could move back in front of her, she instructed him to undo the zip on the side of her trousers. This completed, she swiftly stepped out of them, and in a fluid movement that afterwards he thought must have been practiced, slipped off her knickers (matching the bra, he noticed briefly), before diving into the bed.

Looking up at him, the sheet up to her neck, she asked, "Well, what's keeping you?"

Somewhat flummoxed by the turn of events and the realisation that he'd not really seen her naked yet, Richard found himself undressing almost as if he was on his own. Despite the lack of passion in the last few minutes, he was still fully aroused as he took off his old-fashioned y-fronts. He felt her looking at his erection, not with desire he thought, more like a property developer evaluating the outside of a somewhat dilapidated terraced house. He too got into the bed, making sure that he raised the sheets enough to at least get a good look at her breasts. He wasn't disappointed. Well, not so far anyway.

He put his arms around her and they kissed, her lips parting for his tongue, and his hands started to roam over her body, although she didn't seem over keen to let his hand delve between her legs.

After just a few minutes she simply asked, "Do you want to put it in then?"

With a grin he replied, "Are you kidding?" and raised the sheet to see her naked body for the first time.

Small, pert breasts with dark nipples, a slim, almost skinny body and a mass of black pubic hair. He manoeuvred himself over her, his legs dropping between hers as he moved towards his long craved-for goal. He looked down and the sight of her beneath him was just too much and he realised with dismay that he was at the point of no return before he'd even entered her. He desperately tried to think of something, anything else, but disastrously, the picture that flashed into his mind was Julie, the model, with her legs apart. Before he could redirect his thoughts to anything safer, the orgasm hit and he heard Victoria give an involuntary "yuk" as his semen coated her belly. Frozen in despair, he heard the object of his desire ask him for some tissues so that she could clean herself up.

Richard rolled off and passed them to her before watching in dismay as she wiped herself clean of any trace of him, now clearly no longer worried that he was looking directly at her body.

"Not to worry," she said brightly. "Maybe better another time," as she turned away and turned off the light.

Richard lay there enveloped in mixed emotions of despair and self-disgust at his inability to do the most basic of male things, resentful that she'd so easily dismissed the most important moment of their wedding night. Eventually, he drifted off to sleep but couldn't rest easily, being used to sleeping on his own.

He woke in the morning, as usual with an erection, but this time one which he hoped would see some action. Turning onto his side he was briefly perplexed to find himself alone in the bed until he saw his new wife over by the window, wrapped in a dressing gown and making tea.

"Morning sleepy head," she called over. "Thought I was going to have to wake you so that we didn't miss the boat."

Richard scrambled around to find his watch. Seeing that it was nearly half past eight, he said: "We've got a bit of time, let's have that tea in bed."

"Don't you want breakfast?" she asked, "We've a long day ahead."

"I'd rather have you," he murmured.

"Plenty of time for that later," she replied in a flat voice.

"But it might go better this time," he said desolately.

He could see that she was reluctant, so he patted the side of the bed saying, "We don't have to go full at it. Let's just have a cuddle and see what happens."

She turned away and Richard thought that he'd been rejected, but after pouring the tea, she brought it over and got back into the bed, albeit still wearing her dressing gown. He put his hand under the cloth and slid it up her leg. Without any verbal indication that she might have changed her mind, she lay back, and pulled up the front of the garment.

"OK then, put it in," she said unemotionally.

Wanting so much more than this, Richard put his hand between her legs pressing his fingers into her. He didn't really know what to expect, but this dry, tightly closed valley didn't tie in with what he'd read in magazines. After a couple of minutes of inexpertly prodding away at his unresponsive wife, he climbed between her legs and attempted to enter her. He glanced at her face. She'd turned her head to the side, looking away from him. Maybe it would get better for her when they were properly making love, he thought gloomily as he started a short in and out motion, still with only less than half his length inside. Far too quickly, he felt the unwelcome sensations as he came again.

Not a word was spoken by either of them as she cleaned herself and they got on with getting ready for the day ahead.

No longer virgins, but still no nearer to the knowledge of what making love really felt like.

Eventually she spoke, a simple, "Right, we'd better be going," although in a surprisingly light and happy voice.

Richard may have been forlorn that the much anticipated night of passion hadn't taken place, but Victoria seemed happy with how her life was going.

*

The journey down to the ferry and the drive across France raised his spirits. Bright sunshine and the rolling landscape felt a world away from the grey factory environment of their usual day-to-day lives. They stopped for the first night in France in a small Gîte outside Lyon, enjoying the unaccustomed flavours of the local cooking before retiring to their room. Richard was slightly drunk from the wine and found himself falling asleep before he could think about any other honeymoon activities, and when they awoke the next morning it was already past the official check-out time and they rose rapidly to hit the road.

Afternoon found them pulling up to the unprepossessing hotel booked by Richard's parents in the centre of Mouans-Sartoux, north of Cannes. A small town, with a good mix of medieval and modern architecture, a wide open centre and clean, tree-lined boulevards. They wandered through the streets, enjoying the summer heat and peaceful nature of the place. The bars and restaurants in the centre of the town looked inviting. No need to worry about hotel price meals.

The sun was starting to go down when they found themselves in a small restaurant enjoying a dish of pasta.

Richard laughed.

"What's up?" Victoria asked.

"I was just thinking this is just like the spaghetti scene in *Lady and the Tramp*."

"You old romantic."

"Less of the old, if you don't mind," he laughed back, then, "God I love you!"

"I love you too."

They retired to their room, happy with their day, holding hands and quietly talking about how lovely the meal had been, how lovely the village was, and how lovely life in general was turning out. With a hopeful smile, he opened their room door for her.

Her chattering slowed slightly as she said, "Sorry love, but my period's started. We won't be able to do anything for a few days."

"No problem, Vicky. I can make do with a hand job," he grinned back at her.

"That's okay," she laughed, "but can I nip in the bathroom before you do it? In case it takes you a while this time."

As the bathroom door closed behind her, he wondered whether she'd deliberately misinterpreted his suggestion. He also felt slighted by her jibe at his premature endings so far.

*

The next morning, all such worries were a thing of the past as they shared a leisurely breakfast. He with the Full English, while she said that a single croissant and coffee were enough for her. She didn't want to spoil her figure.

"What do you want to do today?" Richard asked idly, adding hopefully, "Laze by the pool for a couple of hours? Have a wander and check out a café for later?"

"Well… she paused. "I think Cannes has a museum at the castle. Wouldn't mind a wander round it…"

Richard had spent the last two days driving and wasn't really in the mood for driving to Cannes, or for anything too cultural, but it was what she wanted and he felt it would be wrong to reject her request. Especially as he'd been the one to ask what she fancied. "Okay," he replied, trying not to sound too sulky, "let's make a move then."

The inside of the car was oppressive from standing in the full sun since dawn. But five minutes later, with the windows open and a French radio station blasting out a combination of incomprehensible French ballads and British or American rock anthems, he soon relaxed into the half-hour drive. As they drew nearer to Cannes, the amount of traffic increased and they wound the windows up to keep out the exhaust smoke belching from a couple of slow moving lorries that he couldn't overtake, the roads being too windy for him to pass them and his view being obscured by their left-hand drive, low power car. For some reason, this simple problem annoyed him disproportionately and he found himself snapping at Victoria when she pointed out a turning that she thought they should have taken. "Sorry," he quickly said in as contrite a voice as he could. "I'm just a bit tired from the driving."

"Oh," she paused. "I'm sorry, I would have driven, but I thought you were enjoying it."

"No, it's all right. I was enjoying it. It's just catching up on me now, that's all." With his apology following her apology, both avoiding the risk of inflaming the situation, or having to deal with the tension that was starting to develop.

Dispiritedly he carried on driving, making no attempt to overtake even when a clear opportunity arose, and they were soon driving around the centre of Cannes, looking for a parking place. One presented itself on the Boulevard de la Croisette, a wide road separating the town from the beach. Richard unwound himself from the driver's seat and trudged around to the other side to open the passenger door for Victoria.

The two of them squelched across the pavement to look at the glistening seascape, feeling the sun beating down on their pale skin. The vista was impressive with the sun glinting off a sea dotted with yachts and cruisers, and in front, acres of yellow sand that extended for miles to the left and right. While Victoria was clearly taken with the panorama as a whole, Richard's gaze was drawn to the abundance of tanning flesh on show. But before he had a chance to study it in more detail, Victoria was moving back towards the town. Dragging himself away from this sweet shop of delights, he followed his wife as she set off inland. Glancing on and off at a map, she led them through the main roads and back streets until a tiresome 20 minutes later they found themselves outside a substantial old stone building with (for him) the dreaded word 'Musée' over the door.

An interminable age followed as they drifted from room to room while he pretended to be interested in her pronouncements regarding the significance of bits of old cloth covered with equally old paint or pieces of furniture that he would have used as firewood. It wasn't that he was totally uninterested. Under different circumstances the ethnic carvings might have occupied him for ten minutes. But in these muggy rooms and with the entertainment of the beach not far away, he just wanted to get it over and done with.

Three hours later ('Yes', he thought, not willing to utter the heresy. 'Three hours wasted! Three hours that could've been spent on the beach.'), they emerged blinking into the intense sunlight.

"Lunch?" she asked.

"Sounds good," he replied, knowing that any other choice wouldn't go down well.

They drifted along the Promenade de la Pantiero looking at menus outside the numerous cafes and bars. Richard's understanding of French was poor at best so he said he'd leave it to Victoria's better judgement as to the choice of café. Unfortunately for him, her choice turned out to be one that looked way too upmarket as far as he was concerned.

A meal here was going to cost them three or four times what they usually paid back in Berkshire, but she dismissed his objections with, "We're on honeymoon. When else will we be able to enjoy a meal like this?"

"Of course," he replied gallantly, telling his inner objections to sod off. "Let's go for it."

The Head Waiter, clearly spotting that this young couple were neither rich nor local parked them at the back of the restaurant and disappeared off. They didn't mind; it was all part of the experience. Another waiter arrived. Nearer their own age and loaded with leather-bound menus. He passed the first to Victoria and Richard noticed him clearly looking down the front of her dress as Victoria leaned forward to take it. Surprising himself, Richard didn't feel jealous or offended, but instead enjoyed it. It wasn't that he wanted to show off his wife. No, he found himself aroused by the voyeurism. The waiter trying to see something that he shouldn't. Victoria being unaware.

An indecipherable list of foods covered each page. Richard could pick out the odd word, but couldn't find the ones he was hoping for; Frites, for example.

"Straight into main course?" he broached, thinking that he would at least save some of his francs. "Leaves room for dessert?"

"Mmmm," was the only reply, until a while later. "I'll go for the Pâté to start, Magret de Canard as main and think about a pud after."

Seeing the impending overdraft that this would cause, Richard decided to try to mitigate the cost. Buried deep in the main courses, he recognised the word "veaux" which he knew to be veal. He hadn't a clue what the preceding words "ris de" meant, but a bit of light meat should be a safe choice and the price didn't look too bad.

The waiter returned and suggested, "Maybe a kir royale for madam?" Madam concurred but Richard pleaded that he'd be driving later and shouldn't have too much. This objection meant nothing to the good French waiter, who pointed out that one such drink wouldn't be enough to worry the gendarmes. Richard gave in and moments later the couple were toasting each other and the long married life they believed they would enjoy.

The kir started to cheer up Richard and he ordered a bottle of red. It was one of the cheapest on the wine list but when he took a sip, he declared it way better than any of the stuff served at the Kings Head back home. And cheaper as well.

Victoria's starter arrived and a hungry husband watched as she nibbled away at it. She did offer him a taste, but it was barely a forkful. The empty plate was removed and then the mains arrived. Victoria's duck looked magnificent. Browned on top with a crisscross pattern of cuts across, and a healthy selection of colourful vegetables.

Richard's meal did not look anything like the veal steak that he'd been expecting. Grey, shiny and lumpy. He tentatively cut into it and there was no real resistance as it seemed to almost crumble under his cutlery. It smelt almost mouldy, and the taste and texture was not exactly pleasing to his British palate.

He looked over to Victoria and said, "Um, not sure about this."

"Looks okay to me, give us a taste," and she took some off his plate. "That's gorgeous!" she declared.

Willing to demonstrate his ignorance of French cuisine Richard responded, "Okay. It's just that it's not what I was expecting. It is veal, isn't it?"

"Yep, sweetbreads." And in response to his still quizzical look, "You know, like liver or kidneys. I think it's the thyroid or pancreas or something. I'll swap with you if you like?"

Dishes rapidly changed hands before both parties completed their mains, both now happy with what they were eating. Crème brûlée to follow, and coffees after that and married life and a honeymoon in France all seemed pretty good. Even the wallet-emptying bill didn't mar the mood and they were soon walking back to the car hand-in-hand. Richard barely registered the beach as he held the car door open, watching Victoria's skirt ride up as she swung herself in.

An hour or so later, a directionless cruise through the hills got them back to the hotel and they went back to change out of their sweaty dusty clothes. Richard peeled himself out of his damp shirt and jeans and watched as Victoria pulled her dress over her head.

"Thanks for today. I really enjoyed it," she said, smiling at him as she moved to his side, put her arms around him, and with a good-natured, "Ugh, sweat man," brought her lips to his. He put his arms around her, making no observation as to how she felt, but his own feelings became rapidly obvious as he felt himself getting hard. To his pleasant surprise her hand moved off his back and round to his crotch, stroking it gently.

"Shall I save you having to go to the bathroom?" she asked.

Barely able to reply, he just nodded as she sat on the side of the bed and pulled down his pants.

Standing there, still wearing his socks, stiffly erect in front of her, Richard was lost for words and didn't know what to do or expect. She put her hand on the hard flesh and withdrew it almost immediately exclaiming, "Wow, that's hot."

"That's because all of my blood has gone there!" he quipped back.

She put her fingers around it and looked up at him saying, "I didn't think it would be so solid."

"All because of you, my darling," he managed to utter, at the same time thinking how crass he sounded and marveling at her touch being so different from what he had felt when he did this to himself.

"Grip a bit harder and move it up and down," he suggested, delighting in how she did exactly what he needed.

Only a few strokes later he could feel himself getting near. On his own, in the bathroom he could direct the result where he wanted, but here he was split between the ecstasy of what was happening and the worry about what would happen when he came. Where would it go? What if it went on her? Or on her underwear? Seconds later, his concerns were well and truly forgotten as he ejaculated.

"Better?" she asked as she wiped her fingers clean, the rest now wetting the duvet next to her.

"Much better," he found himself saying and then adding incongruously, "Thanks."

"You're welcome sir," she smiled. "I'm off for a shower."

Over the next couple of days they fell into a routine of rising late, having a leisurely breakfast at a café near the hotel (cheaper and better than the hotel breakfast) and wandering around the town before coming back to the hotel pool for an afternoon dip followed by the evening meal in whichever café had grabbed their attention. It was all very relaxed and comfortable and Richard was delighted to find that Victoria's hand could be persuaded to occasionally repeat its stimulating actions, albeit only when she was happy and had drunk a couple of glasses of wine.

They'd been in the town for the best part of a week with only a couple more full days left when Victoria suggested that they go back to Cannes. This time, to Richard's delight, she suggested a trip to the beach. An hour later and they were traipsing across the hot sand, looking for a spot that had all the necessary attributes; large enough for two towels, not near any smokers or kids, near enough to the sea to be able to go in, and at the same time see their bags…

Once the spot was found, and after the British ritual of putting towels around themselves to change into swimwear, Richard was delighted to see Victoria in a new small blue bikini which immediately recalled the one at the camera club a couple of years back.

He felt less of a catch in his old faded trunks.

He noted a couple of well-built local guys looking Victoria up and down with clear approval and once more felt no jealousy or annoyance. Again, just a deep sexual pleasure.

What was missing though was the camera kit; he'd left it at the hotel, not wanting to risk sand or theft, but here he was surrounded by so many photographs in the making (though whether he'd have been able to sit there with a telephoto lens pointing at the local bathing beauties was another matter). But more pressing matters were to hand; sunburn wouldn't be a good end to the day and they took turns massaging sun cream into each other. Bodies suitably oiled, Victoria lay down on her front to develop her tan. Richard sat up on his towel. Beaches weren't really his thing. He got bored sitting there doing nothing except getting too hot, and he wasn't a confident swimmer, so tended to avoid the sea. But this time was different. As his eyes grew accustomed to the glare and was able to stop squinting, he realised that virtually all of the girls were topless. 'Oh for the camera now,' he thought, as he quartered the beach, checking out each woman in turn, comparing breast size, shape, colour, nipples, and occasionally glancing up at their faces. Becoming aware of a growing arousal, he turned onto his front to hide the bulge, all the time still looking out at the people around him.

To his right a woman of about 30 was lying on her back, feet towards him; her bare breasts appearing as flattened peaks beyond. Oblivious to his eyes behind dark sunglasses, she idly raised one knee and scratched at an itch where her bikini bottom met the leg, just giving a glimpse of the pink flesh underneath. Richard was engrossed in the scene when Victoria brought him back to reality asking some mundane question about the route back to Britain. Richard remained on his stomach as he replied, fearing that the state of his shorts would make his other interests far too apparent.

Later, Victoria suggested a swim. Richard's body was a bit more relaxed by now and they soon found themselves in the clear warm water of the Mediterranean, splashing around and delighting in how free and easy it all felt. Returning to the towels, the sun and the light sea breeze dried the water from them rapidly. Victoria looked at Richard's reddening chest and recommended a reapplication of factor 15.

She asked him to do her back and Richard suggested, "Your strap's leaving quite a white line. Why don't you take your top off and it'll all tan a lot better."

The irritation in her reply came as a surprise. "You must be joking. I'm not taking my top off."

Feeling a bit peeved at her tone and her reluctance, he asked, "Why not, virtually every other woman here is topless."

Her tone worsened as she replied, face into the towel, "I might have guessed you'd be ogling them. Is that why you've been ignoring me?" And then, with real venom, in her dangerously quiet voice added, "Prefer the local tarts do you?"

Stuck for any response, he lamely muttered that he only had eyes for her and hadn't meant anything untoward in his suggestion. She received this with a "Hmmm," and then ignored him for the next ten minutes before announcing that it was probably time to be getting back to the hotel. He spent the journey back and the rest of the evening dejectedly reading while she sulkily wrote postcards telling everyone how great a time they were having.

Come the next morning and she was back to her normal self and they spent the last full day much as the first few, in and around the hotel. Richard would have liked to go back to the beach but knew better than to suggest it.

The journey back home was uneventful with Victoria chattering away about their future but Richard had a feeling of foreboding that all might not be quite as he'd hoped.

When they eventually arrived back at their dull suburban flat, so different from what they'd experienced over the last days, both of them were subdued. Victoria disappeared off to tell her family how fantastic the honeymoon had been while Richard took the opportunity to hide in his darkroom and process the safe but unexciting pictures that he'd taken.

She returned late in the evening in good spirits; in telling everyone else how wonderful the trip had been, she'd wiped the negative bits from her mind. He'd cheered up as well, the therapeutic routine of his own sort of negatives having done its best for him. They embraced and said lots of "I'm sorry," and, "No, I'm sorry," to each other. He led her to the bedroom and for the first time in their marriage, she relaxed enough to let him make love to her. And he relaxed enough to actually last more than 60 seconds, although it was still a very perfunctory coupling with a distinct lack of foreplay or any real depth of excitement for either of them.

CHAPTER 3

DURAN DURAN. "Girls On Film"

Over the next couple of years they settled into a comfortable lifestyle; contented rather than passionate. They worked in the same building, walking to work together, meeting every day for lunch, often ignoring their colleagues, and then they would walk home together. Unless they had a very rare evening out, Victoria would spend hers studying for her accountancy exams or watching soaps on the TV. Richard was also studying, but with nowhere near the level of intent as Victoria. In his case it was to become a Qualified Person, a qualification which he needed if he was to advance in the pharmaceutical industry. When he could get away from the chemistry books his time was spent either in the darkroom, or once a week at the camera club, where he continued to indulge his passion for photography, especially at the quarterly life-modelling session.

However, what Victoria hadn't realised about Richard's weekly absence was that he was taking 30 or 40 minutes to make the five-minute walk back from the club's meeting place. She didn't know that he was developing his skills in night-time photography in a way that she definitely would not have approved of.

Late August 1984 and Richard had been walking back from the camera club in the near dark of the late summer evening. He'd been startled when an owl flew across the path just a few paces ahead of him. His eyes followed as it flew into a tree in the adjacent Barclay Park where he thought he could just make out its shape on a lower branch. He went through the park gates, camera at the ready, to try to get a shot.

Having moved away from the light of the streetlamps, his eyes slowly became accustomed to the gloom and he felt sure that the black disc on the branch was his bird. He peered through the lens, but couldn't find it. Moving the lens slightly, the viewfinder lit up with a bright yellow-white light as he inadvertently pointed the camera straight at the lit window of a house overlooking the park. Blinking in the light, he became aware that he was looking straight into the living room of someone's house. A young couple sitting on their sofa, watching the TV. Boring to most people, but to Richard the awareness that he could see them, but that they couldn't see him, raised his pulse as the thrill of it hit home. He watched through the lens, the minutiae of this pair's evening of nothingness. Their scratching, yawning and changes of sitting position exhilarated him.

Not wishing to miss anything, he was loath to turn his lens elsewhere, but after a while let it roam around. The realisation hit him like a lightning bolt; this window on another person's world was far from the only one. Barclay Park was surrounded by terraced houses and their backs were all towards these leafy grounds. A good half of them had lights on, and of these there were probably ten or so that did not have their curtains drawn.

The lens skittered from one window to another while he made mental notes about which to look at again and which looked empty. Soon there were four different windows alternating in their prominence in the viewfinder. Richard was in ecstasy. This was utopia.

All of the upstairs windows that were lit were also curtained, which was a disappointment. But then another flashed out brightly as a light was turned on, visible through an unscreened window. Richard's heart raced as he saw the top half of a middle-aged woman enter the room and pull a blouse over her head to reveal a generously sized bra on a lumpy, overweight body. She moved towards the window, the puffy flesh becoming clearer in the lens, and then, to Richard's frustration, she pulled the curtains closed.

Skimming the camera around the other windows Richard saw plenty more to interest him, although no undressing or anything else that warranted his prolonged attention. He looked at his watch. Victoria would be wondering where he was. He reluctantly broke away from the displays and headed home, excited by the thought of future evenings exploring more, and aroused by what he'd seen tonight. Of course, this arousal went unsatisfied by Victoria. She'd already turned in and he knew from previous attempts that once she was asleep (or pretending to be) no amount of wandering hands, or a strategically placed erection as he cuddled her, would result in anything except a grumpy "go to sleep".

Over the following months, Richard got to know his neighbours, as he called them, very well. He gave each house a number, starting with number 1 to the right of the park gates, as he looked at them from his hidden spot at its darkest point, around clockwise until he got back to the gates where number 42 took its place. A pocket notebook was dedicated to helping him remember who was where and which windows were worth more than a cursory glance. He developed a shorthand so that he could easily record details and ensure that no one else could really see what he was writing about, and if Victoria saw it, she wouldn't realise that "BP 4, MAC, CO, NS, CBT" meant "Barclay Park, house four, middle-aged couple, curtains open, nothing seen, come back to". While BP 32, D!" was a reminder that number 32 had a dog which had started barking when Richard had got near the fence.

Two of the houses became firm favourites after just a few weeks of spying.

No 12 was home to a young woman, all on her own. He'd not seen anything of note yet, but he found her attractive and she spent her evenings reading, cooking or painting rather than watching TV; the predominant activity of the rest of his subjects.

No 17 was occupied by a very average looking couple who were in, he guessed, their 50s or 60s. They were not particularly attractive and again spent too much time sat in front of the cathode ray tube, but these two always left the curtains open and often wandered around semi-naked.

Most weeks, the half an hour was spent looking at not a lot, although this was also tinged with anticipation at what might happen anywhere anytime. Occasional underwear was glimpsed and sometimes, especially at number 17, there'd be someone showing off their lingerie for a little longer. All this was documented in the notebook or with three or four clicks of the shutter if it was something especially worth recording. One evening two months in and number 12 consumed a full reel of film. She'd left a sizeable gap between her bedroom curtains and Richard had maneuvered himself as close as he could to get the best vantage point. He breathlessly watched and clicked away as she undressed and spent a minute or two looking at herself in the dressing table mirror from different angles. Unfortunately, the angle of view meant he could only see her down to the waist, and shortly after she moved out of view and the light went off. Several of the later-developed pictures became the focus for his fevered imagination as he re-lived the minutes while self-satiating his otherwise unsatisfied sexual needs.

The inability to see anyone below the waist when they were in their bedrooms irked him. He'd overcome other problems. Low light levels had been one such difficulty that he'd resolved. In this case by increasing the developing time, which gave acceptable grainy images of low-cut bras and bare breasts. He now toyed with ways of raising the camera above windowsill height. How about mounting it on a monopod held high, with a remote pneumatic release? 'No good; I want to see through the lens,' he'd swiftly decided. 'Climb a tree?' was another thought that was dismissed. Scouting out the park during the daytime showed that years of municipal care had resulted in all the lower branches being neatly removed, and while climbing up in the day would have been difficult, it would be impossible in the dark.

The solution presented itself a couple of weeks later. Arriving in the park, Richard saw scaffolding up the back of number 13. 'New windows or yet another house getting an attic conversion,' he surmised, while debating how to get into the garden of the house and thence up the scaffold to, he hoped, be able to see into number 12. Both 12 and 13, had tall, solid back fences. No easy way over here. The next one along, 14, was lower and he scrambled over relatively easily. He paused. Looking and listening to be sure that his trespass hadn't been spotted. 'All clear,' he decided, his heart pounding with excitement.

Getting into the garden of number 13 was similarly easy; another low fence followed by another pause, before he hoisted himself up the scaffolding to a platform at the top. Richard was delighted to find that his hunch was right. From this height he was able to look down into bedrooms. No longer would walls hinder his view.

Turning towards house 12, he was discouraged, seeing that there wasn't a light on in any of the rooms. 'Should have checked before putting the effort in,' he thought. Number 14, however, showed more promise. He'd previously discounted it as the main bedroom light was never on, but from this new vantage point a lit bedside lamp illuminated a bed, wardrobe, side units and a few knick-knacks. 'No one there at the moment,' he thought, 'but the light is on so things might get better.'

He sat down. A press of the button on the side of his Casio digital watch illuminated the time; "10:06." Richard needed to allow five minutes to get down and out of the gardens, so he really only had about quarter of an hour before he'd have to descend if he wasn't to arouse suspicion back home. Even when she was apparently fast asleep, Victoria always seemed to know what time he'd come in.

10.15 came and went and he'd resigned himself to it being a nothing-happening evening, when a man entered the bedroom of number 14. Richard carefully stood up and looked down at the unaware subject. Forty-ish, he guessed. Clean shaven, wearing a blue shirt with the neck undone, and suit trousers. The man sat on the edge of the bed and removed the incongruous bright red slippers that he was wearing. The shirt followed next, along with the rest of the clothes and Mr 14 stood there naked scratching his back awkwardly. Richard didn't have any real interest in naked men, but looked on in anticipation as he laid down on top of, rather that under the covers. A woman entered. Same sort of age, dressed in office wear. Smart skirt and white blouse. Richard was instantly aroused. She walked over to the man (husband?) and kissed him whilst, joy of joy, placing her hand on his cock. Richard watched in rapture as she casually undressed, smiling at her partner, and making no attempt to hide her body.

So unlike Victoria.

Richard looked through his lens at her; attractive face, long auburn hair, medium height, not slim or fat, just well proportioned. He gazed at her large breasts and light pink nipples and then the flame coloured hair lower down as she moved onto the bed and turned towards her partner, the two of them kissing and stroking each other. Richard's limited knowledge of bedroom activity soon increased significantly as he breathlessly watched her move her head down the man's body and open her mouth to engulf his rigid flesh. Richard may have read about oral sex but he had never even suggested it to Victoria, knowing it to be way beyond her limits.

Another visual first followed as Richard watched her move back up her man. She sat astride him. A position that Richard had never experienced; his occasional sex being solely in the missionary position.

Richard suddenly realised that he hadn't a clue how long this had been going on and lowered the camera to check his watch. 'Shit. 10.37.. Way beyond what he could get away with. At the same time, he couldn't tear himself away from this fantastic display. 'Just have to make up some excuse for being late,' he decided.

As he raised the camera his elbow caught against one of the scaffolding poles.

In abject horror, he saw it start to move. He grabbed at it but only made things worse when he missed, and soft knuckles hit hard against solid metal, sending the pole tumbling in slow motion down to the garden below. The crash from ground level echoed in the otherwise silent darkness. The couple clearly heard it and Richard watched in despair as they parted and the man moved to the window. Richard tried to make himself invisible, backing up against the house wall and tried to ignore the pain from his bruised hand, but in vain. The man's lips moved in a silent shout and Richard knew he'd have to get away fast. The angry target of the camera lens was pulling on clothes as Richard scrambled down the scaffolding, shaking with fear, hampered by the camera bag swinging behind him and the delicate camera hanging from a strap around his neck.

If he was caught it'd be the end of his job, marriage, everything.

His quivering foot touched solid ground just as the garden of number 14 was flooded with light. 'Fuck,' no way could he go back the way he'd come, and the other fences were too high. Trapped. Then a thought, 'Hang on, how did they get all the scaffolding in?' and he realised that this wasn't a full terrace. There was a gap between the houses. Richard dived down the alley and saw a simple gate, bolted this side, unexpectedly easy to undo, and with immense relief he was in the street in front of the houses.

Thoughts of having escaped were short-lived as the front door of number 14 flew open and an angry looking man wearing just shoes and trousers came charging out. Richard sped off down the street with his pursuer not far behind. Shouts of "stop him" ringing in his ears.

Despite having to cling on to his camera and bag, Richard's youth, frequent jogging and the adrenalin released by the chase enabled him to increase his lead. A right turn, then a left and he was out of sight of his pursuer. 'Hide or go on?' he hadn't a clue. The decision was made for him when he heard sirens in the distance and he accelerated towards home. The sirens seemed to be too near as he sprinted into Acacia Close. Fumbling with his keys it seemed to take minutes before the door opened and he fell into the communal entrance hall of the flats. The door shut behind him, and he stood there – rasping breath, thumping heart and drenched with sweat. Despite the danger of the situation, he felt the need to check his precious camera; it was missing a lens cap but everything else looked okay. So far so good. But what now? What if he'd been seen going in the door? What about Victoria? She couldn't see him like this. And how could he explain being this late?

Richard sat hot, sweaty and breathing heavily on the stairs that led up to his flat, collecting his thoughts. Think of the problems. Put them in order. Solve them one at a time…

Most pressing: was the door about to be kicked in by a couple of burly coppers? Surely not. He'd been here a good five minutes and if anyone had seen him enter, then the door would have been tried by now.

Okay. If the exact door hadn't been spotted, had his chaser identified the street? Again, probably not, otherwise there would be flashing blue lights visible through the frosted glass of the hallway window.

'Okay, so I've probably got away with it as far as people outside are concerned,' he thought. 'Now Victoria…'

He went up the stairs quietly and stood outside the door. There was no light coming from under the door so she'd turned in. But then again, that was normal and she might be lying there awake.

He thought about creeping in, but knew her acute hearing would pick that up. Bloody hell. What could he do? He sat on the doormat leaning back on the door, head in his hands in despair until eventually, despite everything, falling asleep.

An hour or maybe more later he awoke with a start, falling backwards as the door opened.

"What the fuck are you doing there?" he heard his wife ask angrily, noting distractedly that she'd used the word 'fuck'. A word not usually in her vocabulary.

His synapses kicked in: "I lost my key."

"You lost your key? Then why didn't you ring the bell?!"

"I did. But you didn't come. You must've been asleep."

A long pause, then in a softer voice she said, "Oh god. I'm sorry. You've been here all this time?"

"Yep."

Suspicion crept back into her voice as she asked, "How did you get in downstairs? And why didn't you press the buzzer down there? That would've woken me."

"Door downstairs was open. You know it gets left like that sometimes."

"Okay, but what about the buzzer?"

He bluffed, "I did try the buzzer. I don't think it's working. I'll check it tomorrow."

He put his hand gently on her arm. "Not to worry love, you didn't make me sleep out here deliberately. But I do need a pee and a shower – it's not exactly the Ritz out here."

"Sorry," she said. Another word that he wasn't a normal part of her vocabulary. Except when refusing his advances.

A while late, freshly showered, he climbed into the marital bed next to his snoring wife. It looked like he'd got away with it, but he'd have to be more careful next time. The scaffolding and Barclay Park might be too risky for the moment, but if normal couples were having normal sex there, then there had to be other places worth checking out…

*

The following Thursday he lurked in the streets to the South of the park. Plenty of lit windows, but no good hiding places to spy from.

The following week the area immediately to the East proved similarly frustrating.

A couple more weeks of fruitless wanderings and poring over local street maps and there was still nothing as good as Barclay Park. He was on the point of giving up on these pastures new, but passing the bungalows in Frobisher Drive for the umpteenth time, he noticed a footpath at the end of them. 'Worth a look,' he thought. The unlit path led around the back of the buildings appearing to be just a rear access for getting rid of garden rubbish. Judging by the overgrown state it was not often used, so there was little chance of being caught. Even better, the fences were low and / or falling apart, giving unrestricted views. The windows were all at ground floor level so there was no need to climb up, and to complete the picture, there hadn't been any dog giving away his presence. This looked promising.

He counted eight houses, so if this was like the Park, then he could expect four or five to be lit up. But here it was all eight. Better by the minute. He couldn't see anyone in five of them at the moment, but numbers two, three and six – all conveniently viewable from one point – had people visible. Two and three were middle-aged couples watching TV ('Why does everyone think TV is the be-all and end-all?' he wondered). But number six was instantly a winner. A girl, a 'teenager,' he thought, in her bedroom, dancing to unheard music. As he watched, she appeared to be gripped by the spirit of St Vitus. Jerking from side to side with a hairbrush in her hand acting as a surrogate microphone. His camera caught a couple of her poses. Unselfconscious, naturally ungainly. She carried on for a good five minutes until stopping and reacting to some unseen stimulus. She appeared to be shouting to someone out of sight before tossing the hairbrush aside and to Richard's amazement and delight, she calmly got undressed and stood there, gloriously naked, oblivious to the perverted lust of the man watching her. The voyeur snapped away as she walked around her bedroom, relishing the sight of her tiny, budding breasts and the downy bush at the top of her legs. All too quickly her light went out and Richard was left standing in darkness with a raging erection that he had to satisfy then and there. His onanism completed, he walked, absentmindedly back down the path, out onto the road, not even checking to see if he could be seen, and back home. Victoria was, as usual, lying in bed, eyes closed. But the last half hour was still imprinted on his memory and he pawed at his wife, desperate for even the most basic of couplings until she reacted with a grumpy, "I'm trying to sleep."

Normally, he would have turned away in priapic despair, but being so worked up, he persisted and to his amazed pleasure, she turned onto her back saying, "Make it quick… You usually do."

Not caring about her insult, he flung himself on top and thrust straight in, his imagination envisioning the body underneath him as an inexperienced, but willing schoolgirl.

Moments later, he came for the second time that evening. This time inside a woman in her twenties rather than onto bare gravel. He rolled off and took little notice as Victoria grumbled about her disturbed sleep, his inconsiderateness and why on earth was he like this this evening?

The next morning Victoria was still in a bad mood, but Richard didn't really care. Firstly, he was used to her mood swings, but more to the point, he had a new subject for his camera.

The photos developed that evening and over the following weeks reinforced his desires as he totally ignored that they explicitly depicted a girl who might not yet be 16 and that his images may be illegal as well as immoral.

CHAPTER 4

1987

Five years into their marriage and Richard was reading the local paper over a Saturday morning breakfast. Angry headlines mirrored the radio news of a murder, not far away, a couple of evenings ago. The police were asking anyone in the area to come forward, reminding them (in case they'd somehow forgotten already) that they might have been coming home from the polling booths that had just seen Margaret Thatcher win a third term in office. The crime had taken place in Kingfisher Road in a house backing on to Barclay Park.

Richard contemplated that if he had continued using that optical playground, he could well have been a witness. Most people would regard witnessing a murder as something horrific, but Richard was not like most people. For him the greater emotion was annoyance. Annoyance that he'd missed it. If he had been there, camera at the ready, his photos could have been spread all over the papers, with him gaining proper recognition for his photographic skills. He was immensely proud of how he'd refined his techniques, pushing the film to ISO 1600 and getting sharp images with a 200mm lens, vibration dampened by a bean bag on a monopod. His hidden crop of images couldn't be shown to anyone, but capturing a murderer in the act would have earned him the respect that he so desperately craved.

Victoria was wittering away in the background, but he wasn't really listening until she pushed down the top of his paper asking, "What do you think?"

"Sorry love," he said, "I was stuck in the paper. What were you saying?"

"I was just saying how everything is settled now. We've both finished college and your pay's more than enough to cover our bills, even with the mortgage now at some stupid interest rate."

Richard, distracted by fantasies of winning press photography awards, agreed with her. She was right, he thought. They both had well-paid jobs and he was enjoying the resultant lifestyle of essentially being able to do anything he chose. Lie in at the weekends (albeit without sex), read the papers, or watch TV. Or he could sit and listen to his small but growing collection of CDs, the new technology making vinyl LPs redundant, on a top-end Philips CD960 player, which at £700 had cost close on a month's salary.

Victoria carried on, "So now would be a good time, wouldn't it?"

"Good time for what?" he asked, still not really thinking it through.

"Kids. We shouldn't leave it too late and we can afford it, can't we?"

The penny dropped. Heavily and without welcome. He had to agree that they could afford it, but there were plenty of other objections. Some of these he could vocalise, but others could end up with him sleeping on the couch.

"Yes, I suppose we could afford it," he said carefully, "but there's not really enough room to bring up a baby, is there?"

"I know that, but that's not a problem. Daddy's already said he'd help us move to a better place."

This was worse than Richard had thought. If she'd already discussed it with Geoff, then it wasn't going to be a sensible discussion between the two of them, but rather Richard against Victoria plus her mum and her dad, who, of course, just happened to be the couple's employer, mortgage guarantor and first port of call whenever they needed help. Okay, so objections re money and housing were not going to win.

"But what about your job?" he asked, "You enjoy it and wouldn't want to give up a career when you've put all that work into it?"

"No problem either," she replied. "I'd just take six months off and mummy's said that she'd love to have a little one in the daytime, so I'd be able to go back to work."

"Okay, that would be good." Richard paused and searched

for other objections. "But what about the way we live? It'd be a big disruption. Keeping stuff out of the way of small fingers, changing what we do and when…." he tailed off lamely, sensing that this argument was going nowhere.

Victoria confirmed this saying, "I know, but it's a small price to pay, and we'll want kids one day, won't we, so better now than later."

Richard was still far from happy so risked alluding to the taboo subject that usually resulted in a multi-day, category-one sulk, "Umm… but I'm assuming that you're not thinking of artificial insemination?"

Unexpectedly, she replied in a bright voice. "Yes, of course I know we have to make love to have a baby. I thought you'd be happy with that!"

"Yes, of course I am," he tentatively replied, adding a dig, "But at once a month it could take years."

"Don't be daft," she laughed back, "it'll be a bit more often than that."

Richard knew his wife well enough to realise that this was not an argument he was going to win today. The thought of occasional extra nookie (he was sure it would only be occasional) mollified him slightly, but it also presented an opportunity.

"Well then, let's start now," he said. This was pushing things. The once a month coupling – if he was lucky – usually took place on Saturday night. Missionary position, no foreplay and with the lights out. Never mid-morning.

"Okay love," she replied, surprising him. "Oh, and I've already stopped taking the pill. I knew you'd like the idea."

For the first time they found themselves in their bedroom with bright daytime sunlight streaming in through the window. Victoria went to close the curtains but Richard stopped her saying, "Don't worry about them. No one can see us."

As they got into the bed, he fantasised about looking in through the window. These thoughts resulted in it all being over even quicker than usual, but much to Richard's delight, there were several more similar interludes over the next couple of weeks as Victoria's headaches miraculously cleared up and she welcomed his advances, no matter what time of the day.

Richard's demeanour changed markedly over this time. He was laughing more and less grumpy. His laboratory team postulated that he might be taking one of the several diazepam derivatives made by the company. Geoff and Lorna Bristow guessed that he was happy at the thought of being a dad.

Victoria conceded inwardly and with some sadness, that her husband was only truly happy when his sexual needs were being met.

A couple of months went by with no sign of pregnancy. Richard was happy with this; no lifelong parasite on the horizon, and he finally had what he felt to be a good sex life. He knew it could be better; their foreplay usually consisted of getting undressed, and they never strayed from the missionary position. He had yet to experience any of the kinks that he'd read about, or had witnessed through the camera lens. He'd tried suggesting some basic variations in the past but this had only resulted in rejection and Victoria sulking even more than usual.

One Sunday morning and they'd had tea in bed. Richard hoped that Victoria would be receptive to another attempt at fertilisation (as she'd started calling it) and wondered if maybe she'd accept some changes if she thought it might help reach her conceptual goal.

He took the risk of suggesting, "Maybe a different position will help?"

"What do you mean?"

"Well…" He thought he might as well go for it. "What about from behind? I'll go in deeper then."

"All right…" she replied, "but take it slowly and be careful."

She turned over and lay on the bed.

"No, stand on the floor and bend over," he told her. Victoria looked over her shoulder with an unhappy look at him, but did what he asked.

Richard stood behind her. Gazing with curiosity at her in this previously unseen position, he ran his eyes down the cleft of her backside to her labia. This position was more explicit and brazen than any he'd seen before. 'Oh, for my camera,' he thought to himself, instantly dismissing the idea. Victoria was horrendously camera shy and had lambasted him in the past when he'd suggested a slightly suggestive photo of her in underwear. He put his hand on the hot flesh of her pussy lips, marvelling at how different she felt in this position. Moving his fingers up and down her slit he could feel it more open than in their usual position. An overwhelming urge took him down onto his knees, his tongue out as he moved towards the enticing pink lips, but before he could get there she stood up and sharply told him, "Don't be so disgusting! You wanted to try this position. Don't spoil it."

"Sorry," he babbled. "But this is normal you know. Most couples enjoy it."

"Well, I don't want to," she snapped again. "Come on, if you're going to do it, do it."

As usual, despite the lack of passion or any involvement from Victoria, Richard couldn't resist and moments later found himself thrusting into her from behind. Bliss. How could it be so different? In ecstasy, he felt himself come deep inside her. 'Oh to do this again and again!'

There were a few more occasions when he enjoyed this euphoria but then the idyll was shattered when just two weeks later she rejected his overtures and said in a quiet voice, "You do know I'm late, don't you."

Richard played it safe. "That's fantastic. But we shouldn't get too hopeful, it's still early days."

It was indeed early days. But those days turned into weeks and Victoria was over the moon when the pregnancy test proved positive. Despite earlier misgivings, Richard started to look forward to being a dad. Victoria's and Richard's parents were delighted at the prospect of becoming grandparents and barely a day passed without someone in the family offering good advice and making plans for their future. Richard's mood swung between happy pride at thoughts of what was to come, together with fear that something could go wrong, and in between, general grumpiness now that celibacy was again the order of the day ("We don't want to risk the baby," she'd said when he suggested recreational rather than procreational coitus).

The day of the first routine ultrasound check arrived and Bristow Pharmaceuticals gave the two of them the day off.

"Take as much time as you need," Mr Bristow had boomed. "This one needs looking after much more than the laboratory does."

The hospital waiting room was a mixture of anxious mothers-to-be and out-of-their-depth fathers-to-be. Victoria was nervous at seeing the bump as a real living person while Richard was distracted, thinking about the costs that were coming their way as he listened to other couples proclaiming the merits of ultra expensive, high tech baby kit that was "absolutely essential" for the safe upbringing of their progeny.

Eventually, their turn came and Victoria found herself lying on her back, belly exposed, while a technician ("Thelma", according to her name badge) effusively apologised for the ultrasonic gel and probe being so cold.

Thelma was very quiet and Victoria asked anxiously whether there was anything wrong.

"Not at all…" came the reply, "all's good… In fact, it's probably twice as good as you were expecting."

There was a pause and Victoria asked, "Twins?"

"Yes. Healthy looking twins."

Richard hardly heard Victoria and Thelma happily discussing the details of the two hearts beating on the screen and the number of limbs. Again, he was divided; delighted that all was well, but conscious that this changed their plans significantly. More cost. More disturbance. More nappies. And, he was sure, more of the burden on his shoulders.

*

Summer 1988 and two perfect girls were delivered. The tired, but radiant parents cried together as they looked at the new members of their family. For once, Richard was genuinely pleased with his lot in life.

They named them Emma and Lucy. Not the first choice names; the new grandparents applied gentle but irresistible pressure for names that ran in the families.

Over the next months, Richard found that he had been right about the cost and the amount of work that this all entailed as they spent all their waking hours (and there were many more waking hours than there used to be) in endless toil. They were both too tired to be unhappy or resentful.

Their cramped flat had to give way for somewhere bigger; an event that took place almost without their input. Lorna Bristow trailed around estate agents bringing back glossy brochures to share with her daughter while Richard was back at work. He came home one evening to be told that Victoria had found the house she liked. The estate agents brochure declared that: "The Willows, Wanstead Avenue, Twyford, is an exceptionally well appointed semi-detached family home in the catchment area for the best school." The estate agent himself recommended that it should be purchased instantly as the price was so affordable. Of course, they ignored all this blurb. What was more important was that it had three bedrooms and was within walking distance of Grandparents Bristow who were putting up a good chunk of the purchase price. It was a foregone conclusion that this was where they'd move to.

But five miles was too far to walk to the Camera Club (not that Richard had been much lately, what with being a good dad and husband) and, as he would have to go by car, he'd also have to give up on his established Thursday evening viewpoints, as parking in some of these roads would be too conspicuous.

"The house looks okay," he started, "but we don't want to move away from here do we? What about our friends and not being able to walk to work?"

She countered, "We'll still see them, and we've got the car so might as well use it. And I don't feel safe with those murders." He hadn't realised there'd been more than the one ('More missed photo-opportunities?' he thought).

"And there's nowhere in that house for a darkroom," was his final objection. Victoria demolished this saying, "You don't really need one. There are plenty of good photo labs around. And anyway, chemicals and babies don't mix."

He could see that this was another argument that he stood no chance of winning, but decided that no matter what, a darkroom would have to be set up soon as possible. There was no way he'd risk his film to someone else to develop, not with some of the pictures that he'd caught. Also, without a darkroom, it would be difficult to justify still having Kodak boxes with their "Do Not Open" labels.

But, irrespective of Richard's lack of desire for a move, it happened anyway.

Number 17, as they preferred to call the house rather than "The Willows", had a small, neglected garden which remained neglected while Richard worked on redecorating first the babies' rooms and then the rest of the property. Victoria enjoyed her maternity leave nursing babies and writing an ever-growing list of jobs to be carried out by her overworked husband. Buoyed along by the early joy of fatherhood, he tackled the list and surprised himself with his D.I.Y. skills to the extent that when he'd finished the urgent tasks, he persuaded Victoria to allow him to convert the garden shed into a darkroom, complete with a lock on the door ("To protect my expensive kit from theft," he had said), and to which he had the only key.

Of course, there were always more jobs to be done, and there was the day job as well.

Before they knew it, four years had gone by. Victoria hadn't returned to work preferring to keep her daughters close at hand, despite Grandma's willingness to look after them. Richard's enthusiasm for white gloss paint and wallpaper had waned as tiredness took over. Slightly resentful that Victoria was having, as he saw it, all the fun and time off, while he did all the work, his mood deteriorated as their lovelife dwindled to all but nothing; she was always too tired, and he was too afraid of rocking the boat to argue his case.

"Besides," as she reminded "Mr Grumpy" one evening when he dared to suggest an early night and a return to Saturday evening routines, "we've got our two gorgeous girls now and we're in love with each other, so we don't have to worry about that sort of thing, do we?"

Richard tried pleading that it was a natural part of a relationship but all he got was platitudes.

He lay there awake growing resentful while Victoria snored beside him.

He mused on it all. Apart from sex, he was pretty happy with his lot. Lovely wife (PMT issues excepted), lovely daughters, nice house, reliable car, good job…

But sex was such a fundamental need…

He was starting to accept that Victoria was not going to satisfy even his most basic of needs. At least, not in the foreseeable. So, what could he do? He started to build up a list of options in his head, along with their pros and cons.

By 1am, the mental list was sparse but thought out.

'Options…' he thought, 'in no particular order…'

'Option One. Accept it as it is… No… Not for much longer.' That was an easy scratch from the list.

'Option Two. Divorce. Meet someone else… No, no way. I'd lose my job, the house, everything.' Another one scratched.

'Option Three. Have an affair. Pluses; sex. Different sex… Minuses; get caught and again everything goes down the drain.' He dwelt on the practicality of it. Having gone straight from a boy's only school to marrying his first girlfriend, he hadn't a clue about chatting up women, let alone where he might meet someone also interested in an affair or where they could go… 'just too many negatives,' he surmised.

The thought of a different sort of negative started him off on Option Four. 'Get out there, watching and taking photos. Watching's almost as good as doing it.' He immediately found himself getting aroused. 'Pluses; I know what to do. I'm good at it. There's little chance of getting caught. I can "have" a lot of different women. There's always the possibility of something different.' This was a good start. 'Minuses; nothing springs to mind.'

The thought of whether it was dodgy in any way didn't rate as a problem.

He also mulled over another possibility: 'Option Five. Pay for it. Pluses; sex, variety. No need to connect with the other person. Less chance of getting caught. Minuses; cost, health risk.' An option he was happy to think about as a fall back. Again, morality had not entered the equation.

But he kept coming back to Option Four. Watching.

Another sleepless hour later and Richard was convinced that being a peeping Tom was the only way he'd meet his needs. Now it came down to the how's, where's and when's.

He hadn't really explored the area around the new house properly yet, despite the length of time they'd been there, but his gut reaction was that it probably wasn't the best of hunting grounds. Most of the houses were larger and detached. There'd be problems with shooting angles and having to look upwards as he'd had to during the early days in the park. Also, there were no obvious hiding places and there was the very real risk of being seen by his father-in-law who liked to walk their dog around the neighbourhood.

So it would have to be further afield. That meant getting in the car. Going by car meant parking. Parking could be conspicuous as a different car in a street might be noticed by some busybody.

And the registration number would lead back to him.

Then there was the problem of when and how to get out of the house. The camera club had worked well in the past, but Richard was sure that Victoria wouldn't be happy with him going off and enjoying himself again when there was work to be done.

Maybe even this option wouldn't work.

He eventually drifted off, without him having resolved any of it, but knowing that there had to be a way to satisfy his needs.

It was to be several more months before fortune smiled.

CHAPTER 5

BLONDIE. "Picture This"

1993

Maypharm became the new name for Bristow Pharmaceuticals after an expensive marketing agency rebranded them, declaring that "Bristow Pharmaceuticals" sounded too northern and that the abbreviation "BP" was already spoken for. The same marketing agency was certain that if Maypharm gave them a substantial advertising budget, then expansion into non-prescription products within pharmacies would reap tremendous benefits for all concerned.

Geoff Bristow had often joked that he was one of the country's top drug dealers who'd never been to prison. He knew pharmaceuticals. What he could make. What sold. Who would buy. And, most importantly, how big a margin he could put on the medicines. He was the first to admit that his knowledge of non-prescription products was zero and he couldn't see his factory starting to make plasters, nappies, electricals or any of the other numerous lumps of plastic and metal that seemed to sell. The only area which looked interesting was non-pharma liquids and powders. On a market research visit to the local branch of Boots (or to be more precise, when buying some hay-fever medicine), he was struck by the large variety of possible products there was. A dozen different bubble baths, numerous skin care creams and lotions and over the counter remedies to treat all of the inconveniences of modern life.

He could see that there was indeed a market for all of these products but didn't have the time or knowledge needed to capitalise on the opportunity, so set up a working group within the company to sort it all out for him.

Trusting family more than the current batch of shiny-suited executives who'd probably bugger off if given a better offer elsewhere, Geoff Bristow appointed Richard as head of the working group, despite his mere 32 years and lack of experience, giving him free rein to do whatever he thought would benefit the company. The marketing guys (whilst quietly rubbing their hands with glee at the option of further advertising spend) told Geoff that this freedom, the lack of any clear guidelines or any defined budget, went against all business principles. But old man Bristow persisted being sure that his son-in-law would always put the company first. Richard put together a small group of Maypharm stalwarts; John and Dereck from purchasing and finance who understood costs, Martin from compliance to tell him what was legal, Jane from the lab, whose ability to formulate new products, he admitted, outshone his own, and of course, Mike and Justin, sales and marketing representatives who would actually have to sell the new range.

Richard relished the challenge. It appealed to his analytical mind and he started to sketch out the possibilities, losing track of time and working late day after day. Like his father-in-law, he ruled out everything except liquids, pastes and pills, before spending time with the team delving into the possibilities in more detail. Between them they honed in on a small number of possibilities. These were ones with acceptable margins, products that Jane felt her team could develop, and which Martin was sure wouldn't land them in court fighting product liability or patent breach claims.

It was Victoria who unknowingly made the key comment.

The committee had zeroed in on four possible new areas.

The first was antacids; an expanding market for lumps of chalk that consumers loved to swallow to apparently eliminate acid reflux and settle their stomachs. Good margins, easy to make, no legal issues and a no apparent problems. This looked like one to go for.

Next was hair conditioners – silicone oils that made hair look glossy and bouncy. Again it had legs; there was a good profit margin and a healthy market demand. But Jane wasn't happy that she understood the chemistry of blending silicones.

Then there was sterilising solution – sodium dichloroisocyanurate powder that could be dissolved in tap water to make a liquid guaranteed to kill 99.999% of germs. Easy one to formulate and make, but John and Dereck's spreadsheet suggested a lower profit margin, especially as Mike reckoned it would need constant advertising spend. Richard being as risk averse in business, as he was in his marriage, scrubbed it from the list.

The last was simple bath and shower product; another range that would be profitable. Products that the laboratory could formulate and stability test easily. The only worry was that it was already a crowded market with numerous competitors.

Richard pulled the team's reports together and spent evenings putting together a report for Maypharm's directors so that they could decide which way to go. He wasn't going to make any recommendations. Better that they shoulder the blame if it went wrong.

Victoria was happy to let him do this work at home. It wasn't a waste of time like relaxing or snapping away with the camera would have been.

Richard completed the presentation and tried it out on his wife. As he expected, she came out with what he felt were trivial or unconstructive criticisms. "I would have used a blue background instead of white," was one. Another was "Why haven't you got the company logo on the slides?"

He was used to her being negative about his efforts and thought the slides were fine, but he still made the changes. Just to keep her happy.

Then she came out with the comment that made him see the task in a new light. "I do hope that those Neanderthals in marketing don't make ads full of girls in showers and baths," she pronounced contemptuously.

'Girls in showers?' Richard loved the vision that sprang to mind. His train of thought carried on down the single track of his daily passion. 'Victoria doesn't get involved in the company nowadays and wouldn't know who makes the decisions. She doesn't have influence… I wonder if I could get away with taking them myself?'

Another night lying awake, but this time imagining auditioning naked models, then working out how he could sway the Maypharm's Directors to go for this as the right product range. And also, how could he get to take the pictures? 'I'm Project Manager so have the authority,' he mused. 'I could get old man Bristow to okay me taking pictures. After all, I've done others for the company in the past.'

The problem would be that Victoria would have a right hissy fit if she knew. And there was always the risk that her dad would let it slip over Sunday lunch round at theirs.

Sleep arrived and in the morning the problem had resolved itself; what if he sub-contracted the photography to someone else? Or rather, told the company that that was what he was doing. He could then enjoy taking the pictures himself and bill the company as the fictional photographer. The invoice would come to him for sign-off and he'd get the payment. No one would know and he'd make a few quid on the side.

Over the course of the morning, the presentation took on a less balanced view of the choices. Margins and sales forecasts took a dip for hair products and chalk pills. Shower and bath on the other hand looked a lot more profitable. After presenting these subtly twisted figures to the board, complete with some suitable differences in tone of voice, Richard was pleased to hear the decision go the way he wanted. And as expected, he was appointed to head up the new business unit.

*

Richard Marsh, Skincare Division Manager, Maypharm Ltd, settled back in his genuine leather look office chair behind his genuine oak veneer desk and picked up the latest status report from the team putting the shower range together.

Richard had been heavily involved in the bits that he understood; he'd spent hours leafing through reference books at the Royal Society of Chemistry's London library, copying down any recipe that he could find to pass on to Jane, claiming it as his knowledge that he passed on "to help her". The result was a range of "me-too" formulations. Recipes for products that had no real Unique Selling Point, but were just as good as others on the market. In this case, shower gels that would adequately clean skin, maybe have some moisturising additive, such as aloe vera, that marketing could latch onto.

Richard left the rest of it to others. The marketing team came up with a brand name "DownPour" ("The capital letter in the middle will make it stand out," they reasoned). Martin did all of the registrations necessary. Engineering re-purposed a couple of 4,000 litre mixing vessels with cooling & heating coils, a Silversen shear mixer and the associated four head filling line.

By September the groundwork was in place and the conversation that Richard had been waiting for took place when Justin from Marketing came to discuss the advertising campaign.

Standing in brown polyester suit and looking like he'd just arrived on a placement from the local polytechnic, Justin reiterated the details from market research that they'd commissioned early on. With a mixture of acronyms and buzzwords he explained that, "We've benchmarked DownPour against consumer expectations of retail placement and the concept is scalable with optimum R.O.I. when focused on several target gender age groups, such as twenty-something women."

Richard maintained a silence when Justin had finished stating the bleedin' obvious and asked, "You mean that anybody who has a shower could be a customer?"

"Well yes, you could say that," Justin admitted slowly, then added, "but we've identified the demographics for optimal –"

"– Hang on." Richard interrupted, "I've got that. We just need to get it under people's noses and they might buy it."

"Yes, but there's a bit more to it than that." Justin didn't look comfortable. "We've got to target the ads to our audience, we don't want to scattergun it."

"You may well be right," Richard smiled, "but really, if it looks okay on the shelf, and if it ain't too pricey, then they'll buy it."

Richard watched Justin deflate. The marketing lad had hoped to build up the need for a hefty advertising budget. The bigger the budget, the more important his role. It now sounded as if there might not be any advertising budget at all. Richard let the unhappy marketeer stew for a moment then dropped the bait, "but I do think that some advertising would be beneficial. As long as it's in line with what I've agreed with the board, of course."

"What do you mean?" Justin nibbled around the hook.

"Well…" Richard wiggled the bait more, whilst starting the process of moving the advertising his way, "they want something very traditional. A mix of magazine and maybe poster ads that people recognise instantly as being for shower gel."

Justin bit, "Well we can do that."

Richard added the final details. "The only restrictions are, firstly that they want to sign off on the story board and, secondly, they've a photographer that you have to use."

"No problem. We can work with that."

Hook, line & sinker.

*

The basic design of the advert, complete with mock-up of a woman in a shower with sponge and product bottle strategically placed, was drawn up by Richard. As far as Justin was concerned, this design came from the Board. He could sort out the detail, the text, the font, pitch size, where to publish and all that, but he wasn't to mess with the basics of it needing a photo of a naked model. Richard also said that he alone would liaise with the photographer that he had been instructed to use, for some reason, omitting to mention that said photographer would be himself.

Then there was the model herself.

Shutting his office door to make sure that he couldn't be seen or heard, Richard started to look for a woman willing to stand naked in front of him. First call were the agencies advertising in one of his *Professional Photography* magazines. Their rates quickly ruled them out, but Richard asked for quotes and photos to be sent to him. The former so that he'd have proof of how much this was costing. The latter purely for his licentious interest.

Moving downscale he tried a couple of the ads in *Amateur Photographer*. The model's rates were undoubtedly lower, but the women didn't instill him with confidence when he started discussing their age and size. Perfect for the local camera clubs, but not really a national advertising campaign.

The thought of camera clubs made him reach for the phone again and he called Dave Fletcher, the camera club member who had always professed to know so much about the modelling industry. After the usual natter, Richard moved onto the reason for the call. "Dave," he asked, "we're looking for a model for some ads were running, but the pros are bloody pricey. Where does the club find its models?"

Dave had the answer. "Oh, we've got our regulars and then there's the amateurs register. It's got their portfolio pictures, rates, specialties, travelling info and just about everything you need."

Despite having enjoyed looking at the girls for some years,

Richard hadn't realised that there was a directory.

"That sounds perfect. How do I get a copy?"

Dave's reply wasn't really a surprise, "Oh, I've always got the latest one. I can send you the previous issue if it's any help."

"Yes. Thanks. You'd better send it to my work address. Oh, and mark it personal if you would."

"No problem mate. I guess your other half wouldn't be impressed?"

"Spot on." Richard admitted.

*

The Professional agency's glossy brochure arrived first. Top quality pictures of perfectly coiffured girls. All of them between 5ft 7" and 6 ft. All size 10 or 12. All between the ages of 18 and 28. None looking as if they had a spark of character. Even without the champagne-lifestyle pricing, Richard would have ruled them out. These girls just didn't do it for him.

The brochure sent by Dave on the other hand was a lot simpler. And more interesting. Still printed on glossy photo paper, but lighter weight and hand stapled by the looks of it. Girls, women, of all ages and sizes. Genuine faces smiled out from the pages. Within the first four or five pages he already spotted a couple who looked like possibilities. Then on page seven, a face from the past leapt out at him. There she was, "Julie White" he read "age 38, height 5ft 4, size 14, areas covered: South UK, Non-nude, glamour & nude work, £20 - £40 per hour + travel." Then a telephone number.

Richard leaned back. This was just too good to be true. She wasn't the classical look of a TV or magazine model, but maybe that would be the hook that made their advert a little different; a more believable image. A normal (but beautiful) woman, in a normal shower / bath rather than one who looked straight out of the pages of an interior design magazine. Plus, as an amateur model, she wouldn't necessarily expect a full make-up and lighting team, so he might get away with being alone with her. And there was the money side of things. Produce an invoice at the prices quoted in the professional brochure, but pay her a fraction of it and pocket the difference.

He reached for the phone. Hesitated. Might he get caught? 'Well, yes,' he reasoned, 'there's always a risk, but I can manage it. After all, nothing ventured, nothing gained.'

He dialled the number and found himself smiling as he heard it ringing at the other end of the line. A few rings later and an answerphone kicked in. "Hi, you've reached Julie White. Leave a message and if you're not selling anything then I'll probably get back to you."

He'd not thought this possibility through and found himself mumbling something to the effect of "Hi, Richard from Maypharm here. I'll call back later." He didn't leave his number. He wanted to call her rather than risk her calling back when he wasn't alone.

A couple more tries during the afternoon were similarly unsuccessful. On the off-chance he tried again, just before leaving the office and this time the call was answered after several rings. A breathless voice at the other end, "Sorry Jo, just got in."

"Oh, hi, sorry, no this isn't Jo. I'm calling from Maypharm." Richard felt stupidly nervous as he said this.

"Oh, sorry, I was expecting someone else. Who did you say you are?"

"I'm Richard Marsh from Maypharm, looking for Julie White?"

"Julie here. Sorry, don't recognise your company. What did you want?"

Richard paused for a second. No going back, he thought. "You've been suggested as a possible model for an advertising campaign that we're doing."

"Me?" She sounded surprised. "You must be mistaken. I don't think I'd be your first choice?"

"No," he exaggerated slightly, "we've seen your portfolio and you're just what we're looking for."

"Oh... well, tell me more then?"

Richard continued, picking his words carefully. "Well, we're launching a range of bathroom products and we're looking for a natural looking model for the adverts. We want a new face rather than the ones who are recognised instantly as representing other products. Oh, and to be honest, our budget doesn't stretch quite as far as others might do. Yet." He was pleased with that last sentence limiting her expectations of big money, but at the same time implying that there could be more in due course.

"Well, thank you. Certainly sounds interesting."

They talked for a couple more minutes during which

Richard promised to send over an outline of what the successful model would be doing.

'Strike while the iron's hot,' he thought and settled down to type her a letter, making it plain that the adverts were to be tasteful and that Maypharm was a reputable company. He finished off by suggesting that, as they had a couple of models to consider, he would like to meet her prior to agreeing any contract. He put the letter in the post, and was now over an hour late leaving the office. Victoria would be tetchy about his lateness, but he didn't care.

Two weeks and two phone calls later their meeting was set up. The location had been a problem. Suggesting going to her home wouldn't look professional, and he didn't want her to come to his office; as far as the company was concerned the photography was being carried out by an independent photographer. On top of this she mentioned having a full-time job so was only able to meet evenings or lunchtime close to her work (although she didn't say what she did, and he felt it wouldn't have been right to ask). In the end, they agreed on a middle of the day meet in a large, anonymous business hotel local to her work where he could hire a business meeting room by the hour. He got there early and made a point of spreading out company brochures and advertising briefs on the meeting room table. He also set up his camera on a tripod and sat back to wait, noting that his pulse was a bit higher than usual, and the room seemed very warm.

A knock on the door and Julie entered.

It had been 15 years since Richard last saw her in the flesh (although her photos had been perused frequently in the intervening period, often held in one hand while the other was busy elsewhere), but he recognised the smile instantly. He held out his hand and introduced himself.

Julie didn't give any indication that she might remember him, but then why should she? It was a long time ago, there'd been a camera in front of his face and she must have seen hundreds of photographers since then.

Richard desperately tried to avoid being obvious about how he was looking at this gorgeous woman, but clearly wasn't very good at it as she asked, "So, do I look okay?"

"Definitely," was all he could reply. Then drawing a breath and forcing himself to get down to business, "let me tell you more about what we're looking for, and you can tell me a bit about yourself."

"Of course," she said before he went on to describe the products and the advert ideas.

"So all it really needs from you is to take a shower and let the camera person do their job," he concluded.

"Well, that's no problem." She smiled, "though I'm still not sure why you'd go for an amateur like me when there's lot more experienced models out there."

"It's just that we're looking for the more natural look," he repeated. "Someone who's not already associated with other products. Someone that could be thought of as, well, sort of neutral, you know, not looking like they were just doing it for the money."

"Uh-huh. Where and when's the shoot?" she asked.

"Depends on your availability. Assuming that we select you," Richard hastily added, wanting her to be keen to please and go along with him.

"I've got a full-time job. Is that a problem?" Julie asked.

This fell in well with a plan that Richard had been hatching to get what he really wanted; just him behind the camera watching her in her own shower.

"Yes, that could be a problem…" he hesitated, deliberately raising the stakes. "Our usual studio and camera guy are only available in the daytime…" He paused again as if the problem was insurmountable, then added, "I mean, well, I could do the camera work if there was no other option. I'm qualified and do a lot of our company product shots already. But studio is a bigger problem. Unless you know anywhere?"

"Um, I don't know any studios set up for this." She too paused, but there was no objection to him taking pictures he noted.

"You'd think it'd be simple wouldn't you…" he sighed. "All we need is a natural, homely looking bathroom shower…" Another pause. "I'd even suggest my own house, except that it's being decorated at the moment…" He let the possibilities hang in the air, letting her add her own suggestion.

"You could use mine, I suppose." She didn't look confident about the idea.

"Well, maybe." ('Don't sound too keen,' he cautioned himself.) "It's not really the sort of thing we do… But it should meet the brief for looking natural. And with some strategic lighting… Yes, it could work, I guess."

"All right then." She accepted the idea.

Richard struggled to hide his elation. She'd just agreed to let him watch her in the shower in her own house. No need to hire a studio. No need to get anyone else involved. She was already on the backfoot and he was sure, on the day, he'd be able to persuade her to pose however he wanted.

A bit more discussion re details and he magnanimously announced that as she looked good, and as she was willing to help with the set, he'd pass on the other candidates and the job was hers. A model release form would be drawn up and posted to her and he'd see her, at her place, next Thursday evening.

*

The Marketing Team was told that a photographer and model specified by the Directors had been lined up. The Directors were told that the Marketing Team had found a photographer and model to suit their advert. Richard was confident that neither would discuss it with the other.

Thursday came and he told Victoria that he was going to go to camera club.

"So I'll have to do the girls' bedtime, the washing up and all the tidying," she grumbled.

In a rare moment of forcefulness he replied, "Look. I've not been for yonks. One evening won't hurt."

Julie had given an address in Wanhill, a small village 5 or 6 miles away and well off the beaten track. 'The Old Barn' did have some old stone walls, but was predominately recent masonry, large plate glass windows, and modern wooden beams. It stood in a small courtyard together with one other conversion, 'The Old Granary', which also bore only a passing resemblance to any past life.

Parking his unwashed and ageing Ford Mondeo next to a gleaming red MG, Richard felt a twinge of jealousy. If he'd not been trapped into marriage with Victoria, this might be his lot in life. He conveniently ignored that by marrying her, he'd got a well-paid job, a lot of financial help from in-laws, two daughters and a lifestyle that a lot of other people would have coveted. He unloaded the camera and lighting kit, plus the small bag of shower products that the lab had made up that morning. He'd suggested increasing the sodium lauryl ethyl sulphate by 15% and adding 1% glycerine to give a longer-lasting foam. He didn't want Julie covered in suds, obscuring his view, but thought it might help with some of the photos as it covered the bits that shouldn't be on display in family magazines.

Of course the doorbell was a fancy pull rod affair that produced a pealing somewhere inside. And, of course, as the door opened, the obligatory well pampered, presumably pedigree, Labrador rushed out to jump over any visitor. Less welcome was finding the door opened, not by Julie, but by a middle-aged, red corduroy jeans wearing man. "Hi, you must be the photographer," he boomed, "come on in." Richard noted that no handshake was proffered, photographers being too low in the food chain he guessed, feeling annoyed.

"I'm Lawrence, Julie's husband. Come on through."

The house was as expensively furnished as Richard had

guessed it would be, from the outside appearance, and he continued to feel irked by the sight of what he couldn't have. But on the plus side, as far as he was concerned, no sign of stuffed toys, kids, affection, or real life here.

Lawrence led the way up the stairs to where Julie was fussing around, tidying up an already immaculate bathroom.

"Hi," said Richard, and then being stuck for anything further to say, added unnecessarily, "I'm the photographer."

"Yes, of course, I know," she grinned, but also looked a bit relieved. Maybe Richard had inadvertently broken the ice.

The paperwork was sorted out and Richard made a pretence of looking at the shower from every angle he could think of. In reality, he'd decided as soon as he'd arrived upstairs; he'd take pictures from the landing, through the open bathroom door with a small amount of telephoto to bring Julie out from the background. The glass shower doors would be open and out of frame, so that it looked like she was in a walk-in shower (or that the viewer was in the shower with her). The spray from the shower with the doors open might have been a problem, but the bathroom was expensively fitted out as a wet room with floor drain as well ('It would be,' he thought).

"Just be yourself," Richard instructed Julie, "Pretend I'm not here. As you shower, just turn forwards and backwards so I can get a variety of angles. Keep picking up and putting down the product bottle so that I can get more angles, but always with the label outwards. Use the sponges and try to keep lather levels high."

"Easy," she said. "What about my nips and bits? How do you

want me to hide them?"

"Oh, don't worry about that. Just carry on as you would do normally and we'll crop the pictures later on so that nothing's showing."

"No probs," she replied. "Give us a couple of secs."

He just about managed to stop himself saying that he would've been delighted to enjoys secs with her…

Julie started undressing while Richard continued his pretence of preparing the camera along with the lens, flash and a couple of fold-out reflectors to even-out the light. All the while he was looking at Julie's reflection in the mirror as her clothes came off.

"Anything I can do to help?" Lawrence said, not really sounding as if he was willing to shift a finger, but reminding Richard that he was there.

"No, but thanks." Richard replied in an offhand manner. "But, without meaning to be rude, can I just ask that you keep back a bit?" What he really meant was 'bugger off and let me lust after your wife in peace,' but that probably wouldn't have been a good choice of words.

Julie stood there naked. Richard looked at her. Purely in a professional way, of course. She'd gained a few pounds, but was still a beautiful, voluptuous woman. Her breasts still well shaped, nipples slightly erect, pubes lightly covering the area that he lusted after. A few lines and creases, but that was fine.

"Okay then," Richard managed to croak, covering this with a cough. "In your own time."

Julie got into the shower. Pulled the door shut without thinking and then apologised as she opened it again before turning-on the water in front of an already turned-on cameraman.

"Like this?" she asked, striking a pose.

"No, just shower as if I wasn't here."

Richard watched and snapped away as Julie soaped and sudded her body. Turning this way and that, turning her head upwards as the water streamed over her. In just a couple of minutes a reel of film had been used. "Just need to change film," Richard called and she turned off the water.

"Take a moment out." Richard suggested. "I need to move the reflectors as well."

Julie sat on the closed toilet lid as he fiddled around the bathroom. The mirror on the wall slightly steamed up at the edges. Just like Richard.

"Um, excuse me." Richard addressed Lawrence. "Could you do us a favour?"

"Of course, what is it?"

"I need another reflector. I think there's one in my car." Holding out his keys Richard asked the unwelcome chaperone, "Could you take a look?" He knew full well that there wasn't one in the car, but the search should give him at least some time alone with Julie.

"Yah" was the only response as Lawrence went off and Richard suggested to Julie that they do another set.

Richard lined up an angle using the mirror. It worked well for him. He felt as if he was spying on the woman in the shower. He felt himself growing hard, but wasn't worried whether it might be noticeable as Lawrence was out of sight and from this angle, Julie couldn't really see him. Or so he thought. As he finished the next reel of film and suggested another break, she looked at him with a grin, pointedly looked down at his crotch and laughed, "I take it you're happy with what you see?"

He felt himself blushing deeply and stammered out an apology.

"No need to apologise!" She was still laughing. "I take it as a compliment."

Before Richard could think of anything to say, he heard Julie's husband coming up the stairs behind him saying that he'd not found the reflector.

"That's all right." Richard said over loudly and without turning around to Lawrence. "I think I can manage without."

"All okay love?" Lawrence addressed Julie.

"Yes…" she replied, and then with a knowing grin directed at the still embarrassed voyeur, "He was just paying me a big compliment."

She added, "I vaguely remember you giving me compliments once."

Lawrence laughed, not realising the slight directed at him. "No need now love, you know I think you're perfect so I don't need to say it all the time."

Julie gave Richard another smile and, he thought, a wink.

Another couple of reels of film and Richard felt that much as he'd love to carry on all night (in more ways than one), stringing it out any longer would look suspicious. He called an end to the session and packed up his kit, while watching Julie dry herself and put on a dressing gown.

The three of them went downstairs and as Richard loaded up the car Lawrence disappeared off, happy now that he didn't have to stand guard.

"Thanks again," Richard said to the wet-haired Julie, "I think we got some good shots. Oh, and a cheque will be in the post shortly."

"I enjoyed it…" she replied, adding with a grin, "and I know you did as well."

Lost for words, Richard climbed into the car and just called out, "See you again."

He thought she replied, "Anytime." Or was that just wishful thinking?

*

The only problem now was sorting out the money. He needed a company name, address, and bank account in order to invoice Maypahrm. It all had to be anonymous and not traceable back to him. Having had no experience in committing business fraud (although he saw it rather as a way of getting paid for work that he'd carried out), these were all problems that he naïvely hadn't expected. The banks wanted proof of address and identity and to get a company name there were similar issues with the Companies House application form. After exhausting the proper procedures, Richard decided he'd have to involve someone else, someone who might know how to sort it. A less than ideal solution, but necessary if he wanted both the money and no forensic trails left.

He called Dave Fletcher, ostensibly to thank him for the model directory. After the usual pleasantries, he dangled a hook. "Dave, without your help, we wouldn't have found this girl and would have ended up spending a lot more money. I think we should pay you a finder's fee."

"No need, it was nothing," Dave pretended that he wasn't interested in the money.

"No, we really should do this. Even if it's only a hundred quid." Richard had thought long and hard about how much to offer. Too little and Dave wouldn't be interested. Too much and Richard's profit suffered.

"Hundred quid? That's generous… And it would be useful." Dave was biting.

"Great." Then dropping his voice a bit and talking in a deliberately hesitant way, "but I've realised that there could be a problem… We've got plenty of budget for the model and the like, but there's not a budget for a finder's fee. I mean, it all adds up to a total that's okay for the company, but if there's not a budget line, then it's bloody difficult to get the cheque raised…" Again, a long pause, during which Dave just said, "Oh."

"Tell you what we could do…" Richard said in a brighter tone, pretending that the idea had only just occurred to him, "It's not strictly kosher, but I know you're trustworthy, so what if we said you were the photographer, send you all of the money and you send me all but £100 back?"

"Sorry, not quite with you mate." Dave sounded doubtful. "I can see that if I send you the cash, you can pass it on, but how am I supposed to ask for it?"

"Simple," Richard explained. "Your car business is just called D. Fletcher Ltd isn't it. It doesn't say car sales or anything, so just make up a bill on your company headed paper. Add 'Trading as Dave Fletcher Photo Services', and 'cheques payable to D. Fletcher'. I'll get it authorised here. You get the cheque and when it's cleared, send the balance to me."

"Well, that would work I suppose… Give me the details and I'll do you a bill. Nice doing business with you."

*

The photos were perfect and were split into two piles; a set to go to Marketing for them to play with, and a larger number kept back for Richard to look at as he played with himself.

Two months later, with strategically placed text and judicious cropping to avoid the slightest trace of an areola or pubic hair, the adverts appeared in the national press.

Julie's first inkling of her impending notoriety came when she arrived at work. As she walked in, the receptionist laughingly asked if she'd had a good shower that morning. In ignorance of the reason, Julie just answered with, "Morning Charlotte, yes thanks."

John, her boss, "just happened" to be standing by her desk when she got there. He looked her up and down and with a distinct leer and said, "Hadn't realised what you look like without the office wear."

The penny only dropped when Janet, one of the few in the office that Julie considered a friend, wandered over with today's copy of *The Sun* and putting it down on her desk open at the advert, commented: "Page 3's got nothing on you girl!"

By the end of the day, Julie had split her colleagues into groups:

Firstly, the fantasist men who thought that she'd drop her clothes for anyone and anytime. They were swiftly disabused of the notion. One with a slap which he fully deserved.

Next, a smaller number, mainly women, who found the advert offensive. Some would say so to her face. More would mutter in the background.

The third group were those who simply ignored it. Not making any views obvious.

The remainder liked it, thought it was good or were just simply okay with the idea.

There was no logic to which group people would fall into, as evinced by calls that evening from Mum and Dad ("Love it! Our girl modelling in the papers."), her brother ("Bit tacky sis."), an old male friend who'd never made a pass in the past ("God, you've got a body there. Can I come around with my camera?"), and a neighbour who thought that somehow her appearing like this would lower the property prices.

Lawrence didn't mention the advert until Julie placed it under his nose at dinner. His only reply was something to the effect of how good their bathroom looked. He wondered why she stomped out of the room in disgust.

In the long run, of course, it made little difference to her on a day-to-day basis. No sudden multi-million pound modelling contract, or in contrast, an appearance in the stocks on the green. The ads, or variants of them, appeared on a regular basis for a while, but the majority of her acquaintances soon tired of commenting. There was the occasional glance from a stranger in the street who thought that they recognised her from somewhere, but the events soon slipped into distant memory for most people. Not for Richard though.

PART 2

REVELATION AND
RESENTMENT

CHAPTER 6

The mid-1990s brought the internet to the masses and Richard realised how wrong he had been about sex in general, and about sex with Victoria, in particular.

Large desktop computers had been in use at Maypharm for a couple of years when Mike, a new PhD graduate, suggested hooking one up to the World Wide Web so that they could communicate with other researchers to speed up product development. Old school cynicism about this new technology was rapidly quashed when they completed a new product formulation project in a quarter of the time it would have usually taken. Richard, not thinking of anything but work (for once), got Mike to give him a tour through 'usenet.sci.chem' where all of the communication was taking place and was pleasantly bewildered by the amount of information available, not to mention the willingness of complete strangers to help with technical queries.

Mike explained and talked through the different types of newsgroups, and in passing, joked: "Just don't open up the 'alt. sex' directory tree, it'll put you off your lunch for good!"

Of course, any mention of sex caught Richard's attention and he immediately decided that another usenet-connected computer was needed. Purely for work, of course. This one would be in his own office and out of sight of other people. Mike prepared a crib sheet so that Richard could look around this repository of all and sundry without constantly asking for help, or, more to the point, anyone knowing what he was looking at. A press of a few keys and the distinctive warble of the dial-up modem heralded his first foray into what would soon develop into an addiction.

Until this time, most of Richard's sex education had come from glimpses through his late-night lens. He'd built up several Kodak boxes of prints of undressing or undressed girls, women and couples (a man on his own wasn't worth the film cost in his opinion). There were a few of couples having sex, usually under the covers or with little visible detail. He'd not managed to see anything really clearly since that evening in Barclay Park when he'd so nearly been caught. He also had a small collection of top shelf magazines, but censorship in the UK was still strict and *Playboy, Fiesta* or *Mayfair* didn't show anything explicit. Yes, there were numerous stories and reader's letters about all of the variations and kinks of foreplay, but Richard's limited practical experience made these difficult to imagine.

Through extensive research into the 'alt.sex' newsgroups, his understanding of the human body and what it could do, rapidly progressed. Unfortunately, this also led to a growing perturbation over his own lack of experience and resentment with Victoria for her unwillingness to indulge in anything beyond a very occasional Saturday night quickie.

There was another problem.

Sunday lunchtime and as usual Richard, Victoria and the girls, now both bright, energetic six year olds, were over at the Bristows. Richard enjoyed these escapes from the drudgery of day-to-day married life. Lorna Bristow was a good cook and good company. She also had no problem with her husband and son-in-law disappearing off to The Royal Oak for an hour or two before lunch ("I'll be dishing up at two!" she'd always tell them, knowing full well that the men wouldn't leave the pub until closing time half an hour later, and that they wouldn't sit down to eat until closer to three).

Old man Bristow tended to avoid talking shop at the pub, after all, they had plenty of opportunity during the week, but this time he raised something as soon as the two men were alone.

"We might have a problem, Richard." He started. "I was walking through the lab a couple of days ago and Mike looked like I'd just caught him up to something. He was on his computer and started pressing buttons as soon as he saw me. I know nowt about computers but know he was up to summat."

Richard just nodded, thinking it was a good thing that Geoff hadn't seen what was on his own screen a lot of the time.

Geoff continued. "It might not be anything. But he's been a bit off since we turned him down for the Lead Chemist role… You don't think he could be talking to another company do you?"

"Well, anything's possible," Richard replied non-commitally. "You're right though that he's not been himself lately. Not sure what I can do?"

"Sound him out," Bristow mused. "But do it gently. I've arranged for a specialist to come in and check all the computers. He might find something, but you're closer and should be able to spot anything odd."

"Of course, happy to help. This specialist, did you say he's checking everybody's?"

"Yes. While he's in, he might as well look at them all."

Richard was worried. Not about possibly losing Mike though. Richard's loyalty was primarily to himself and secondly to his family. Anyone else, including members of his staff, was way down the list. Besides, this chemist was a bit too bright and ambitious for Richard's comfort. If his development work carried on the way that it had to date, then Richard's own lack of competence would become a bit too apparent.

Richard was worried about discovery of his own computer usage. The numerous folders of extreme pornography (all obsessively labelled with the genre and source) could land him right in it.

"But we don't need him to check the others do we?" Richard pressed. "Quicker and cheaper if just the one?"

Geoff Bristow had already made up his mind. "You're right we could save a few quid, but I'm going to get them all checked just to be on the safe side."

"Good idea Geoff." Richard had to go along with the bosses' decision. "Just thinking about it though, there's a lot of sensitive tech and commercial info on them, and there's a lot of hazardous material in the lab, so we can't have someone in there on their own. We might be able to trust him to keep data confidential, but I'd feel a lot happier being present when he's in my lab."

"That's good of you Richard, but you don't have to."

"It's no problem. I can give him a hand. He won't know anything about our work and might miss something. Besides… I took Mike on and if I've made a mistake, then I'd rather sort it out myself. When's he due?"

"5.30, next Friday."

"I'll be there."

"That's good of you Richard. Thanks."

*

Richard spent the week moving his favourite images onto discs labelled 'formulations' and with other similarly bland or technical titles. He also checked out newsgroups to research how to wipe a computer. There were ways, but he was still worried that something could be found by an expert, or that a completely clear drive would look equally suspicious.

The light bulb moment came on the Thursday evening back at home. Feeling in need of some stimulating images for his own self-gratification, Richard picked up one of his Kodak boxes and opened it, only to find unexposed white photographic paper. After a reflexive, "Oh shit." at the thought of ruining an expensive load of paper by letting light in, he realised that this might be the solution to the problem. Just like mixing up the boxes, could he swap his computer with a clean one before the investigator arrived?

The plan was simple, but still had risks. What if Mike's PC did have something suspect on it? He'd just be swapping one dodgy computer for another. Could he check out the computer before swapping? Technically yes, but he didn't have the skills to find something hidden.

'So, do I know of a computer that is definitely clean?' he pondered. 'Of course; Jo's'. As the lab secretary, Jo was in full view all of the time and anything untoward would have been spotted instantly. While anyone might have something dodgy on their computer, hers was by far the lowest risk. 'Okay, I'll have Jo's' he decided. 'She gets Mike's and I'll just have to take the risk that if there is anything incriminating on it, then it's a problem that I'll have to sort separately. Mike gets mine and so be it, he'll have to be the scapegoat.'

5pm Friday arrived and Richard watched Mike and the rest of the team taking off their white lab coats and getting ready to go home.

"I'll lock up," Richard announced. "Got a bit more to do. Have a good weekend all."

Left alone, Richard looked at his watch. Just 25 minutes before the analyst was due. Should be plenty. He'd already disconnected the tangle of wires at the back of his own computer and now got to work on Mike's. Easy to do. But Jo's proved more of an issue. The first cable connector he tackled was held in place by two screws and while one came undone easily, the other firmly resisted his fingers. "Bugger this," he swore quietly, "have to come back to it. Must get the others sorted."

He felt perspiration starting to build as he carried his own black box over to Mike's desk. More from stress than effort. Computer, monitor, mouse and printer were quickly connected and to all appearances, this was now Mike's machine. Mike's real unit now needed to go to the secretary's desk but as he was carrying it over he heard the sound of the lab door opening.

"Fuck" he swore under his breath. He couldn't put the box anywhere in sight in this state; it wasn't connected up. He turned into his own office and put it on the desk, before coming out to greet the visitor, closing the door behind him.

"Evening," came a voice. "George White from Whitesand's looking for Richard Marsh."

"That's me," Richard replied. "I'm just finishing a bit of lab work. Can you come back in ten?"

"Don't worry, I won't get in your way. I'm here to look at the computer hardware. You are expecting me, aren't you?"

"Oh, yes. Sorry, a sample came in late, which is why I'm not quite ready for you. I just need a few minutes if you don't mind?"

The answer was given with surprising firmness, "I'll work around you. I can see one unit over there" – he was looking at Jo's – "I'll start on that one" – and immediately made his way over to her desk.

Richard could see he was beaten. 'Fuck, fuck, fuck,' he muttered inwardly. 'I'll have to have Mike's instead. Haven't a clue what's on it… But must get it connected up quick.'

"No problem." He said out loud. "I'll just be in my office here if you need me."

"Not playing with test tubes? I thought you were busy on something?"

"Oh yes," Richard was flustered, but managed to counter. "The reagents just need a few minutes to react. Just avoid the workbenches over there…" he pointed vaguely at the far end of the lab.

"Will do," came the distracted reply as George sat at the secretary's desk and turned on the computer.

Richard nipped back into his office and pushed the door shut. Connecting the cables he debated his next step. Should he check out Mike's computer? But then, if he did find anything, what could he do? If there was a lot, there's be no way he could safely sort it out. Even if there was just the odd file, could he safely delete it without there being any trace?

Before he could start to think about the answers, the door opened and George White stuck his head around and pointedly asked if Richard could help him.

"Of course," Richard replied following him over to Jo's desk.

"Can you talk me through this one?" George asked. "What exactly does this unit get used for? And, I need to know about these contacts…" – he pointed to a list on the screen – "to know if they're work related."

Half an hour later and the computer, and by extension Jo,

was signed off, all clear.

"Right. Next one," George instructed. "I've got two more on my list. Yours? And Laboratory Development? Point me in the right direction."

Richard decided it would be better to drop Mike in it straightaway and indicated the computer that had, until recently, been his own, watching nervously as it was fired up. Again the specialists fingers tapped away at the keyboard. Richard was about to escape back to his own office when he heard George say, "Oh dear. This isn't good. Mr Marsh, you'd better come and take a look."

Richard watched as his pornographic images were brought up onto the screen. Simple nudes, couples in extreme positions, close ups, some of his favourite ones, ones that he was sure he'd deleted, a deluge of flesh that was accompanied by George White's negative comments, "Definitely not right. Much worse than I've seen for a while. Oh dear. Oh dear…" Then, "I've seen more than enough. Let's finish off with your one."

"Do you still need to? We've covered the main ones?"

"Yes, strict instructions. Check them all. You may know what you've done with yours, but I have to check it in case anyone else has used it."

Richard's pulse raced as he watched the computer on his desk being turned on and checked. Deafening silence. Should he leave? He turned to go out of the door, the tension becoming too much for him.

"Hmmm…" he heard George say.

Richard turned around. He couldn't see what was on the

screen, just this snooper looking intently at it. "That's not good," he heard, and his heart sank. "Have a look at this."

Richard reluctantly made his way around the desk and looked at a screen covered with letters, numbers and symbols.

"This isn't right," George said.

Richard didn't know what was going on, and wasn't sure whether he wanted to. "Sorry, not with you," he said neutrally.

"Look…" George pointed at the screen, "this drive's nearly new but there's already bad sectors on it. Didn't you spot that it was struggling? And you must have lost data?"

"Is that all?" Richard asked far too fast.

George didn't notice Richard's manner and replied, "That all? Well it is serious. But yes, that's all."

Richard struggled to hide his relief as he watched the inspector continue to type for a couple of minutes and then turn the computer off. They talked briefly about what George had found and the report that he'd be sending to Mr Bristow, saying that one machine (Richard's) had a corrupt disk and a second (Mike's) corrupt contents.

Richard led him out of the building before returning to his office, sitting there for a good ten minutes recovering his composure. 'So far, so good,' he thought. 'Now to deal with the fallout. Get in quick…'

He picked up the phone and dialled the Bristow's home number. Lorna picked up and Richard had to pass some time in inane conversation with his mother-in-law before he could talk with Geoff.

"You were right," Richard got in fast. "You'll get the report from your consultant in due course, but I thought it best to let you know now. I'm going to have to let Mike go."

"What did they find?" Geoff sounded resigned. "Has he been leaking data? Who to?"

"No, it's a different problem. We've not lost anything. Well, we won't if I'm careful with how I handle his dismissal."

"Sorry, not with you?" Geoff queried.

"It wasn't work related. Unfortunately, he was accessing pornography."

"Oh. Well, I suppose we should be glad in some ways." Geoff sounded relieved. "I'll just have to deal with him on Monday."

This was not what Richard wanted. Mike would, of course, deny everything and could potentially drop Richard in it if he pushed for further examination of the computers. "No, leave it with me," Richard insisted, "it's my department."

"Okay. But if you need any help, just let me know. And how are you going to stop him going to a competitor?"

Richard had an answer lined up. "We've got a confidentiality agreement with him as part of our standard employee terms and I'll tell him that as long as he keeps to this, then we'll give him a good reference and a payoff. But it'll probably have to be something like six months' salary if we're going to stop him going straight to the competition."

"You know I don't like buying people off." Geoff sounded reluctant, "But I'll leave it to your discretion. Look, you and I both know that as long as he can keep schtum about the latest lab work for a few months, we'll be alright. Just try to minimise the cost and hassle please."

"Will do." A relieved Richard said, and then to tie up the last loose end, added: "There was another minor issue."

"What now?" said Geoff, irritated.

"My own computer has a technical glitch and it's still within warranty. No big thing, but I'm going to have to send it for repair."

"Is that all?" Geoff replied, unknowingly echoing Richard's earlier reaction. "I'll leave that with you."

"Thanks, no problem." The final pieces of Richard's hastily drawn up plan clicked into place. He could swap the computers back, copy Mike's work onto his own, and take some of the credit for the development work. Mike's box could go off for repair, come back clean and usable for the next member of staff.

Sacking Mike could be tricky. Richard couldn't tell him that they'd found porn. Mike would know this to be a lie and could cause problems by challenging his dismissal. Similarly, Richard couldn't use the much-used line that money was tight, 'last one in, first one out,' and so on. No, Maypharm had recently posted good profits. What about a reduced departmental budget? Again, not a winner as he wouldn't be able to advertise for a replacement chemist without the risk of Mike seeing it and taking them to court for unfair dismissal. Richard would have to think of something over the weekend...

Moving on though, he'd have to cut out his work-time perusal of stimulating images. Maybe get a computer at home? He'd have to find a way of keeping the contents away from his wife and daughters, but that shouldn't be too much of a challenge.

The weekend went by all too fast and soon Richard was

addressing the unlucky chemist.

"Morning Mike, hope you had a good weekend," he started, pressing on before Mike could answer. "Look, I'm sorry, but we have a bit of a problem."

"Problem?" Mike didn't look concerned.

"Yes. I'm afraid so." He paused for effect and then produced printouts of some of Mike's work. "Can you have a look at the experimental results on the second and third pages?"

Mike took the papers. After a couple of minutes he started to look worried and then said, "This isn't right. The acetic results at the end don't tie in with my assays here…"

"That's what I thought," Richard said. "Your conclusions aren't supported by the raw data."

Mike didn't know that Richard had got in early in order to change some of the dozens of lab results and blustered, "Yes, I can see it's wrong. Ur, I'll go back to my lab books to check it."

"No need," Richard replied. "I've checked a couple already and there were more discrepancies. Too many. Look, I don't know if this is just transposition errors or whether you've felt it necessary to change raw data to suit your results, but it's not acceptable." Richard couldn't give the dejected chemist a chance to argue his case so ploughed on. "I'm really sorry about this Mike, but we're going to have to let you go."

Mike started to protest, but Richard put his hand up to stop him. "I know this is a disappointment for you," he said with some degree of understatement, "but it's not something we can do anything about. Look, I like you and can see you're a good worker. You've got a great career ahead of you if you can take this all on board."

Again, he stopped Mike from replying and went on, "I don't like seeing anyone leave us, and we try to be as generous as we can. There's a healthy severance payment. Subject, of course, to a couple of minor points."

As he hoped, the prospect of a pay-off deflected Mike's line of thought over the argument he was about to put. Instead, he just asked, "What points?"

"Well, a chemist with your qualifications isn't going to have any difficulty getting another position, but we have to take into account that you have a lot of confidential information in your head."

Mike, already feeling that his professionalism had been called into question, protested, "What? You think I'd pass it on?"

"No…" Richard had again got this reply lined up. "I know that you can be trusted, but the compliance team here don't know you, and they require you to sign a further non-compete agreement. If you're happy to do that, then the settlement would be a full six months' salary instead of the four weeks which is all we have to give you legally."

Mike could see that a simple signature would gain him five months' salary. He'd also made contacts through the '.sci' newsgroups and was as sure as he could be that he'd find something in a matter of weeks. Maypharm was okay, but Richard was a shitty boss as far as Mike was concerned. He accepted the terms.

Documents were signed and Richard moved on, free of any taint from the affair. He didn't really care that he'd cost a young man his job, or his employer a significant amount of money. He was in the clear and his mind was already wandering as he glanced through the meeting room window towards the receptionist bending over to pick something up, oblivious to Richard's lecherous gaze.

*

Richard went on to buy a Packard Bell Computer with a Pentium processor working at a hefty (for the time) 133 MHZ, complete with 1.3 GB hard disk, 15 inch CRT monitor, DVD-ROM drive, external modem, and numerous features which sounded good when pushed by the sales rep who could see a healthy commission on the horizon.

Back in his study, after several hours of work, swearing and sweating; opening large boxes, crawling around the floor connecting up wires, loading software, looking up error codes in incomprehensible instruction books, deleting software, reloading software, phoning the shop and following their instructions, it was eventually all working.

Checking that his family were otherwise occupied (they'd given up watching the new toy being installed some time ago), Richard closed the door and resumed his perusal of the ever-growing world of internet porn.

Evenings of optical stimulation led to fresh and arousing images being at the front of Richard's mind come bedtime. Bedtimes when Victoria continued to reject his advances. Bedtimes when he lay in the dark wondering how it could be that every other woman he saw online was willing to do this, that and everything else, whereas his wife was about as sexually willing as a pre-menopausal nun with a hangover.

Going to the camera club once or twice a month was the maximum he was getting away with, and on the way home there would be about half an hour at any one of the dozen or so sites that he'd now identified as giving good bedroom views. Increasingly though, he was finding the glimpses caught through the lens inferior to the online pictures taken by other voyeurs.

CHAPTER 7

BOBBY GOLDSBORO. "Summer (The First Time)"

A general malaise had settled on Richard, when in the spring of '98, Victoria unexpectedly suggested that, as the girls were now ten and less of handful, "How about having another holiday in France? Rather than another year of wet Devon?"

"Great idea!" Richard responded enthusiastically, thinking of the beach babes of Cannes. "What had you in mind?"

"Well, Mummy and Daddy are renting a place in Normandy in July and said there's room for us as well."

Not what he had in mind. He'd never been to northern France (apart from driving through Calais on honeymoon) and thought it wouldn't differ much from the wet, overdressed, British beaches. Staying in a house would mean no rest from domestic drudgery and sharing it with the in-laws would definitely inhibit Victoria from anything sexual in case the occasional squeak of a bedspring was heard by her parents.

On the other hand… it should be cheaper. Maybe the in-laws would babysit some of the time, and if Victoria had already discussed it with them, it was a fait accompli and he'd be safer accepting it.

"Sounds good," he replied, unable to smile at the obvious happiness this brought to Victoria's face. They'd both been a bit tired and generally down for a while. A holiday would do them good.

*

As usual, Victoria took over the planning. Richard went off to work each day and on his return would find some detail or other sorted. New shorts, T-shirts, sunglasses and other essentials all miraculously appeared out of nowhere and before he knew it, they were driving into the car park of Folkestone Eurostar terminal.

"You going to take the girls to the loos while I sort out the headlamps?" he asked.

"Yep. You've got the beam deflectors haven't you?" Victoria replied.

"Uh, no. Didn't you get them?" An innocent question, but Victoria was in a mood again.

"No, you were going to get them," she snapped. "Couldn't you even remember that one thing?"

Richard felt the mood deteriorating further and went off

to buy them from the terminal shop. Purchases of two sets followed. He put the first on in the wrong position and then found that they couldn't be reused, prompting further derision from Victoria. A further £5 and ten minutes later the family sat in the car. The mood subdued.

Their boarding slot was called and they drove towards the train. Getting nearer, Richard saw height barriers over the road. One comparatively high, the next lower and the last lower still. All, he knew, were just above the height of their car. An ill-judged sense of mischief settled on him as he sought to rekindle the holiday atmosphere.

He called to the girls, "Those barriers look a bit low. I hope the car doesn't hit them."

Having gained the attention his passengers, he accelerated, laughing inwardly as they went under the first bar and the girls and his wife instinctively ducked. Still accelerating, the second barrier resulted in the same reaction. As they reached the third, Victoria screamed.

As he knew it would, the car passed under easily.

"What the fuck do you think you're doing?!" she yelled at him; language that she never would usually employ, especially in front of the girls.

"What do you mean?" he retorted. "There was plenty of room."

"That was stupid!" she continued, visibly upset. "If you think that was funny, then you're even more ignorant and emotionally retarded than I thought."

Richard could only manage a quiet, "Sorry," and the rest of

the journey was completed in tense silence, only punctuated by occasional comments from the back seat about how silly daddy was.

*

The house was set above the eastern side of Arromanches. A solid, two-storey detached family house built in the last 30 or 40 years. Yellow-grey stone walls, white shutters and flat garden, complete with a small swimming pool cut into the hillside. Inside was comfortably furnished with four bedrooms and bathrooms. Geoff and Lorna were already settled in, having arrived a few days before and they showed the new arrivals around as if it was their own home. Luggage unloaded and wardrobes filled with holiday wear, the six of them walked down the hill to the town centre with Victoria chatting to her mum, the girls with their grandad and Richard trailing slightly behind. It wasn't as bad as he'd expected. About 30C in the shade and in bright sunlight Richard could see the sea twinkling half a mile away. They passed a few small shops and arrived in the market square. Geoff pointed out the D-Day museum and a couple of restaurants that he'd already been to.

"It's bound to rain one day," Richard declared. "Let's save the museum until then. I'm sure the girls would like a look at the beach."

The beach had a few sunbathers and kids on it, as well as some people looking at the huge concrete remains of the Mulberry artificial harbour built by the Allies after the D-Day landings. Impressive structures, even with the somewhat objectionable smell of rotting seaweed inside them.

Geoff Bristow pleaded a need for something to drink and the three generations retired to a seafront restaurant for burgers (Emma and Lucy), salad (Victoria), moules (Lorna) and steak (Richard and Geoff), plus a couple of carafes of red and white wine.

The evening was spent in convivial conversation and eventually they all turned in. In their bed, Richard slid his hand up Victoria's thigh.

"You've got to be joking after what you did earlier," she snapped at him. Clearly her good mood was reserved for everyone else.

The next day was spent in Arromanches. They all went to the museum (no one but Richard wanting to wait for a wet day), but even he had to admit to finding it interesting with its eclectic mix of militaria. Then to another bar / restaurant for further liberal quantities of food and drink. Richard didn't even bother trying anything at bedtime. Victoria's body language was not positive.

The long sands to the east, codenamed 'Gold' during the Normandy Landings, were their next destination. The six family members, plus beach kit, couldn't all fit in one car so they split up and Geoff led the way with Victoria and the girls as passengers, while Richard followed with Lorna.

Richard and his mother-in-law got on well and chatted often, but it was rare that they were able to talk without others around.

Shortly into the drive, Lorna spoke quietly, "I hope you don't mind me asking this, and I don't want to put you in an awkward position, but what does Geoff talk about when you're with him in the pub and at work?"

Confused by the question, Richard replied, "All the usual things I suppose, Lorna. You know, work, family and all that. Why'd you ask?"

"Oh, I don't know. It's just that he's been a bit, well, secretive and quiet lately. There's nothing wrong with the company is there?

Richard didn't know of any company issues, and said so, adding, "He seems the same as usual to me."

Lorna changed the subject, talking about the girls and Richard made no attempt to bring it back to her husband's behaviour, but as they arrived at the beach, Lorna turned to him and quietly said, "You won't mention our chat to him, will you?"

"Of course not. I'll keep mum." He smiled at this pun.

Long and wide, the beach was clean and the sand warm underfoot. They set up the usual towels, chairs, and all of the excessive accoutrements that are somehow needed to survive just a few hours of doing not-a-lot. There was a smattering of other families spread around and before long Richard and his daughters were enjoying a game of beach tennis, with him losing against the two of them.

Later he found himself alone; the in-laws were both snoozing in deckchairs and the others down by the water. He wandered off for a mooch along the beach, enjoying the peace and tranquillity so lacking in his day-to-day life. He was also enjoying passing a bit closer than he should do to the occasional topless sunbather and regretting the lack of a camera, when he realised that the couple directly ahead were both totally naked. And there were other naked couples and singles further on. This was more like it.

Walking on, he discreetly looked at the various bodies, while reflecting that sunglasses were a great way of watching without being too obvious. Despite this, he became conscious of frowns from some sunbathers as he went by. Realisation hit; here, wearing trunks made him the odd one out. He should take them off to avoid causing further irritation. He wasn't too worried about anyone seeing him naked, but what if he got an erection? 'Worth the risk,' he thought as he stripped off, 'just to see more.' It felt odd. It felt very odd. Cool wind on bits that were never usually exposed and, if anything, he felt his penis shrivelling rather than getting embarrassingly big.

Walking further into an area where there was plenty to look at, he used the shorts as a makeshift, albeit very small, towel and sat down, marvelling in how free and natural it felt.

A good ten minutes later, while engrossed in trying to make out the details of someone who was just a bit too far away for him to see clearly, he was startled by a "bonjour!" from behind him. Turning around, he found himself looking directly at a neatly trimmed pubic triangle less than a metre away. He looked up, shielding his eyes from the glare of the sun, which hit him from just to the side of the owner of the pubes. A woman of a similar age was saying something in French. "Excuse-moi, je ne comprehends," he tried to say in schoolboy French.

"O, you are English?"

"Yes, Oui, sorry my French is not good."

"Non, I should say sorry for – uh – disturbing you." Her French accent making the words sensuous.

"No," he apologised again in the British way. "It's fine. How can I help?"

"I'm sorry," she repeated. "I was just asking if the, um, how you say, chien, um dog, is yours?" She pointed at a nondescript mongrel snuffling around a few metres away.

"No, not mine," he replied, surprised at how his body just about managed to avoid embarrassing him. "Why do you ask?"

"I am worried, what is the word? It is lost?"

"Oh, I see, No, it's okay. I saw it with the people over there…" He pointed.

"Merci," she replied. She looked as if she was about to walk away, then hesitated. "Je, I mean I am Christine."

"Richard, pleased to meet you." He smiled. "Are you local?"

"Oui, very close. And you?"

As their small talk continued, she moved around more in front of him. Richard desperately tried to avoid being obvious as he glimpsed the opening between her legs parting as she sat down. He could feel a slight stirring so tore his eyes away. 'Don't look there,' he said to himself, 'look up,' and then felt even more at risk as his eyes ranged across her pert breasts.

Trying to avoid being obvious, he placed one arm across his exposed crotch. She noticed the movement and laughed saying, "I think you are not so used to naturiste?"

Flustered again. "You're right, it's not very common in the UK."

"C'est bien. It is natural. You Anglais are too, um, worried!"

Despite his best attempts, Richard felt the beginnings of an erection. He tried to think about something, anything else, but the old joke was right, an erection is like the theory of relativity; the more you think about it, the harder it gets.

He could see Christine looking directly at his penis, a grin on her face, as it grew. She laughed, "You are married? Non?"

"Yes, I am," he admitted.

"Well, your wife is a very happy woman I think." She smiled. "He is very healthy. Malhereusement, my, um mari, husband is not so healthy."

"Thank you," Richard managed, then amazed by his own lack of discretion, "but I think my wife would like your husband. My wife does not like a healthy husband."

"Oh, Je, I am sorry to see this, it is a pity."

"I think your husband is very lucky." Again, Richard surprised himself being more forward than usual and making no attempt to hide that he was looking at her breasts. He continued, "If I was your husband, I would be very healthy all of the time."

"And I would be happy," she laughed, "but now, excuse-moi, I must continue my walking."

"That's a shame. I am enjoying your company. Will you be here again? Maybe tomorrow?"

"Maybe yes, maybe non." She smiled as she got up. "Au revoir."

"Au revoir…" he replied happily to her bare bum as it wiggled into the distance.

After five minutes, he felt that the swelling had subsided enough for him to be able to stand up without embarrassment.

A further quarter of an hour and he was back to the family's pile of towels trying not to grin too much. Geoff and Lorna were still basking in their chairs and Victoria was playing some ball game with the girls. Spotting her husband, she said something to her daughters and waved for him to come to her as she walked towards a quieter part of the beach.

"You've been a while," she said. "I was getting concerned. Anything up?"

"Not now," he couldn't resist replying.

She gave him a quizzical look and went back to the girls.

The rest of the afternoon and evening progressed as if nothing had happened. Family games, a meal at another restaurant, Richard and Victoria playing cards before turning in for the night. Getting undressed, Richard was thinking back over his earlier encounter and didn't care that Victoria could see that he was aroused. As usual though, she just ignored it, and his needs.

They went back to the beach the next couple of days, and on both of them Richard smoothly extricated himself for another walk along the beach. Plenty to look at, but no sign of Christine.

The following day was cloudy and Richard's suggestion of the beach was dismissed. Instead, they spent the day walking around Bayeux and some of the massive military cemeteries in the local area.

Their break in Arromanches was drawing to a close when they returned to Gold Beach for the last time. Richard didn't really expect to see Christine again, but he could hope. He walked the length of the beach several times over the day, but as before, not a sign of her. They all returned to the house for showers and to get changed before going out to eat.

Sitting around a large table in yet another bar-cum-restaurant, Richard reprised their break in his head. He'd been wrong; it was a great place to be, the accommodation had worked well and the company – especially the unexpected local company – had been great. His reverie was disturbed when the waitress came over and smiling, handed out the menus. It hit him like an express train when he looked up and realised that it was Christine.

As she handed him a menu she smiled, saying, "Menu monsieur? We have some healthy plates if you like…"

No one seemed to have noticed his reaction to seeing the waitress, or thought anything odd about what she'd said, and they all got down to choosing their masticatory targets for the evening. Christine returned to take their orders, deliberately leaving Richard's to last, the others now chatting amongst themselves.

"And what would monsieur enjoy?" she asked, teasing.

Richard would have loved to come back with a quip about having a French hen and plenty of stuffing, but didn't dare in case it was picked up by anyone else. Instead, he simply chose a fairly standard dish whilst discreetly trying to indicate to her the door labelled WCs opposite. She took the menus and orders to the bar and then to Richard's delight made her way through the door as he'd hoped. He excused himself from the table and went through the same door to find Christine standing at a washbasin on the other side, playing with her hair. On seeing him enter, she smiled and without a word walked into the cubicle marked "F" leaving the door wide open. He followed her into the small space, and shut the door behind them. His heart was going nineteen to the dozen and he didn't know what to say or do. He needn't have worried.

Christine took hold of his hand, lifted her skirt, and pressed it between her knickerless legs. Richard's fingers burrowed deep inside her as he felt her undoing his zip. In seconds, his trousers and pants were round his ankles and she was gripping his rigid cock, hand moving up and down.

"You have un préservatif?" she whispered. 'Preservative??' He thought, 'What the fuck does she mean?'

"Er…" was all he could manage to say.

"Préservatif," she repeated, "for sex."

Click, he realised she meant condom. Oh fuck… "Non."

"Ahh, okay. Seulement la pipe, monsieur?"

Again, not a clue, but so what, "Er, yes, oui."

Somehow he found himself standing there, his back against the cubicle wall looking down at her as she bent over his groin, his hand over her naked backside with his fingers dipping into her vulva, her lips kissing the tip of his penis. In ecstasy, he felt her lips slowly envelop his erection, taking it into her hot mouth. It was all he could do just to remain standing as he felt her start to suck, moving her mouth up and down, her tongue stimulating the end, and her teeth gently grazing against his glans. Her hand moved around his balls and he couldn't hold back. He came urgently in her mouth.

She carried on sucking for a moment or two before standing

up, looking him directly in the eyes and licking her lips. Without a word she rearranged her clothing, opened the cubicle door and left, closing it behind her.

Richard stood there, trousers around his ankles and senses battered by the events. Coming back down to earth, he pulled up his pants and trousers, flushed the loo and opened the cubicle door, only to come face to face with Victoria. The blood drained from his face. How long had she been there? What had she seen?

"You do know you're in the ladies, don't you?" She laughed, seemingly unaware of the earlier events and relishing his error.

"Oh god, I wasn't was I?" he pretended, glad that such an error would disguise his discomfort and knowing that it would probably be the basis for more than the odd taunt in the future. But so what! Bloody hell was it worth it!

Over the course of the evening, Christine continued to act in a friendly and professional manner with all of the customers, but she and Richard managed to surreptitiously catch each other's eye from time to time. The Bristow / Marsh table had finished their main courses, and another good quantity of wine, when she arrived bearing dessert menus. Arriving back at Richard last again, she carefully opened it for him at an angle so that only he could see her thumb holding a small piece of paper. Surreptitiously, he took the note and slipped it into his pocket. He couldn't get away with looking at it at the table, so took himself off to the conveniences again.

It was a business card for the restaurant. On the back, handwritten, "Encore?" followed by a smiley face, a telephone number and an address. It was signed "Christine xxx." Richard tucked the card back into his pocket and returned to the table. Eventually, the bill arrived and, as usual, Geoff Bristow pulled out his credit card to pay.

Christine asked, while looking at Richard, "I hope everything was good?"

"Definitely," replied Richard. "I wish we could come back soon… but we go back to UK tomorrow…" hoping that Christine would understand both his desire and his apology.

She did: "You will be welcome toujours. Anytime."

That night, lying lonely next to Victoria as she slept, Richard relived the brief moments of the evening over and over in his mind. How her body had tightened around his fingers as they entered her, the feel of her lips on him, so much more sensual than anything he'd felt before, how intense his orgasm was, and how she'd looked at him afterwards. A camera would have recorded only a fraction of it. It was the feelings that he wanted again. Craved.

'Sorry Victoria,' he thought in the darkness of torment and loneliness. 'If you won't do it, then I'm going to have to find someone else who will.

CHAPTER 8

THE WHO. "Who Are You?"

Back in Twyford, Richard fantasised about ways he could meet Christine again, whilst knowing that it wasn't to be. He looked at the restaurant card that she'd given him. "Sorry love," he said quietly as he went to crumple it up, but then changed his mind and hid it away in his desk.

Back to the perpetual quandary of how to meet someone new. Someone just for sex, whilst also keeping his marriage and life steady. Going with a prostitute was still bottom of the list as there were too many risks compared to the comparatively limited experience that his money would buy. Having an affair was still risky, but potentially a lot more fulfilling. But a risk worth taking? At the same time he didn't have any idea of how to meet someone. 'Surely there must be some way,' he frequently found himself musing. Unable to resolve the problem. Richard poured himself into the routine of work, looking after the family, Sunday lunch at the Bristows, and when the chance arose, after-dark camera and online forays.

Meanwhile, another storm was brewing.

Richard had forgotten about Lorna Bristow's holiday enquiry about her husband's conversations and activities until one evening in August, after the girls had gone to bed, Victoria said, "Mummy's worried about daddy."

"In what way?" Richard replied.

"She thinks he's up to something."

"What sort of something?"

"She doesn't know." Victoria paused, nibbling on the end of a fingernail. "She's worried that there's a problem at work. You don't know anything do you?"

"No, nothing springs to mind. But she did ask me the same thing when we were on holiday. I would have told you, but she asked me not to."

"So, the company is safe, you think?"

"Definitely. I've seen the latest figures. They look fine. And I can't see your dad fiddling the books. Can you?"

"I don't know what it is…" another long pause, "but I've been thinking."

This was a phrase that Richard always feared. "I've been thinking," usually preceded a major problem or change in his life, and was usually something that he could do nothing about beyond suffering in silence.

Victoria continued, "The girls will be at moving up to

secondary school shortly and I don't need to be here all day. I think I should return to my old job. If there's anything going on, I'll soon spot it."

Richard didn't like this. He'd end up doing more housework, and more to the point, there was a significant reason that he didn't want her back in the accounts department.

He broached the first of these worries, the safer one. "Okay, but you do an awful lot around the house. How will you find the time for it all on top of work?"

"Oh, I'm not worried about the cleaning and so on," she replied. "We can do that together," confirming his worry.

The bigger concern was that while searching for anything that Geoff was up to, Victoria might come across his own well-kept secrets. Several accounting fiddles that she must not find.

Richard had seen how easy it was to sign off a dodgy invoice when he'd used Dave Fletcher to launder the modelling fee some time back. Since then, there had been a steady succession of small invoices which he'd forged and then signed off. The amounts weren't large; just the odd hundred quid here and there to pay for subscriptions to XXX porn sites and for additional reels of film and paper so that Victoria didn't know the true extent of his hobby.

The current Maypharm accounts team just accepted his purchase orders and signed off invoices at face value. Victoria was another matter. Richard knew her to be far more diligent and inquisitive, and if she was actively looking for something wrong, then the "Roger Francis" account could be his downfall.

Roger Francis was the name that Richard had used to open

a bank account that Victoria didn't know about. Roger Francis Ltd was the name of the company on the invoices. Roger Francis didn't exist.

The account had taken some work to set up. Richard had needed a name and address that couldn't be traced back to him but that would pass the bank's security checks.

He'd realised how to get a name when watching an old spy film. Going through the "Deaths" column in the local paper, he found an announcement for a man of about the same age as himself and purchased a copy of the birth certificate for the man, Roger Francis, from the Registrar's Office.

The address had been easy. All he had had to do was pop into a newsagents in nearby Reading, who for five pounds per month, would hold any mail addressed to "Roger Francis" for him to collect later.

Next Richard printed off a photo of himself and attached it to a passport application form. The photo had to be signed on the back by a qualified person who could confirm that it was a true likeness of Roger Francis. Richard's qualifications were sufficient to do this and Richard duly certified that Roger existed. This was, potentially, the only risky part of the process so far. But over several years of signing other people's passport applications, Richard had never been contacted by any official to check the declaration.

With a passport, birth certificate and address, Richard had sufficient to open a bank account in the name of Roger Francis.

The original motivation was money, but the thrill of being someone else, someone unknown and anonymous for his subversions and perversions, had also given Richard the appetite to extend the identity. He'd taken a driving test under the new name and generally amassed all the pieces of paper needed to establish this whole new identity.

The Roger Francis account was more than good enough to pass the day-to-day scrutiny of Maypharm's accounts team. But if Victoria was actively looking for something amiss, then the account and the whole of Richard's alternative persona were at risk.

Unfortunately for all concerned, four weeks later Victoria resumed her job at Maypharm.

*

Driving home from work a couple of weeks after Victoria's return to work, she suggested to Richard that they stop and have a drink at the pub. This was out of character; Victoria usually wanted to get home and relieve her mum of childminding duties and get back to being queen bee.

"Let's find a quiet table," Victoria suggested and they cosied up in the far corner of the pub. But this wasn't a prelude to deeper physical contact. Instead, Victoria quietly told Richard, "I've been looking at the books."

"Okay. And?"

"And I think there's a problem."

His heart sank. "Right, what's the problem."

"Well, actually I think there's several problems." She looked away from the table. "I think that a couple of people have been fiddling expenses, but that's not the main thing."

Richard just nodded, waiting for whatever bombshell was about to be lobbed at him.

"You know daddy does the weekly suppliers visits?" Victoria continued.

"Yes," he replied, breathing an inward sigh of relief. Not something to do with Richard Francis Ltd.

"Well, are they all in the same place?"

"Sorry," he replied. "What do you mean?"

"Are they all in Milton Keynes? Or do the supplier meetings take place elsewhere?"

"Well, I think Arcalside are in Milton Keynes, and they're one of the big ones."

"Yes, I know," she sounded stressed, "but Daddy visits other suppliers as well, doesn't he?"

"I guess so. What are you getting at?"

She spoke quietly. "It's just that he's always staying at a hotel there. Virtually every week."

Richard pondered, "Arcalside's a big supplier. They've come from nowhere to being our main supplier of excipients in only a year."

"Yeah, I saw that. But that's only a fraction of what we buy…" She looked down at her small glass of wine. "It gets worse. He always stays at the same hotel out in the middle of nowhere. The hotel bills just have a total for everything and don't break it down into room and food, and so on, but it's always a lot. Couple of hundred per night."

"Well…" said Richard cautiously. "What do you think?"

"Well, he's either getting backhanders from Arcalside, and I can't see that being enough to warrant a weekly visit."

"Or?"

"Or he's seeing someone up there."

The silence hung in the air as she looked at her drink.

"I don't think your dad would do that," Richard said, thinking the opposite,

"I don't know what to think," she said in a small voice, trying to keep back the tears. "What should we do?"

Richard noted that it was "we" rather than "I." Whether that was good or bad, he didn't know.

"Well," he considered, "we shouldn't go making accusations without any evidence. Don't say anything to your mum…"

He thought it over. If Geoff Bristow was caught having an affair, then the family repercussions would be bad. On the other hand, he thought 'if I can rescue the situation, then I'll be well and truly in everybody's good books… pay rise… wifely nookie…'

"Tell you what," he said, "although I don't think he would do anything wrong, I'll have a quiet chat at the pub on Sunday. Sound him out. Can you hold back saying anything to anyone until after then?"

"Yes… thank you," she replied quietly.

They finished their drinks and returned home to the normal hullabaloo of two ten year olds and their doting grandma, all oblivious to the forthcoming storm.

Later, in bed, Richard felt Victoria's hand move onto his leg. "You can, if you want to," she said.

*

Sunday came. As did Richard when, for the first time ever, Victoria initiated wake-up sex. After this she reminded her husband of the conversation he needed to have at the pub. Clearly, the sex was just a way of stopping him from pulling out of the chat.

"As if I could forget," he smiled at her; the post-coital endorphins overwhelming his foreboding.

Richard tackled his father-in-law after the second pint, when he hoped he'd be more receptive to what was to follow.

"Geoff… Not sure how to put this…"

"Put what?" Geoff somehow managed to say at the same time as sinking another large mouthful of Brakspears Bitter.

"Look. I don't want to bring this up. But I think that there's something you ought to know…"

"Uh-huh?"

"I'm sure that it's nothing, but I think Victoria may have misinterpreted something that she noticed at work. It's something to do with your stays at Flitwick Manor?" Richard stopped to let Geoff react.

Eventually the reply came, "Right. I see."

An age later, Geoff continued, "I can trust you, can't I?"

"Yes."

"What's she said?"

"Just that you stay there a lot more often than you should do."

"Yes, but is she saying that I'm doing anything in particular?"

Richard thought before replying. "She doesn't know. She just thinks that there's something wrong. Look, she wanted to talk to Lorna about it, but I said I'd talk to you first. You know, in case there's an innocent explanation."

"Thank you. I really appreciate that. It's good that one of you two is willing to talk to me." Richard basked in the faint praise that was coming his way. Geoff looked at Richard. "I'll be straight with you. Yes. There's problems at home. You know that. If Victoria is anything like her mother, then I guess you have the same problems… I'm surprised either of us have kids…"

Richard felt now was the time to go into man-to-man mode. An angle that didn't fit with him usually, but needs must.

"Yes. You're right. I guessed that was where she got it from." Richard dived in further. "So, you're having an affair?"

"Yes."

"Want to get it off your chest? Or should I avoid that part of the problem?"

"No, I'd like to talk about it. Strictly between you and me though."

"Of course, Geoff."

There was a long silence which Richard broke, asking: "So who is she? How did you meet?"

"Name's Dawn. She's one of the reps at Arcalside. Lovely girl. She's the one who came to see us, to introduce them. We just hit it off from first meeting."

Richard realised that he knew who Dawn was. He'd seen her a couple of times in the early days of the Arcalside business when he'd had to discuss technical specifications and QC with them. He guessed she was still in her thirties? Young enough to be Geoff's daughter. She looked okay, but not the sort he'd expect his father-in-law to go for. "Umm… what's the situation? Is this a brief fling that we can sweep under the carpet?"

"You mean, am I going to continue seeing her?"

"Yes, I suppose that's the question. And also what do I tell Victoria?"

Geoff finished his pint. "I'll need something stronger first. Mine's a large scotch on the rocks if you'd like to get them in." He passed Richard the money.

With new drinks in place, Geoff Bristow went on. "Right. Situation is that, to put it bluntly, she's the best thing to have happened to me since god knows when, and I'm not going to give up my happiness because my daughter's moral code is stricter than Mary Whitehouse's."

Richard was temporarily distracted by memories of how the anti-permissive society campaigner Mary Whitehouse's name had been hijacked for a pretty good (in his opinion) soft-corn porn magazine. Richard had a copy of *Whitehouse* hidden away. In Kodak box number four, if he remembered rightly.

Geoff continued. "Do you think that Victoria can be persuaded to not say anything?"

"Not if I know my wife," Richard apologised. "And even if she said that she'd keep quiet, knowing her, she'd still manage to let it slip. Accidentally, of course."

The two men sat in silence.

"So, if you're still going to be up at the crack of Dawn," said Richard, trying to put some light into the conversation, "the cat's going to get out of the bag sooner or later."

"Yes."

"I can probably get Victoria to hold back for a while. Maybe a week or two. But sooner or later, you're going to have to come clean."

"Hmm."

"Unless…" Richard allowed the silence to build, then continued, "Unless, that is, I can persuade her that you're not having an affair?"

"Good luck in that!"

"No, I'm serious. What if I persuaded her that you had a genuine reason for being there so often?"

"Such as?"

"Well…" Richard smiled a little, "Just as a suggestion. What if Maypharm were in the process of buying out Arcalside and only you and the Board were in on it at the moment? There'd be plenty of reasons not just for being up there, but also for your silence about it…."

Geoff thought for a moment. "Bloody good one… Yes… maybe Vicky would swallow it. You'd have to swear her to silence, supposedly to protect the deal… I can go on up there for a while, then find another way of seeing Dawn, and then just say that the deal fell through…"

Geoff paused again and grinned at Richard. "God, you're devious! In a good way that is. Thank you! I think this calls for another double. On me."

The two slightly drunk men staggered back to the dinner table half an hour later than usual, grinning and talking over-loudly about some idiot that they'd seen on the pub TV. Victoria looked expectantly at Richard and he gave her a thumbs-up sign. Not knowing whether this meant, "Yes, all's okay," or, "Yes, he's up to something," she walked over to Richard, grabbed him by the arm and hissed, "I think a couple of minutes fresh air may be in order, darling?"

Richard let himself be led to the garden, whereupon he gave his overjoyed wife the excellent tale that he and Geoff had dreamt up.

"Of course, I won't say a word to anyone!" Victoria promised before giving Richard the longest kiss that he could remember in recent years, before adding, "You stink! I think we should keep the two of you off the wine at lunch."

Victoria drove them home later and Richard spent most of the evening asleep on the sofa. Later, there was another first when Victoria rewarded him for the second time in one day.

*

It didn't last. Monday, and legs-together mode resumed as the norm. Richard was undoubtedly the blue-eyed boy at work, but back home he was back to being Mr Unnoticed (except when something needed doing).

It went dramatically downhill just before Christmas. Lorna Bristow got a card in the post with a jolly Santa on the front. But inside was a simple message that brought her world down around her ears. Under "Merry Christmas," printed in neat handwriting, was added, "Can you ask your husband to stop fucking my wife, then we can all have a Happy Christmas and good New Year."

Lorna thought briefly that it must be a joke. But deep down she knew.

An unprepared Geoff came home that evening to find the house empty and a single Christmas card in the middle of the table, together with a handwritten note from his wife: "I assume this is true. Finish it and we'll say no more about it."

Geoff sat there for the rest of the evening and eventually went to bed alone. Shortly after turning out the bedroom light, he heard the front door open and footsteps on the stairs. From the landing, Lorna said, "Leave the light out," and she entered the bedroom. She broke the dark silence with, "Well?"

Geoff had spent his adult life being the boss at work but intimidated at home. Finally, something had happened which forced him to change it all.

"I'm very sorry Lorna," he said unemotionally. "I did try. But however this works out, I am going to continue seeing Dawn."

"So that's her name is it? I don't need to know more."

"What are you going to do?" Geoff asked.

"What are we going to do, you mean," she replied. "*We* are going to have Christmas as normal and pretend nothing has happened. Then you are going to leave." Without giving him the chance to reply, she concluded, "I'm sleeping in the spare room tonight. You can tell me what you are going to do tomorrow."

Geoff left for work without seeing his soon-to-be-ex-wife. On getting into his office, he called Richard in and explained the situation.

"It's up to you how you handle it with Victoria," he said, "but Lorna wants what she calls a normal Christmas before the shit hits the pan properly. Thank you for all your help. I do appreciate it."

Richard felt he'd come out of it well with his boss, all things considered. His mother-in-law didn't know of his collusion, so that was okay. The girls would get over Grandma and Grandad's change in circumstances. Victoria was the difficult one. In the end, he kept quiet until Boxing Day, when he suggested to Victoria that they go for a walk while the girls were around at the Bristows, and broke the news as gently as he could. He claimed that Geoff had duped him as much as he had duped Lorna and insisted that he was totally in the dark until now. This being a story that Geoff had said he'd happily back up as a small thank you for Richard's earlier silence.

"But why did daddy do it?" a tearful Victoria asked.

"I'm sorry, but he told me that it was the only way he could be happy sexually."

"You fucking men!" Victoria snapped. "You're all the same. Like dogs! One sniff of a cunt and you'll go for it. Sod the consequences! Sod anyone else!" She angrily snatched her arm away from his and stomped off ahead.

Richard knew this mood all too well. But he also knew that left alone, she'd eventually calm down and everything would be back to normal, as if nothing had happened.

CHAPTER 9

THE PET SHOP BOYS. "It's A Sin"

Spring 1999 and Geoff moved out of his spacious marital home and into a flat ten miles away in Reading. The bachelor pad was soon also occupied by Dawn when she left her husband. Geoff and Dawn reached out to Victoria but she didn't want to know. She would talk to her father (no longer "daddy") at work, but avoided him elsewhere whenever she could. Of course, it wasn't that simple, as Geoff wanted to maintain his relationship with his grandchildren.

Lorna continued to live in the house that she'd shared with her husband and Victoria spent increasing amounts of time around there with the girls, occasionally even staying overnight. "Mummy needs me," being the usual reason.

Richard began to feel even more irrelevant than he had done

in the past. Victoria said that he was always welcome to go with her to Lorna's but he always seemed to be the one left out of the conversation. The unnoticed one in the corner.

The already occasional missionary position on a Saturday night had become a once-in-a-blue-moon event, but Victoria's absences with her mum did have the advantage of giving Richard more opportunity to go off on the prowl.

Increasingly, digital photography was taking over from conventional film. Richard resisted the change. As well as being a luddite at heart, he didn't believe that this new technology could give him anything as sharp and detailed as he got from his tried and tested Ilford film. This changed when at a camera club presentation, the local Nikon agent showed a photo of an illuminated clock tower, taken from quarter of a mile away at night, using the new Nikon D1. The image was way better than Richard could achieve with his current kit and he found himself tempted. That is until the price was mentioned. Around £5,000.

Richard came away from the evening with a strong desire to own a D1. On the usual post-club spying detour he realised that such a piece of kit would open up numerous low-light and far-away bedrooms which were, at the moment, closed to his hungry view.

Sitting in his office the next day, he pondered how to raise such a sum. There was no way Victoria would allow such an expense from the joint account and the Roger Francis account was down to just a few hundred pounds due to some recent online pornographic excesses. He was still well in with Mr Bristow, but didn't want to ask him for help. The departmental budget would more than cover it, but even if a camera was wanted in the lab, they could get by with one which cost a lot, lot less.

But maybe part of the departmental budget could be 'borrowed' or diverted…

Richard's previous fiddles had all been three figure sums, as any expense over one thousand pounds had to be countersigned by Geoff Bristow or another Director. 'So, one large fiddle or four or five smaller ones?' He wondered. There was just as much work in doing it, irrespective of value, so one large one should be easier. Apart from the countersignature issue, there'd also be four or five times less chance of a dodgy invoice being spotted, especially with Victoria now scrutinising all company invoices.

'What is there that the lab might spend £5,000 on?' he wondered.

'Consumables?' This was how he'd got some of the previous invoices through. Order up a load of glassware and keep the money. No auditor had ever asked how many beakers they had, and even if they had, he'd just say there had been some breakages. But 5K in consumables. No way he'd get that through.

It would have to be capital expenditure.

Computers was the first thought, after all, they were just anonymous grey boxes which could have cost any amount. But… there was no justifiable need for a new one.

Hi-tech lab equipment then? Gas chromatography, mass spectrometry, HPLC, all of these were pieces of kit that had five or six figure price tags. But they were all very noticeable items and ordering one and it not arriving would certainly be spotted.

This wasn't going to be easy.

Still pondering, he was interrupted by a knock on the door and Sarah, one of the junior lab assistants that he'd taken on – not so much because of her CV but because of her ample cleavage – came in.

"Sorry to disturb you," she said, "but the second benzo HPLC is playing up."

"No problem. I'll come and sort it out."

This piece of kit was one of two used to measure the level of benzodiazepines in their sleeping tablets. Unfortunately, it kept going out of spec. Really it should have been sent away for refurbishment or replaced ages ago, but he'd been putting this decision off as a refurb could be a couple of grand and replacing it, ten grand plus.

The obvious fiddle struck him: 'Get it refurbed and tell everyone that it's a new piece of kit when it comes back. Keep the difference. Could it work?'

Richard spent the afternoon working on the HPLC. He could have fixed it in half the time, but wanted to check it over more fully. Apart from a serial number, what difference would there be between the new and refurbished kit? Refurb would cover all working parts but it wouldn't deal with cosmetic differences, such as the scratches on the side or the small dent on the rear panel. If this was a car, then these sort of telltale signs would be easily covered…

Another light bulb moment…

Camera club Dave, who'd assisted with the modelling fee invoice, ran a car dealership. He'd be able to get the casing looking like new. 'Would he help again?' Richard speculated. If so, he'd have to know at least some of the details, but Richard had known Dave long enough now to know that he wasn't averse to the odd under the table deal. After all, most of the camera club members were driving cars from Dave's dealership; some having bought bargains without any VAT receipt, others driving cars whose histories were more than a little suspect.

Richard spent some days and a couple of phone calls getting everything in place.

Wesley Instruments quoted Maypharm for a new HPLC at £22,438. This was signed off by Geoff Bristow without any hitch. Maypharm's purchasing manager raised an order to go to Wesley Instruments Ltd and gave it to Richard to send off.

He put the order in the shredder.

The refurbishment company quoted D. Fletcher Ltd £3,400 to service a Wesley HPLC. D. Fletcher ltd placed their order and the lab benzo HPLC was hand delivered to them by Richard. They replaced all of the serviceable parts and called Richard to come and collect it.

They sent their bill to D. Fletcher Ltd.

The fully serviced benzo HPLC was delivered to the car dealership, where a technician, in return for a generous backhander, did the equivalent of knocking 70,000 miles off the clock of a car, returning an unscratched, undented, new looking Wesley HPLC to Richard, which he then delivered into the lab early one morning before the staff arrived.

Richard ordered some spares from Wesley Instruments. When their invoice arrived, it was scanned and Photoshopped to turn it into an invoice for a new Wesley HPLC, complete with bank details for Maypharm to pay into.

These bank details related to a certain car dealership's bank, rather than those of Wesley Instruments.

Maypharm paid £22,438 (+VAT) into the D. Fletcher car dealerships account thinking that they were paying Wesley Instruments.

D. Fletcher Ltd paid the refurbishment company £3,400 (+VAT)

The difference, £19,038 (+VAT), less an agreed commission, was paid into the Roger Francis' account.

All parties were happy with the deal, especially Richard, when he used some of his ill-gotten gains to buy a brand new Nikon D1.

*

Next Thursday, Richard didn't even bother with the camera club. He spent the whole evening night-testing the capabilities of his new piece of kit.

The results far exceeded his expectations.

He started off on a footpath behind a row of pre-war semis, all of which had gardens the length of an Olympic swimming pool. It was only just dark, but still dark enough for him to be invisible to anyone indoors. Looking through the viewfinder, he could see into both lit and unlit rooms. A woman watering a pot plant became his first test shot. Immediately though, there was a problem. Instead of the gentle click from a well-engineered shutter, a loud "beep" and the screen on the back of the camera lit up like a Belisha beacon. Richard retired to his car to play with the camera's settings. He didn't want to risk doing anything that might alert his unknowing targets.

He wasn't used to the menu system, but soon the camera was reset for night-time fun. It didn't make any sound, and it no longer lit up.

He returned to the footpath and spent a glorious half hour watching people in their homes, all of them unaware of the voyeur outside. There wasn't much happening. 'Maybe a bit too early,' he thought. But still, he'd got a nice one of a woman trying on a couple of blouses. Pity she was wearing a bra, but hey, you can't have everything. He tried a couple more locations with equally good results and was convinced that this camera would do him well for the foreseeable future.

Driving home, he noticed a Ford Fiesta disappearing off down a woodland track. Normally, he would have ignored this. He'd tried watching couples in their cars before, but it was always too dark. But maybe with the new camera?

He parked up and walked back to where the car had entered the woods. There was just about enough moonlight to enable him to make his way carefully down the track, trying to avoid barely visible mud and puddles.

Turning a corner, he could just about make out the car a little way in front, parked side on to his view. The windows were open (a plus in his view, having been defeated by steamed-up windows in the past) with the radio or CD player quietly playing Oasis. Through the lens he was pleased to find the light from the dashboard was sufficient to be able to see a young couple snogging. The guy's hands were on the girl's jumper, treating her breasts as if they were stress balls. Richard continued to watch as the lad pulled the jumper over his girlfriend's head, and wonder of wonders, the bra came off. There was just about enough light for Richard to make out her hard nipples and he pressed the shutter for a sequence to enjoy later.

As he watched, he saw the girl stiffen. She hadn't realised they were being watched, had she? Richard was ready to make a retreat when he heard the two of them start to argue. He couldn't make out the details, but she was obviously angry at something and it sounded like she was threatening to report him. It sounded like to the police? The lad's voice was more pleading than angry, but when Richard again raised the camera to take a closer look, he could see that the guy's hands were around the girl's throat. 'This is serious,' he thought, wondering what on earth to do. Years ago, he had wanted to witness the Barclay Park murderer. Now he didn't know whether to intervene and risk getting hurt, get out of there, or carry on watching. The voyeur in him won out and he took more pictures. She was still shouting, but clearly in difficulty. Richard stood his ground and watched her go silent and crumple before his eyes.

All was silent within the car. The headlights came on and the engine started. If the car turned his way, then Richard would be clearly visible to the driver. He turned and threw himself into the undergrowth, not caring about where he landed. Lying in the middle of the thicket, he saw the lights disappear off.

Richard extricated himself and checked his precious camera.

All looked okay. He walked carefully over to where the car had been. No sign of anyone there. He wasn't sure if that was good or bad. He didn't want to find a body or someone hurt, but on the other hand, he wanted to know the fate of the young girl.

Coming out of the woods, he could see that he'd picked up some scratches and mud that might be tricky to explain away. Luckily though, when he got home, the house was in darkness with a note on the hall table. "We're at mummy's. Pie in fridge if you're hungry."

Richard took the opportunity to clean himself up and went to bed, still not certain whether he'd done the right thing or not. One thing was for sure though; he wasn't going to take his pictures to the police. Explaining them would have been impossible and most likely dropped him in it with his wife. He eventually drifted off to sleep suffering weird dreams involving him strangling Victoria in their bed while some faceless stranger looked on impassively.

The next morning he listened to the local news, but there were no reports of any murder or assault. Nor was there over the next few days, or in the papers. If it wasn't for the photos, he would have doubted anything had happened. But the evidence in front of his eyes showed a topless young girl, clearly either dead or unconscious. Either way, surely it wouldn't go unnoticed and unreported.

*

The gender gap in the Marsh household widened as Victoria,

Lorna, Emma and Lucy spent more and more time together. Richard increasingly found himself left out, albeit usually through his own lack of interest in the girls' extracurricular pursuits, which currently revolved around ballet and music lessons. He was bored at home. He was also bored at work. He'd been in charge of the laboratory for years and was fed up of the same routine QC tests, the drag of product development and the monotony of compliance checks. Back home his sex life wasn't just boring, it was non-existent. The only times he was really happy were when he was alone in his study listening to prog rock at full blast, or when he was looking through his camera lens at people doing the things that he wanted to do.

Boredom breeds resentment. Increasingly, minor irritations became major issues. Coming home from work and trying to park the car, for example. He'd frequently come into the house muttering about the trouble he had had finding a parking space or why couldn't other people use their driveways.

Victoria's lack of interest in these problems irritated him further. Add in her lack of time for him and his resentment levels increased day by day.

Most couples would have sorted out their problems by talking about them or by having a row. But Richard and Victoria had never had any other relationships. Neither of them had ever had a real argument with a partner, or been dumped, or dumped anyone else. Victoria wasn't particularly worried; she had her family, house and work, and didn't need any more intimacy than she already had. Richard wanted so much more, but didn't have the life skills needed to sort this relationship out and was afraid to try.

Instead, he sat and stewed on the unfairness of it all.

Left on his own one evening, sitting at his PC, Pink Floyd coming out of the speakers, he made his way through his favourite porn sites. But tonight, even these didn't lift his jaded mood. He opened a new tab and typed into Ask Jeeves: "How do I have an affair?"

The page of results included one headed simply, "Married but bored? Find a lover today." He clicked on it and found himself on a dating website. He'd looked at a couple of these in the past, but they hadn't interested him, being all about finding a husband or wife. This one was different. 'wedbutlooking.com' promoted itself as a dating site for people who were already attached.

He clicked on the "Browse members" button and was taken to a search page with drop down boxes for his preferences. Was he looking for a male or a female? Easy; female. Location: Just leave it on "England" for the moment. Age, height, build: All left blank. He might have an ideal for all of these, but for the moment, he just wanted to see what there was out there. He pressed "SEARCH".

"724 results" he read at the top of a page full of pictures of women and their profiles. A couple of head and shoulders pictures, the rest showing parts of bodies, mainly dressed or in underwear, plus a couple of breast shots.

'Looks interesting,' he thought and clicked on "Julie, 47, Greater Manchester."

A larger picture opened up. A well-rounded woman wearing

a floral dress with a plunging neckline. He couldn't see what her face was like, the picture was cropped, presumably so that Julie could maintain her anonymity. "Hi, I'm a happy-go-lucky mum of 2," he read, "looking for a w/e, younger man who can make me feel like a woman again. Love 'O' but not into w/s or pain. Daytime only."

Richard knew from his porn perusals that 'w/e" meant well endowed, 'O' was oral sex and 'w/s" so-called water sports. He clicked "CONTACT MEMBER" to be greeted by a page saying, "Subscribe to create your own profile and contact members instantly."

He checked out more profiles, finding plenty that looked interesting. 'Why haven't I looked before?' he asked himself, 'It's all here.'

The noise of the downstairs door opening brought the session to a rapid end as he closed the tab and brought up his security page. A safe page that he'd opened ready in case he needed it. Victoria came into the room with a "Hi love" and on seeing the estate agents website open on the screen, asked: "Looking for something new?"

"I was," he replied truthfully.

It was a maddening couple of days before he had another chance to safely go back onto 'wedbutlooking.com'. This time though, he wanted to take it further. He'd already planned a profile and taken a photo of himself, smartly dressed and at an angle that, he hoped, showed his "fine physique", whilst conveniently obscured his face.

Having found the site, he spent half an hour signing up

(money from Roger Francis's account, of course), uploading a photo and typing in his profile. He made a note of the sign-in details and hid them at the back of the drawer. Back to the search page, he just searched within 25 miles of his RG10 postcode this time. 14 profiles came up.

"Jane, 42, Reading," was the first. "5ft 4, size 14, 36C," all sounded fine. According to her profile, she was, "looking for a similar age man" (tick), "must be local" (tick), "available daytimes" (he was sure he could wangle something), "w/e" (he assumed so, based on the porn sites he'd seen) "well built" (he thought so), and "would only do safe sex" (Tick).

"CONTACT MEMBER." Click. 'Now what to say?'

"Hi, I'm Roger" – he'd already decided that he should use his false name – "I'm 39" – no harm in knocking a couple of years off – "and am local to Reading. I'm free to satisfy your every need during the day." Not being able to think what else to put, he just added, "Hope to hear from you soon, Richard x." He was about to press the "SEND" button when he spotted his first rookie error and he deleted the "Richard" from the end, substituting it with "Roger". 'Could have been awkward,' he thought to himself as he clicked on "SEND".

Not sure on what to do next, or how long a reply would take, he browsed several more profiles, wondering whether he should reply to them. He decided not to. Best to just meet one woman at a time. 'Then again…' he thought, as he read about "Michelle, 38," also from Reading, who professed to be an extremely attractive and vivacious woman who loved giving and receiving 'O'.

Halfway through typing his version of who he was and what a fantastic match he'd be for Michelle, Victoria walked into the room.

He'd been so engrossed in his attempts to get laid, he'd not heard the front door.

"Hi love!" she said brightly as she came in.

Richard had made another rookie error; he'd not got his safety page ready. He clicked quickly on another tab at the top of the screen very much hoping that it was the BBC or Maypharm's website, both of which he'd been looking at earlier.

Unfortunately, just as Victoria looked at it, the screen was filled by a pair of naked breasts.

"For god's sake," Victoria sighed as she turned and left the room.

"Just tits. Could've been a lot worse," Richard muttered as he closed down all of the tabs, including the unsent reply to Michelle, and went downstairs. He was expecting Victoria to be upset or angry, but she just carried on for the rest of the evening as if nothing had happened.

Later in the dark of the bedroom, she said, "I know I'm not always enough for you, but you wouldn't do anything, would you?"

"Of course not darling," he lied, relishing the fact that she'd actually given him a chance to talk about a usually taboo subject. "It was just, well, you know I have needs…"

"I know you do." Her voice was still unusually apologetic. "But you wouldn't go elsewhere like dad, would you? You know I could never forgive you if you did."

"Of course I wouldn't Vicky. I can honestly say that you are the only woman I've ever slept with." This was the truth after all; He'd been very much awake when Christine had given him his one and only blowjob. And even then, he thought, 'That wasn't really sex, was it? It didn't involve penetration.' The Clinton defence.

"Good," Victoria said, relieved. "Though if you have to look at mucky pictures, can you do it elsewhere. I don't want anything like that under my roof."

"Of course, love."

He thought about seeing whether this sudden openness would extend to a quickie, but before he could make any move, his wife turned onto her side away from him.

*

Another two days went by before Richard could get back to 'wedbutlooking.com'. He waited expectantly while the site loaded, then went through the log-in process and opened his mailbox. One e-mail. "Welcome to wedbutlooking.com."

Just an administrative one. Nothing else.

Over the next three weeks, whenever the opportunity arose, Richard carefully went through all of the search results for women within 25 miles, sending mails to all of them. Then to everyone within 40 miles. Four times he excitedly opened replies. "Jane, 47, Wokingham," simply said, "No." "Sarah, 32, Slough," was slightly more expansive, "Hi Roger, thanks for your e-mail, but I'm no longer looking." Another Sarah, this time 36 and from Wokingham, was more dismissive with a, "too old," and finally "Chloe, 44, Reading," sent a naked picture of herself, legs wide apart, and said that she'd love to meet Roger and give him the best fuck of his life, and that it would only cost him eighty pounds for the hour.

He persisted in browsing and replying for another month, but with similarly poor results.

CHAPTER 10

PAUL WELLER. "Wild Wood"

The sheer quantity of images on the internet and the high quality of his digital photographs had resulted in the older film photos being neglected until one evening, when clearing out a drawer, Richard came across the original ad for DownPour. Julie's smiling face as she held a bottle of it in just the right place for it to be both prominent and conveniently obscure her breasts, prompted him to dig out his pictures from when he first met her. Once again, the images of her naked and open-legged resulted in a very satisfactory few minutes in the bathroom.

The next day, digging through the files in his work desk, he managed to find her details from when she'd modelled for Maypharm. He had a healthy stash of illegally obtained funds in his account, a high-spec digital camera and a desire to recreate some of the early photos, so why not call her to see if he could hire her again? This time just for himself? He remembered that she worked in the day, or had done so when they'd met previously, so best to make it an evening phone call. Luckily, Victoria was due to take Emma and Lucy to and from music lessons tonight, so there'd be a couple of windows of opportunity.

Richard fidgeted through teatime, wishing the minutes away until the women would leave him alone. Typically, they took ages getting coats, violins and everything else sorted, but the door eventually closed behind them and he watched as the car disappeared out of sight. He felt more alive than he had for months as he picked up the phone and dialled Julie's number. It rang and rang, and his heart sank, until just as he was about to put the receiver down, a woman's voice at the other said, "Hi, Julie White"

"Oh, hi Julie, not sure if you'll remember me, Richard Marsh from Maypharm."

"Richard! How could I forget! That DownPour ad is my biggest claim to fame."

"Glad to hear it, how are you?"

"I'm good, you?"

The usual pleasantries carried on for a moment then Richard went on, "Anyway, reason for my call… Wondering if you'd be available for another modelling session?"

"Not like the last one I hope? I'm probably a bit too old now!"

"No, not like the last one, and I'm sure you're just as attractive."

"Flatterer." He could hear the smile in her voice, "So what's it to be this time?"

"Well, I must admit it's just for me. I've been developing my skills at figure photography and wondered if you'd be available for a one-to-one session."

"One to one's are always good." Was she flirting?

"Good-oh. I could rent a studio, but would rather come to your place again. If that's okay?"

"No problem. I'd be pleased to have you here." Surely that double entendre wasn't accidental?

"Let's do it then. When's good for you?"

"Oh, anytime really. I'm here, or can be, any day."

"Not working then?" Richard asked,

"No, I'm a lady of leisure. My husband earns enough to keep me nearly in the style that I'd like to become accustomed to."

"That's good. How about next Monday? Say, um, two in the afternoon?"

"Yes, that's okay for me. Is there anything you'd like me to have ready? Any particular type of outfit?"

"No, we'll have a naked session, if that's okay?" was Richard's attempt at a similar double entendre.

She laughed. "Naked's good. And what about backdrops and lighting?"

"No, none of that. I'd like to go for natural light and I'm sure we can find some suitable locations around the house."

"That's good. And as for the money side–"

"Don't worry about that," Richard interrupted. "I'm happy to pay whatever your standard rates are."

"Excellent, so I'll see you Monday?"

"You'll see me Monday."

He hung up with a grin on his face. Monday was only a few days away. Not long to wait. It would give him enough time to come up with an excuse to be out of the lab that afternoon. 'I'll say that I'm going to see a supplier. That should do it,' he thought.

The weekend was spent in the usual round of shopping, chores and Sunday lunch with Lorna. The anticipation through Sunday evening left Richard feeling more randy than usual. Victoria, as usual, rebuffed his bedroom advances but for once he persisted, cupping a breast in his hand and stroking the nipple. The nipple reacted nicely, hardening. Victoria reacted not so nicely, pushing him away without a word.

In the morning, Richard felt very mixed emotions. He was thoroughly pissed off with his wife, but at the same time excited, anticipating the afternoon.

Work dragged that morning. As he'd thought, his story about visiting a supplier was accepted without question and, eventually, he was able to get out of the door. Even the 30 mph limit on the roads seemed to be designed to make his journey take forever, but just before two, he finally found himself pulling once more into the courtyard in front of 'The Old Barn'. The front door opened as he was taking his camera bag out of the car and a smiling Julie invited him in.

Richard didn't know whether a now fashionable kiss on the cheek, or a handshake was more appropriate, so he did neither, instead following Julie into the light and airy main room.

"Good to see you again," she started.

"You too," he replied, stuck for what to say next. He needn't have worried, Julie was happy to chat away about how the last photoshoot had brought her a degree of fame, albeit at a very local level.

"I've actually stopped modelling now," she added, "but happy to make an exception for you."

"Thank you, I'm really glad of that."

"Can I get you anything? Tea? Coffee? Or would you like to get straight down to it?"

Richard was still unsure whether her choice of phrases accidentally had a double meaning or not. Especially when she added, "How do you want me?"

"Well…" he replied, "This room's pretty good, but if you're going to be nude, then you might not want to be right in front of these windows."

"I'm sure the neighbours have seen it all before," she replied, "but you're right, might be a bit distracting. Want to take a look around?"

A short tour of the house later and Richard suggested, "I think the main bedroom would be best. Good light and plenty of space."

"Sounds good to me too."

They went back to the bedroom and he started to sort out his camera kit. '28 – 70mm zoom lens should cope with most eventualities,' he decided. 'Stick it on wide angle for full-length shots and the zoom will get nice detailed close ups. No need for flash; enough light coming in through the windows. Although a bit of fill in might help to see into the cracks', he smiled inwardly at the thought.

"Oh, shouldn't we sort out the paperwork?" he asked.

"Sorry?"

"You know, the money side. I don't even know what I'm paying you yet."

"You're not!" Julie chuckled, "You did me a massive favour with the ad. I owe you one."

"Thank you. But I really don't mind paying–"

"No, this is my way of saying thank you, and you'd be rude to refuse my thanks, wouldn't you."

"Okay, thank you for your thank you!"

"Anyway… Straight to nude? Or some as I am? Or?" Julie asked.

"How about a bit of everything." Richard replied, "Pretend I'm not here and you're getting undressed for bed. I'll only say anything if I need to."

"Okey dokey."

Julie walked around the room, looked out of the window (which gave Richard a great hard light side-shot of her face), and then moved back to the bed. His mouth went dry as she undid the zip down the side of her dress and slowly pulled it over her head. He clicked away while she stood and turned, this way and that, dressed in just a thin white bra and knickers. Her arms went behind her back and she undid the bra releasing her breasts. She smiled as she slowly took off the last item of clothing, Richard's camera getting every movement as the briefs were gently tossed aside. He saw that she no longer had a bush of pubic hair, instead being beautifully waxed or shaved. Again, she turned side to side, looking at herself in the dressing table mirror, then turned to Richard and smiled. "Was that okay?" she asked.

"Very much so," he replied. "How about you lie down."

Without a word, she draped herself along the bed, her experience of modelling becoming apparent as she moved through her repertoire of poses. Richard moved around, up and down, getting as many different angles as he could, every so often suggesting a slight movement, or change in expression.

"You won't remember," he said from behind the camera, "but this isn't the first time I've taken pictures of you like this."

"Of course I remember. The advert."

"No, of course we both remember the ad. No, what I mean is that I've taken pictures of you lying down in these poses before."

"Have you?" she looked confused. "When was that?" Her questions punctuating poses, "And, more to the point… why don't I remember? You haven't been drugging me have you?!" she laughed.

"No, nothing like that. But you modelled at my camera club."

"Oh right, well that makes more sense… when was that?"

"Believe it or not, 20 odd years ago."

"Bloody hell. I bet I looked different then!"

"Just as gorgeous, I can assure you. In fact," he continued, "that was why I picked you for the ad campaign."

"Well I never…" Julie went quiet thinking back over the years. "I was a lot slimmer then."

"Maybe, but I think your figure is better now."

Julie moved again and the Richard added carefully, "But you

had a few different poses back then."

"Did I? In what way?"

"Well… my favourite picture from that session–"

"What, you still have some pictures of me from then?" Julie interrupted incredulously.

"Of course, they were some of my best ever! But the one I like most–"

"Yes."

"Is a black and white, side lit picture…"

"I don't need the technical details," she grinned. "Just tell me why it was so good, then maybe I can try to get into it again."

"I'd love that. But, well, basically, it was a picture of you holding your, um, pussy lips open with your right hand and with your left middle finger hooked inside you."

A pause then, "Fucking Hell! I remember that night! You were the lot who paid me to stay for an open legs session!"

"Yep, although I think you called it 'continental' at the time."

"Bloody Hell!" Julie grinned, "I really enjoyed myself that evening." She paused, remembering. "There was a slimeball who tried to get me to flash my bits earlier in the evening and he paid for me to stay on."

"Yes, that was Dave. He's still at the club. And he's still a slimeball."

"And there was a poor sod of a kid who didn't know what to do."

"That'd be me!" Richard grinned.

"Fucking hell! You're joking!"

"Nope."

"God, I wound him, sorry, I mean you, up terribly. You were as red as a beetroot. You hadn't had much experience then I guess?"

"No, none."

"Well I never…" She grinned again. "So was I good education?"

"The best. I never had a teacher like you."

"I'd hope not!"

"You were really sweet though," Julie said. "Most of them tried to touch me up or get my number. You were about the only one who treated me with any respect."

"Umm thanks. But I think it was more to do with being shy. I would've asked for your number if I'd had the courage."

"Maybe. But you wouldn't have got it! I wasn't into underage virgins," she joked.

"Well, I wasn't underage." He smiled back at her, meeting her gaze.

A pause, then, "So, remind me, what pose did you like?"

Richard didn't need to answer. Julie lay back raised her knees and then parted them, before moving her hands down between her legs. Richard watched with breathless joy as for the next ten minutes Julie slowly masturbated herself to orgasm. His camera captured every detail, the movements of her fingers and the wetness of her vagina. Her semi-closed eyes looking sometimes at him, sometimes at the ceiling. The red flush that appeared at the top of her chest, and her neck and face as she cried out in elation, climaxing.

Her breathing returned closer to normal and she smiled at

him. "I didn't do that at the camera club, did I?"

"No, that was amazing. I've never seen anything like it."

"Well, not in front of your camera?"

"No never. Not at all."

"Sorry?" Julie raised her eyebrows. "You've never watched a woman play with herself?"

"No," he admitted. "In fact, I've never seen a girl orgasm."

"What! Get away! You're married aren't you?!"

"Yep."

"And your wife hasn't had an orgasm in front of you?!"

"Nope."

"Sorry, you're kidding, aren't you?"

"No, she just doesn't like sex."

"No way! Every woman likes sex."

"Not this one." Richard paused before going on, "We were both virgins when we met. Sometimes I feel like I still am one."

"But you're not, are you. I mean you have a sex life?"

"No, well not with anyone apart from my own right hand." Somehow he felt he could tell Julie anything, even the details of his dismal own sex life. "The occasional missionary position is the maximum I can hope for. In fact, apart from missionary, well, she's only ever let me try one different position. And that was a long time ago."

"No way… But why?"

"I don't know. I really don't. I mean, I'm willing and able. We get on alright in everyday life. It's just the bedroom. I mean, she even turns the TV off if there's a sex scene on it…" he trailed off.

"So me doing this…" Julie pulled herself wide open again, "is something she wouldn't do?"

"Definitely not."

"What about this?" Julie rolled to her side and Richard wondered what was going on as she opened the top drawer in the bedside unit. She delved around and brought out a vibrator. A pink, slim plastic tube about five inches long with a rounded end.

"Definitely not!" Richard said again. "In fact, I've only ever seen one used in pictures."

"Well, today you can take some pictures if you like?"

"I like."

Again she lay back with her legs parted, but this time her orgasm was reached in just a few minutes as she ran the tip of the buzzing toy over and around her clitoris, arching her back as she came. When she had settled down again, she looked him in the eyes, then pointedly dropped her gaze to the front of his trousers.

"I guess you enjoyed that nearly as much as I did? Judging by the bulge I can see there?"

"God, yes. Umm sorry."

"No need to apologise. I'll take it as a compliment. Why don't you show me…"

Richard was stunned. Had she really just said that?

"Ur… sorry?"

"Stop saying sorry! Get that cock out. Now!… Or maybe you don't want to?"

"Oh, I want to."

"Good. Well get on with it before I change my mind!"

Richard put down the camera and started to unbuckle his belt. Julie's hands gently stopped him and she took over, undoing his trousers and pushing them down his legs.

"Well, take them off," she instructed.

As elegant as an elephant trying to carry off a complex ballet move, Richard bounced from foot to foot, first trying to take his trousers off over his shoes, then fumbling around to get the shoes off, then eventually the trousers. He stood there in his briefs. Despite the faffing about and Julie's laughter, he was still as aroused as he could ever remember.

"Now then…" Julie smiled and pulled the front of his pants down. "God! That's a good one!"

"Eh?"

"I bet you weren't afraid to go in the showers at school!" she shrieked.

"It's not that big is it?" Richard's knowledge of the average size of the male penis being somewhat skewed by his viewing of professional porn stars and their abnormally large appendages.

"Well, I've seen a few, and that one's way up there!"

She put her hand around it and he felt himself go weak at the knees. Seeing him become unsteady, Julie pulled him down onto the bed beside her.

"Let's get the rest off," she said a bit quieter, and between them they stripped off everything else that Richard was wearing.

"I like," she said and lowered her lips onto his erection. For only the second time in his life, Richard gloried at the feel of a woman's mouth around him. He was close to coming in her mouth when she took it away saying, "Not yet big boy. My turn."

She rolled onto her back and widened her legs, before repeating, "My turn."

Richard knew what he was supposed to do, but was nervous.

"You'll never believe this," he said, "but I've never done it before."

"I had wondered. But don't worry. It won't bite."

Richard maneuvered himself so that his mouth was inches away from her moist, pink opening. A tentative lick and he tasted a slightly salty sweat.

"Go on" she said quietly, and he started licking up, down, around her opening and over the clitoris. She brought her hands down to hold herself wide open and in a low voice softly instructed him what to do, where to concentrate his efforts, how much pressure to exert, until with a shudder and cry she started to orgasm yet again.

"Don't stop!" she pleaded as he endeavoured to keep his mouth over her bucking body, her inner thighs gripping his head so hard that his ears hurt until she loosened her grip and he surfaced, breathing heavily.

She grabbed at the open drawer, pulling out an unopened box of Durex, which she tossed to him.

"Now fuck me!"

His fumbling fingers tore off the cellophane wrapper. Innocence again: he'd never used a condom before but somehow managed to tear the foil square open and roll the sheath down over his erection. He briefly thought about suggesting some new (for him) position, but as she lay there, legs apart, he decided to just go for it. He slid himself between her legs and thrust in as hard as he could, relishing how hot and tight she felt around him. The two of them writhed on the bed. He couldn't last, this was just too much, and he came deep inside her.

They lay there sweating, still entwined. After an age, he pulled out and lay back. Julie kissed him on the lips and then the chest before reaching for a tissue and gently removing the condom. To Richard's continuing surprise, she then ran her tongue all over his now flaccid penis before lying next to him, taking his hand in hers.

They lay in silence. Richard didn't know what to say. 'Should I say thank you?!' he wondered.

Julie broke the silence. "Do you want the good news or the bad news?"

Richard couldn't care less what the bad news might be. This had been the best afternoon of his life!

"Bad," he grinned

"Well, the bad news is that my husband's going to be home in half an hour."

"And the good?"

"I want to see you again. If that's okay with you?"

"Okay? You bet!" he replied lamely.

He realised that he probably smelt of sweat and of Julie. "Can I use your shower?"

"Of course. You know where it is don't you?" Rachel giggled.

They shared the shower. He started to get another erection while drying each other. Julie kissed it right on the tip saying, "Next time... Now get a move on before my husband catches us."

Driving away, Richard found himself singing along to the radio. Looking forward to a much better life.

*

"What's up with you?" Victoria asked as he walked in the door, "Pissed or won the lottery? And why's your hair wet?"

"Aren't I allowed to be pleased to see my beautiful wife and daughters after a crappy afternoon in Southampton? Where, by the way, it's peeing down?"

"Okay, okay, point made," Victoria said with a smile. "It's just good to see you happy for a change."

The next day at work was a blinder. He got everything done in a fraction of the time usually taken and enjoyed it. In the afternoon, he called Julie and they agreed to meet again Friday morning. Richard got an erection just talking with her.

This time it was an emergency dentist's appointment that got him out of work. Richard surprised himself at how well he played the role of 'man with severe toothache' to Victoria and his work team and he was soon parked in Julie's courtyard. No camera this time. She let him in and the two of them kissed passionately, hands wandering and bodies responding. Richard had the forethought to buy a packet of condoms this time and within five minutes of his arrival, one was in use. He came far too soon, but neither of them minded. There was time for more. And more followed.

Over the next couple of hours, the condoms were all used as she introduced him to yet more new experiences. He didn't know how she managed to arouse him so often, but didn't care either. He didn't know how many times she'd come, but it seemed constant. Finally, they came to a point where both were incapable of further arousal. They were, to put it simply, knackered. And finally, after all of their physical excesses, they started to use their mouths and lips for talking rather than for stimulating each other.

"Wow!" was the limit of Richard's intelligent conversation.

"Yeah," Julie's.

Back at work, Richard was in a dream world, smiling so much that Sarah asked him, only half jokingly, whether he'd been sampling the company drugs larder.

Taking time out from the lab was going to be an issue he realised. The odd couple of hours now and then could be explained away, but what he wanted now was at least a day a week that could be spent extending his portfolio of positions.

He couldn't go to work for another company. His marriage to Victoria was the real basis of his success here despite his mediocre ability. Similarly, their lifestyle was effectively bankrolled by the Bristows. He'd been reminded more than once that losing Victoria would result in him losing his job, home and virtually everything else that he valued.

Could he change what he did in Maypharm? He could do the current job blindfolded and, if he was honest, a lot more effectively if he tried. Completely changing his role would mean having to work harder and might expose his weaknesses. No, he'd have to think of something else. Maybe have a word with Geoff.

Unfortunately, for the moment he was going to have to make do with shorter sessions and they'd have to be mainly outside of working hours.

Victoria was still only putting up with him going to the camera club once or twice a month, despite her ability to be out several nights a week. Increasing club visits to every week would be pushing it.

Sarah came in to ask about some laboratory reagents that she'd requested a while back. Richard had forgotten to order them but came up with the excuse, "Sorry Sarah, I should have said, they're out of stock at the supplier. Might be another week."

As she left, he made a note on a Post-It to order them a.s.a.p. Sarah was getting her coat on, but it was only twelve? 'Oh yeah,' he remembered, 'she's got college this afternoon.' The obvious thought struck him and he was soon online looking up day-release college courses that he could enrol onto.

Reading College was the nearest; local and with a wide range of courses. He read through the long lists of business, management and science courses. "NEBOSH National Diploma in Occupational Health and Safety. 1 day per week. Full-year course." 'Sounds ideal' he thought. No difficulty to get that past old man Bristow. He started to print off the course details when he realised the problem with this course, and also all of the others under these work headings; they all had examinations at the end. Signing up would be okay, but in a year's time, he'd be in the proverbial when the expected qualification failed to appear. 'Could I forge a qualification?' he briefly wondered, then dismissed the idea as being too difficult and risky.

Other courses then…

The rest of the afternoon was spent looking at courses at Reading, Slough, and several other colleges. No daytime courses, but quite a few evening courses which would allow him to be out of the house for three or four hours and didn't involve exams. He needed one that Victoria would be happy for him to attend (i.e. a "useful" subject, not just for his own pleasure) and that she wouldn't be able to test him on. If it was helpful at work as well, then that'd be a bonus, as then he might be able to leave work early 'to make sure I get to college on time'.

He eventually decided on Conversational French at Reading College.

Later in the car with Victoria, he brought up the subject, "By the way, you know we're doing a lot more work with Cosion in France now."

"Oh yes," she replied, not really paying attention to the conversation. She had more important things to think about (like Emma needing a new school jumper).

"Well," Richard continued, "I'm having to deal with them on the phone a lot now," – which was true – "and their lab manager speaks bugger all English," – which was a total fabrication. Monsieur West having been born and brought up in Peckham before moving to France in pursuit of a girlfriend that he'd met at university.

"Uh huh." (Victoria was thinking, 'jumper has to be the blue one'.)

"Well. It's important that we understand each other, and as he's not doing anything about it, I thought it a good idea if I improved my French."

"Oh.. yes." ('Better get a size up, the speed she's growing.')

"So I've enrolled for language classes."

"Sounds good." ('M&S have them in.') A pause, "Sorry what was that?"

"French language. It's Wednesdays at the Tech."

"Oh, okay." (Victoria thinking, 'Did I miss something here? He never wants to put any effort into learning. Or anything else really.')

"And you're usually round your mum's on a Wednesday, aren't you."

"Yes. Sorry, do you mean this is after work?"

"Yes, half six to ten o'clock, I think, every Wednesday. Don't worry about dinner though. I can get something to eat there."

Victoria was sure that something wasn't quite right here, but Richard had been in a much better mood over the last couple of weeks, and maybe he was actually going to get his arse into gear and start taking an interest in something other than himself… "Oh, yes. Okay then, sounds good. Maybe you'll be more help on our next holiday."

Richard smiled. She'd swallowed the story. He'd be able to enjoy Julie swallowing something else every week. And to cap it all, a reference to potentially going back to France? Maybe he'd get the chance to look up Christine and practice his newly gained oral skills with her?

Julie was delighted that Richard had found a way to be free. For her part, she could get out anytime. Her husband paid her no attention nowadays (including in the bedroom) so she just had to say that she was going to see a friend and he gave her carte blanche to go wherever and whenever she wanted.

Richard booked a room at a small hotel just outside Reading under the name of Roger Francis and their next rendezvous was set up.

He arrived in the car park first. Should he go in and wait for Julie in the room? 'No, best not to,' he decided, 'she would have to go to reception and ask for the room number and that would look odd, and might be embarrassing for her.' Instead, he sat in the car. The only one in the car park. Julie arrived five minutes later and the two of them kissed. They walked into the hotel together, he nervously, she enjoying the thrill of an illicit encounter.

"Oh hi," Richard said to the receptionist. "Booking in the name of Mr & Mrs Francis."

"Yes sir." She confirmed the details of the reservation adding, "Do you need any help with your luggage?"

Richard hadn't thought of this and was stumped how to answer, but Julie just replied, "No, it's okay thanks."

"Will you be wanting breakfast?" was the next question.

"Um, no, it's alright thanks," Richard replied, thinking that not staying there all night might be a problem. Handing in the key, checking out and so on. Would he have to come back in the morning to sort it out? If so, that'd be difficult to say the least. How would he detour on the way to work – with Victoria in the car – or nip out to do it later? Then another idea, "Actually," he said to the receptionist, "we may have to leave very early. Can we pay now? And just leave the key here when we leave? We'll pay cash for the bar or anything else."

"Of course sir," the receptionist said with a smile, handing him the key.

They went up to the room and Julie burst out laughing. "Oh that was funny! You're so not used to this are you?"

"Nope," Richard replied. "You know how inexperienced I am. But the girl on reception… she must have cottoned on that we're not married?"

"And? She won't care," Julie said. "Probably sees it every day."

"What if she comes to check on us?" Richard asked.

"Why on earth would she? We're not breaking the law. And half the hotels in England would go bust if they forbid unmarried shaggers. Besides, she's cute. I'd just invite her to join in…"

"Eh?!"

"You heard me… You could have your first threesome."

"What?!"

"God, you should see your face! Don't worry, I'm just joking." She then lay on the bed, saying: "Now let's have some fun."

By half eight both of them needed a rest. They lay side by side, Richard's fingers wandering, gently stroking her tummy.

He looked at her, mentally comparing his lover with his wife. Apart from being a similar height (both of them slightly shorter than him), they were very different. Where Victoria could have almost passed as a man if she had dressed that way, Julie's curves and substantial breasts made such confusion impossible. Julie smiled where Victoria scowled. Victoria had short straight dark hair where Julie had bounteous curls of mousey-coloured hair which tumbled over her shoulders. Victoria had a bush of dark pubes, Julie was shaved. Julie was extrovert and bold while Victoria was afraid of her own shadow. Richard much preferred every one of Julie's features.

More to the point, sex with the two of them couldn't be more different. Victoria reluctantly tolerated it, taking no real part and not getting any joy out of it. With Julie he felt there was a connection between them while they did it. She enjoyed it. She suggested things. Her limits appeared, well, unlimited. She was unshockable.

Until this point, all of their time together had been spent either attending to each other's erogenous zones, or discussing (usually with some disbelief) Richard's lack of experience. This time Richard made the effort to ask Julie more about herself. She was happy to answer every question he put.

Virtually everything about her upbringing was different from Richard's. Unlike him, she'd been brought up, along with an older brother, in a solidly working class household on the coast. She'd enjoyed going to the local co-ed comprehensive where she'd found no difficulty in losing her virginity with a classmate at the age of 15. A university education followed, studying both the French language (useful for giving Richard some new French phrases when he went home from his "evening class") and French kissing. Having left home for Uni, she stayed away afterwards, renting a flat in London and taking a variety of jobs, mainly administrative, around the city. She'd met Lawrence when temping at a stockbrokers whilst asserting her own political view that capitalism was evil and that the only stocks that should be allowed around here, were the medieval sort where you were chained up and subjected to being pelted with rotten fruit. Julie and Lawrence's relationship had been turbulent for the early years until he left his job in the City so that they could have a better life in the Thames Valley. She'd found being a rich man's wife unfulfilling and so had gone back to work until being made redundant a year or so back. Since then, she'd been trying to decide what to do with her time. And then Richard had come along.

She also brought him up to speed with her own sexual history from age 15 on. She was proudly promiscuous until she met Lawrence. By her own estimation, she'd probably had some sort of experience with around 30 or 40 men of all ages. Some long term, other's for just one night, or, in several cases, just five minutes. Oh, and she'd dabbled with a couple of girls as well. But sex with Lawrence, while good in the early years was, like Richard's situation, now non-existent. Lawrence had wanted children. Julie hadn't and this caused some friction between them. Lawrence had basically told Julie that unless children were on the cards, he'd keep his semen to himself, thinking that her need for sex would eventually make her change her mind. It hadn't and they'd both raised the stakes too high to be able to go back easily to how things were before. Julie now suspected that her husband was having an affair with a girl with, as she put it, "a tight cunt and an even tighter arse," adding, "he tried my arse once. That's something I'll never do again."

Richard found himself slightly shocked by things Julie said, but he also wondered if she was saying some of them deliberately, just to see his reaction. Then she provoked a different reaction by suggesting, "It's way too long since I've had your tongue on my clit."

He moved down the bed, "Happy to oblige, ma'am," he replied.

"Don't talk with your mouth full," was the last thing she said for some time.

The clock was approaching ten o'clock and Richard reluctantly pointed out that they needed to get themselves sorted to go. "I'll need a shower," he added, "but got to keep the hair dry this time."

"You're starting to sound like an experienced cheating husband," Julie replied.

Dressed, they looked around at the bedroom. The state of the bed was testament to the activity it had seen. A long kiss and they left the room. Going down in the lift, Julie briefly lifted up her skirt, showing him a complete lack of underwear. They walked out past reception, Richard being relieved that it was unmanned as he left the room key there.

The lovers parted in the car park, each to drive to their respective uninterested spouses.

Julie got home to find Lawrence snoring in bed. She climbed in and meditated on the strange twist of fate that had seen her enjoying herself more now than she had done ever since meeting her husband.

Richard got home to find Victoria watching TV. "Enjoy your French?" Victoria called, as he took off his coat.

"Best French ever," came his reply.

Richard called Julie from his office phone having checked first that no one was around to overhear. They chatted for a moment and Richard suggested the same hotel for their next liaison. Julie said she'd love it, but, "I should just flag up, I'm due shortly, so games may be off the menu. You'll just have to make do with a blowjob!"

"Well, as long as you don't mind making it a couple of them, I'll be happy," he smirked back.

"No problem. But if we don't need a bed, maybe we can go out for a drink or meal instead? Somewhere where we won't be known, of course. And don't worry. You'll still get your blowjobs."

"Sounds good to me. I'll have a think. Pub grub?"

"Yes please. And your special cream dessert to follow."

"I'll make sure that there's enough to fill you."

He was just putting the phone down when Sarah came in to ask about the lab reagents which still hadn't arrive, mainly because Richard had again forgotten to order them. 'Shit,' he thought to himself, 'can't afford to keep making mistakes like this, and a couple of seconds earlier and she would have heard too much.'

Richard acknowledged that he was way behind the times when it came to the latest trends in electronics. In particular, he'd been resisting the growing interest in mobile phones. According to the paper, one in three kids under the age of 18 now had one, and both Emma and Lucy had been pestering for some time. But having an affair and trying to communicate by home or office phone was horrendously difficult and risky so maybe it was now time to accept defeat and get a mobile.

In the end he bought five. One for himself, another for Julie so that the two of them could more easily engage in social intercourse, as well as sexual. The others were for Victoria and the girls. He knew that if he came home with a new phone just for himself, there would be an outcry from the girls about how could he deny them one and then get one for himself. The five Nokia 3210s (all different colours to prevent them getting mixed up) came to an eye-watering £499.95, plus a tenner pay as you go credit each for Victoria, Emma and Lucy, and a more substantial thirty pounds credit for his and Julie's. As expected, there were screams of delight from the girls. Victoria was a bit more reserved. She didn't really like answering phones, but more to the point, she was again concerned about Richard's out of character actions.

Wednesday came and Richard and Julie parked up next to each other in the car park of The Dewdrop Inn, a small comfortable old-fashioned pub deep in Forestry Commission woodland outside of Maidenhead. Before getting out of his car, Richard scanned the car park, just in case he recognised anyone else's vehicle. No problem. He went around to Julie's car and opened the driver's door for her. "Why thank you, sir!" she laughed.

After a toe tingling kiss, Richard suggested a short walk before they went into the pub.

"What you really mean," deduced Julie easily, "is that you

want me to suck you off behind the trees."

"How could I refuse such a politely put suggestion," he grinned.

They walked a short way into the woods and he turned to her. A long snog and he could feel a reaction down below. She felt it too as she pressed herself into him. They kissed more. Richard thought he detected a movement in the trees behind Julie. Deer? He wondered. Then he caught a faint glimpse of a figure, no more than 10 metres away, hiding in the undergrowth. Someone watching him rather than the usual other way around. The thought excited him. He moved Julie's hand down to the front of his trousers, not that she needed much persuading, and turned the two of them slightly so that he could be sure the figure in the trees could see what was happening. With the lights of the pub car park behind them, he felt that they'd be illuminated well enough for their watcher. Julie pressed her hand against him and Richard said quietly, "I think it would like some fresh air. Don't you?"

She unbuckled his trousers and they sank to half-mast. Pants rapidly following. Their tongues entwining while her hand gripped his hard cock. Richard moved his mouth off Julie's and whispered into her ear.

"There's something else I should mention. "

"What?" she asked.

"Well, I've not had a chance to say this before. What with us being so busy… but I do have a very minor kink."

"Oh yes?" she sounded interested rather than worried.

"Yes, if I happen to see a bedroom with the curtains open, I might occasionally look in."

"Well, if that's kinky," she replied, "then I'm a total pervert. I'd look in every time."

"Good… And how do you feel about someone looking in your windows?"

"Well, I'd probably put on a bit of a show for them. As long as it wasn't a coachload of course!"

"Well that's good, because I think we're being watched now. Don't look, but we have company to my right."

"Well, I hope he's enjoying the show!"

Julie moved down into a crouching position and started to suck Richard's rampant rod. He casually looked to the right, out of the corner of his eye, yes, certainly someone watching. The thought of what the unknown person was seeing took Richard over the edge and he came, legs shaking and barely able to stand.

"Fucking hell!" was all he could utter before they tidied themselves up and they went into the pub.

A few minutes after they'd got to the bar, the door opened and a young lad, all on his own came in. Probably no more than 20, tall, slim and boyish looking.

"Do you think that's our voyeur?" Richard asked.

"I hope so," Julie replied. "If we sit over in that corner, we can see where he plonks himself, and if he goes somewhere where he can still see us then he probably is."

"Good idea."

They took their drinks over to an empty table and sat on a long bench seat between the table and wall. Sure enough, their lad sat himself at a nearby table, facing in their direction, while pretending to look at a magazine that had been on the bar. Julie dropped a hand under the table and started to caress Richard's leg, her hand moving higher up the thigh until it started to gently tease the zip of his trousers. No doubt about it. Try as he might to hide behind his copy of *Country Life* ('what 20 year old reads *Country Life*?' Richard thought), the lad's eyes were definitely trying to peer under the table. Richard looked around. There were only two other couples in the bar and they wouldn't be able to see what was going on due to tables and chairs in the way.

"You're hard again," Julie whispered.

"You surprised?"

"Let's see what happens now." Julie brought her hand up from under the table and looked across to the lad. "Are you on your own there?" she said to him, just loud enough that he could hear but not attract the attention of the other diners.

He looked around him, as if he thought she might be talking to someone else, "Er, yes."

"In that case, would you like to join us?"

"Er, yes."

An encouraging smile from Julie with an 'it's okay' nod from Richard and the youth walked over. He was about to sit on the opposite side of the table when Julie said to Richard. "Shift along a bit," and the two of them made space so that the younger man could sit on the other side of Julie.

Sitting in the middle she said, "I'm Julie, this is Richard," almost formally.

"Mark," came the shy reply.

"Hi Mark." Richard said and they started small talk about the pub and where Mark came from. Julie gave Richard a grin and suggested that he move the table forward a bit. All three of them could now see each other's laps.

Richard said to Julie, "I hope that you're thinking what I think you're thinking?"

"And what might that be?" she replied, and in a graceful movement dropped both her hands down. One onto Richard's leg, just above the knee. The other hand similarly placed on Mark's.

"You got it!" Richard grinned.

Julie kept up the small talk while stroking both the men's legs. Her hands just getting to the tops of their thighs before dropping back down. Mark's conversation had all but dried up. He could answer yes or no questions from Julie, but anything longer appeared to be beyond him. She moved both hands upwards, pressing against both trouser fronts, up and down. A moment later and Mark uttered a very quiet "Uhh." Julie kept her hand on his crotch for a moment before taking it away. His bright red face beamed at her as he excused himself to go to the gents.

"I think he enjoyed that," Julie said.

"Almost as much as I did," replied Richard.

A few minutes Mark returned and blurted out, "Thank you."

"Our pleasure mate," Richard replied. "And if you're still here in an hour or so, you never know, there might be a bit more to see outside."

"I hope so," Mark said, then sensing that it might be politic to give the couple some room, he went back to the other table.

"I really enjoyed that," Richard repeated.

"I did too," Julie replied.

They chatted over drinks and a light meal. Time was getting on and Richard was keen to finish off the evening as it had started. They got up to go, giving a simple nod to Mark and left the bar. He joined them outside shortly after and the three of them walked into the woods.

"Sorry, but you can't touch me," Julie instructed Mark, "but you can watch." Once again, she gave Richard a fantastic blowjob and Mark a visual lesson in the delights of the older woman.

Once more Julie was greeted by a snoring husband on her return home. Once more Richard was met by Victoria's enquiry about the French class.

"We were working on how to deal with constructions involving 'you', 'me' and 'him,'" he truthfully replied.

CHAPTER 11

SUPERTRAMP. "Long Way Home"

Richard was called to Geoff Bristow's office. They talked most days, but usually it was during the Chairman's daily walk around. For Richard to be summonsed was unusual. He set off down the corridor, trying to think what he'd done wrong recently. 'Unlikely to be Julie related,' he thought, 'Geoff would talk to me out of work. Shouldn't be anything to do with the apparently brand new HPLC; I would have noticed anyone looking at it. Missed something in QC? – always possible, but that could be deflected onto a lab worker.'

Still unsure, he knocked on Geoff's door and entered the office.

"Morning Richard, how's you?" An affable greeting much to Richard's relief.

Small talk about home and work, ("How're my girls? All okay in the lab?") was followed by Geoff sitting back and looking directly at Richard.

"Richard, due to the family ties, you've not had the frank annual appraisal that other staff here get."

This didn't sound quite so good after all. Richard just nodded his head.

"But I think it's time we had a chat about your future here."

Richard thought that this definitely sounded bad.

The Chairman continued, softer. "The thing is, since I met Dawn, my life has changed. You've probably noticed it, but I'm a happier person. I get in later and leave earlier because I want to make the most of my time with her. To be frank, I'm looking at how and when I should step down."

Richard didn't like the sound of this at all. A new Chairman would certainly not let him get away with half of what he did. In a considered tone he said, "I can understand that, sir." He rarely used the word 'sir' but felt that a bit of subservience wouldn't go amiss here. "But on the other hand, you run this company exceptionally well. To be honest, it would go downhill without you... oh, and you're limited as to what shares you can sell, aren't you? So if the company struggled, as it would do without you, then you could lose everything too." Richard wasn't sure if he'd taken the scenario too far and stopped to let Geoff reply.

"Thanks for your belief in me, but you're wrong. I'm just a figurehead. It's the team underneath me that keep the ship sailing. The thing is, I need to hand over to someone who'll keep my family's interests at heart as much as those of the workers and other shareholders." Another pause while Richard just nodded.

"I've not told you before as it might have affected your work, but I've been keeping an eye on you." ('Ouch,' thought Richard)

"And I like what I see now." ('What?!')

"You were coasting until recently. I know your responsibilities aren't exactly exacting. But I was happy to leave you in charge of your area. A good pair of hands. But you weren't showing much drive." ('Is this praise or criticism?')

"But over the last few weeks you've been like a new man. I don't know what it is. Monkey glands?! Whatever it is I could do with some of it." ('If only you knew!')

"And I was impressed that you're taking on learning a new language for your own pleasure." ('You're right, I'm getting a lot of pleasure from my lessons.')

"Richard. You need to be aware that I'm considering you as my replacement." ('…..!')

"Well, I'm not sure what to say," was Richard's reply.

"Don't say anything. To anybody that is, including Vicki. She may be family, but I don't want her to know. Yet. Carry on as you are now, keep your nose clean, and you'll be Chairman. I'd still be in the background guiding you. As I've got the controlling interest of shares, don't think you have to sweet talk Lorna or anyone else. Just keep it to yourself."

"Thank you Geoff. You can count on me. Just let me know if there's anything I can do."

"Just carry on. Oh, and make sure that Lorna doesn't poison the girls against me. In fact, yes, there is one small thing… Dawn and I will be getting married. No date sorted yet. After all, my divorce hasn't even gone through yet. But when we do, I want my granddaughters as bridesmaids. Lorna will try to scupper it I'm sure, but as and when, I'll be relying on you for your help."

"Well, of course."

Richard privately agreed that the future betrothal of Lorna's ex-husband to "that conniving, money-grabbing harlot," as Lorna had so succinctly put it only last week, would be akin to leaving the big red nuclear missile launch button in the middle of a primary school playground.

Richard resumed his work with renewed energy. Work was completed faster and with more accuracy. Laboratory reagents were ordered and delivered when needed and the additional efficiency freed up some of his time. He considered signing up for a management course, but that would have been just a bit too much like real work.

Geoff Bristow meanwhile was pleased with the progress of his son-in-law and started looking at extra small tasks that could be sent his way, different from what he was already doing. Let him get a feel for the work of the other departments.

"Can you take a look at the current rules regarding employee pensions? Just let me know if we're doing it all right." This was to get him involved with HR.

"Can you take a look at what we're paying for magnesium sulfate. See if you can find a more cost effective supplier?" Richard was now working with Purchasing.

"Can you take a look at the CCTV coverage. Are we secure?" This led to an evening walking around the site with one of the security guards. An evening Richard found extremely instructive, as he learnt the capabilities of the cameras and what they could be watching without him being aware.

Richard thrived at work and continued to spend Wednesday evenings, and occasionally other times when he could, doing his best to maximise the profits of local hotels and condom manufacturers.

He and Julie had got into a routine, a routine that they were very happy with. Three out of four Wednesdays they found a hotel room somewhere. So far they'd worked their way through half a dozen and the receptionists hadn't give them a second glance, and payment upfront with the key in the box at ten had worked well. On the days when Julie was "off games," as she put it, they'd find a pub and have a meal out. Usually with starters and dessert al-fresco. It was still early days, but they were enjoying every minute and there was no sign of the fun ending.

Victoria, on the other hand, was growing concerned. Why had Richard changed so much? He was looking happy. He'd lost weight and was singing in the car. But he was evasive when she asked him questions about work. Lorna had noticed it too, mentioning it to Victoria in passing. Something was fishy.

*

A Monday morning in late November and another call to the Chairman's office. Richard was relaxed about them now; Geoff's requests for him to do something different were actually quite interesting.

"Richard. How's the French going?"

"Bien sur, monsieur!"

"Good. Whatever that meant. Anyway, I'd like you to put your new skills to the test. You know Cosion?"

"Yes, they're our supplier of some of the actives?"

"Yes. Well, as you know, we've had a few quality problems with their raw materials."

"Don't I know it, we've had to double the sampling rate on the SSRis."

"Exactly. Well, at the moment, it's borderline whether we'll continue using them."

"I didn't think there were any other European manufacturers of those actives. And getting them from India or China would take a lot of paperwork."

"Exactly. So I want to fire a warning shot across Cosion's bows. Wake them up a bit."

"What had you in mind?" Richard asked.

"Well, officially we're supposed to audit them on a regular basis, but we've been accepting their ISO certificates as being enough."

"Well, usually it is."

"I agree. But on this occasion, I think it's time for a proper supplier review. I want you to go over there and do a full GMP and compliance audit."

"That's quite a lot of work you know…" Richard hesitated.

"Yes, but if you go out on a Monday, you could get it done and over in three days, back Friday."

"But a week out? And it's not going to be cheap? And

Victoria's not going to be happy with me leaving her that long."

"We manage without you much longer when you go on holiday. And the cost is a fraction of what we stand to lose if Cosion screw up much more. Don't worry about Vicky. I'll have a word with her."

"Okay. I'll start to look into it."

In reality, Richard had no objection at all to a week in France. This sort of audit was easy work and the thought of a week away from family and his usual work… Yes please. More to the point though, what if he could take Julie? A full week of sleeping together – they'd not even managed one night yet. The possibilities were endless…

Victoria's reaction also surprised him. She was gushingly happy when they met later that day. "Daddy's just told me!"

"Told you what?"

"About your trip to France, of course."

Richard didn't know why she was so cock-a-hoop about being deserted for a week. "I thought you'd be pissed off about it," he said in all honesty.

"Of course not. He explained why."

"What do you mean?"

"That this could be your first step to going on the Board, of course!"

So the old man had given Victoria part of the bigger picture. Nothing about his own retirement, but the carrot that Victoria's husband may be about to get more status.

"Oh that." Richard pretended to laugh it off. "That may be yonks away yet."

"Yes, but it looks like it'll happen, doesn't it. And we'll be able to move to a bigger place with the money, and…" She rabbited on excitedly on. Richard didn't really want to move again, but if it kept Victoria happy…

Victoria suggested an early night. Having his needs satisfied elsewhere, Richard didn't give it a second thought until she snuggled up to him and put her hand on his penis. Richard didn't know what to do. Victoria would smell a mighty big rat if he declined, but wouldn't having sex with her mean being unfaithful to Julie? But then he was already being unfaithful to Victoria with Julie. A few moments later, his body made up his mind for him as his cock hardened reflexively from Victoria's touch. What if he pushed his luck a bit? If Victoria took umbrage then he'd not have to do anything further. If she let him do something more, then that would be a win… In the meantime though, his hand was between her legs. He'd learned a lot from Julie and stroked Victoria's clitoris with a more appropriate speed and touch. For once he felt her body responding.

"Put it in," she said, "please." Something he'd never heard her say before.

"From behind?"

She hesitated, but got out of the bed and bent over. Words weren't necessary as he entered her, even now mentally noting that her skinny frame meant that this was nowhere near as sensual or comfortable as when he did the same with Julie. Her bones rubbed hard against him as he moved in and out, but no matter how good or bad this was, nature took over and he found himself coming inside her. He stood there for a couple of seconds, his legs shaking, and pulled out. She turned back around, sat on the bed and reached for a tissue before opening her legs wide to matter-of-factly clean away any evidence of what had just occurred.

"That was nice," she said as she turned away to sleep, leaving him confused about just where their relationship was.

*

Richard had texted Julie (another new skill) about the France trip. "Hi love, how do you fancy a week in Paris with me?" he'd typed. No text-speak abbreviations or lack of punctuation for Richard.

"Yes pls! when," was her reply.

"Next week if you can get away with it? If not I can make it later?"

She texted back immediately. "No probs call me wit details."

They plotted between themselves and Richard liaised with the French company, Cosion, not mentioning that he'd have someone back in the hotel. Geoff had suggested flying, but sorting out two tickets, which would have to be booked separately, was too complicated. Instead, he elected to go for Eurostar again. Just place a booking for the car and no one here would know how many passengers were in it. The four star Terrass Hotel in Montmartre looked a good base for a dirty week away. Pre-paying for a double meant that he could settle the bill for any extras with cash from the Roger Francis account, and Maypharm wouldn't know anything.

Victoria packed him a bag over the weekend, emphasising to him exactly how many pairs of socks, shirts, pants and so on, she'd put in. He looked at the bag and wondered if she thought he was going away for a month, but hey, better to have too much than too little. And it was December, so jumpers and the like would be needed.

Whistling quietly, Richard left on Monday morning waving back at his smiling wife and children. He drove to the secure parking lot at Heathrow Airport where Julie had left her car having told Lawrence that she was off to Paris (true), flying (false), with a group of girlfriends (very much false). The secure parking meant she didn't have to worry about the car while they were away. After all, how would she have explained it going missing from some backstreet in Reading?

Richard loaded Julie's suitcase, half the size of his, and they drove at a leisurely pace to Folkestone, enjoying the luxury of being able to chat without a looming deadline. Nearing the train, Richard spotted the three height barriers that had caused such a problem with Victoria some time ago. 'Let's see how different Julie is' he decided and sped towards the bars. As expected Julie instinctively ducked, but this time he was delighted that the reaction was a laughing, "You bastard!"

The car on the train, they reclined the seats and continued chatting. Richard happy. The conversation was so natural and free. They had so much to talk about; not just family and work. No subject was off limits and Julie's knowledge was deep and extensive.

They savoured the long straight French motorways. No

potholes. The 140 km/h limit was a more comfortable speed than England's slightly lower 70 mph. They sailed through the flat open countryside, eventually getting to the multi-lane motorway around Charles De Gaulle airport before a short urban drive through Paris's noisy traffic to pitch up outside the Hotel Terrass. A porter came out to take their bags as they unwound themselves from the seats and went in to check-in. No problem here being Mr Marsh and Mrs White. Richard even thought he saw a smile of approval from the receptionist. Car keys handed over (parking was sorted out by the hotel), they went up to their room.

It was a comfortable double room with a panoramic view across Paris to the Eiffel Tower. But the view could wait. Richard started undoing Julie's blouse and they were soon making a mess of yet another bed.

That evening they ate in a small restaurant on Rue Lepic before moving up to the bar on the hotel roof. Looking out over Paris by night, Richard felt a warm glow inside him despite the chilly December air.

That night they slept together for the first time. Richard didn't know whether Julie snored like Victoria; the travelling, food and drink, followed by an energetic reverse cowgirl screw meant that he was asleep almost before he shrivelled inside Julie. She cuddled up to him and they slept solidly. Richard awoke to feel Julie's mouth around his morning glory erection, his vision was obscured; her pussy being inches above his mouth. They sixty-nined before Richard took her from behind, her hands each side of the uncurtained window, her breasts swinging with every thrust, visible to anyone who happened to look up at the front of the hotel.

Richard left her with a kiss at breakfast when a waiter came to tell him that the car from Cosion was waiting outside.

A top of the range saloon (Citroen; French, of course), took him to a gleaming factory on an industrial estate just outside Le Perephique. Monsieur Steve West introduced himself and they spent some time discussing the merits of London vs. Paris. There wasn't much of a debate. Richard had already decided that he loved being here. With Julie.

Steve casually mentioned, "Oh, by the way. Sarah? From your lab? called yesterday afternoon. Asked if you could call back. Said it was quite important."

Work didn't know that Richard had a mobile, and only Geoff had the number of his hotel.

"Thanks. Is it okay if I call them now?"

"Of course."

Steve showed Richard to a phone and left him to make the call.

Sarah picked up. "Morning Richard. Or should that be bonjour? Sorry to disturb you but I've got something a bit odd here and thought I'd better talk to you."

"No worries. What is it? More duff raw materials?"

"No, nothing like that. It's an odd one. You know the new HPLC we got? Unit four?"

Richard sat down before answering carefully. "Yes, I know the one. What's up with it?"

"Well, it was reading a bit high yesterday so I thought I'd

reset the zero. I couldn't get it to equilibrate and thought there must be an air bubble in the main pump. So I did a flush and that didn't sort it. Then I thought it might be the lamp."

'Get on with it,' thought Richard, but said out loud, "Sounds fair enough."

"Well, the odd thing is that the lamp housing had burnt through."

"It can happen."

"Yes, I know. But this one had the old style housing. You know the ones that were phased out precisely because of burn out. They're a hazard. If we'd been using a low flash eluent, it could have gone up."

Richard didn't need this. There was a real risk that his refurbished unit might be discovered. "Mmm yes, I see your point. But not to worry, you don't need it until I'm back, do you? I'll take a look then."

"Yes, that's all fine, but what about the other units? That's why I wanted a chat. Should I quarantine all of the them until they've been checked out?"

That would not be a good idea. Taking them all apart would only serve to highlight the issues with his fraudulent one. "No, no need to do that. As it happens I checked all of them when we got the new one. The lamp housing was one of the reasons we made the update and I assumed that because it was a new one, it would have the new housing. I guess that they had some old ones to use up?" Richard was saying too much and reined himself back. "No, carry on as normal with all the other units. Put the broken one on my desk and I'll check it out next week."

"I don't mind–" Sarah started,

"No, I insist," Richard interrupted.

"Okay boss. Will do. Enjoy La France and this one will be waiting for you on Monday."

"Au revoir Sarah."

A close shave. Too close, in fact. But it would have to wait until he got back. The worry that Sarah might still do something nagged at him during the audit. Others might have realised that he was distracted, but the guys here hadn't met him previously. The day's work came to a close and Steve said that he'd got a meal lined up for them out on the town this evening. Richard politely declined saying that he had work to do back at the hotel. The car arrived and took him back.

Richard opened the door to their bedroom.

"What took you so long?" Smiled Julie, lying on the bed dressed in just a pair of stockings and a suspender belt.

"Does it matter?" replied Richard undoing his shirt. "I've got something else nice and long which needs to say hello."

Another meal out. This time on Rue des Abesses, just as good as the night before. Julie nattered away telling Richard about her day wandering around Montmartre and Sacre Coeur, clearly happy with it all, despite being on her own. They finished the evening back in their room doggie style before drifting off. Richard got up briefly in the night to answer nature's call. He tried to be as quiet as possible but Julie was awake on his return.

"You okay?" she asked.

"Yeah. Just needed the loo. Sorry I woke you"

"Oh don't worry about that. I wake if a spider walks across

the wall. Slightest sound is all it takes."

"Well, as you're awake…"

The second day of auditing started and Richard was more with it this time. He spotted a few silly errors in the supplier's paperwork, but nothing serious.

"I'll just record them as minor non-conformances," he said. "Unless you can correct them before I go tomorrow?" Which they agreed to do.

But on a walk around the site that afternoon, he had a nagging feeling that something wasn't right. The plant was all good quality and clean. Too clean? He went back to the batch sheets and compared them to the goods received and dispatch notes. The quantities didn't tie up.

"Steve, look, I'm probably being thick but I don't understand where these numbers come from?"

Steve actually looked worried. He tried to explain that it was probably down to a disparity between the accounting and the manufacturing software using different databases, but that didn't wash with Richard. His analytical brain was telling him that there was something wrong. He just couldn't quite see it. Richard pointed out discrepancies one after another and could see Steve being slowly worn down.

Steve knew there was a problem. A big one. But he wasn't a corrupt businessman, simply a poor sod out of his depth and desperate to get himself out of the mire.

Richard tried again. "As it stands, I'm going to have to give you a total fail on the audit. And on that basis, Maypharm won't be able to buy from you."

"Can we talk privately?" Steve asked. "Off-site and off-the-record?"

Richard followed Steve to the front desk where they were signed out. Steve led the way to a nearby bar. "You're right Richard," he started.

"What do you mean?"

"That there's a problem with our products and paperwork."

"I gathered that much. Go on…"

Richard listened as Steve admitted that Cosion weren't actually making the ingredients. They were buying in products from outside of France and simply repacking them. As far as Richard was concerned, this was as bad as it could get in terms of compliance. Maypharm were buying products that were supposedly made in Europe and complying with European norms and standards. What they received was products with no audit trail that could be contaminated or not comply with all the regulations that they were expected to meet.

But what to do about it?

The correct action would be to report back to Maypharm, Cease trading with Cosion and chase them for refunds on stock-in-hand and damages for products already supplied. But then Maypharm would also be expected to report their own lapses to the UK authorities and could be in line for a hefty fine, or at least, a lot of paperwork.

Or, he could try to sort it out at this end so that no one in Maypharm knew anything? But that would put him in the gun sights if it went tits up. He'd need something in return.

"Steve. Look. From my point of view, as long as I can be

assured of the quality of your products, then that should be enough. But your recent deliveries have included some pretty poor material."

Steve sensed that a compromise might be possible. "Well that's easy. We've been using three suppliers and I know which one is sub-standard. We can cut them out, but lead times may increase."

"I can live with lead times," Richard answered. "But my own problem is that I'm expected to go back and confirm that your products were made in Europe…"

"Talking hypothetically," Steve said, "if our products were up to spec and there was suitable paperwork in place, then you'd still use them?"

"Hypothetically. Of course… But I'd have a problem."
"Hm?""

"Problem is, why would I pretend that products were European made when I knew they weren't?"

"Because Maypharm would get good product and at a good price."

"Yes, but I'm not Maypahrm, am I? They'd get the benefit of a good margin but muggins here would be taking the risk…"

Steve said tentatively, "So what you're suggesting is that you should enjoy some of that benefit?"

"Not suggesting. Just pointing out that it's a problem for me."

"Okay," Steve said with a small smile. "I'm going to have to have a discussion with my boss, but hypothetically again, if for example, two percent of the invoice price was available as a consultancy fee?"

Richard did a quick calculation. Maypharm were spending just under a million pounds each year with Cosion. Two percent of one million equals twenty thousand.

"It's an interesting idea," Richard conceded, "but two percent would be a lot less than I'd lose if I lost my job over this."

"Five?" Steve suggested. "But we'd have to put Maypharm's prices up by the same amount…"

"I don't think a price hike would be an issue. Not if a certain auditor had instructed you to use more expensive methods, for example. But I do have an idea…"

Steve waited.

"I'm guessing it costs you quite a lot to send your sales rep into us?" Richard asked.

"Well, I suppose so, he's based here in Paris."

"So, if I could save you that cost. And get you better margins. And secure the business going forward. Possibly even increase it. Might that be of interest?

"Of course."

"I've a good friend. Roger Francis. I'm sure I could persuade him to be your local rep and he'd sort all of this out."

"Taking on a new employee would be expensive," Steve objected.

"No. Should be cost neutral, as he'd work for commission only. Say somewhere a little north of five percent?"

Steve grinned. "You're a devious sod Richard. I like it."

"And you're the second person who's called me that recently. Sounds like we don't need to carry on with the audit tomorrow. Sounds like I've enough to sign everything off as satisfactory."

"Agreed." Steve held out his hand which Richard shook.

"Just one other thing." Richard asked. "Can I ask a small favour?"

"Of course."

"Can you back me up by calling my office and giving them the opposite story; that the audit's taking longer than expected and we won't finish until the end of Friday?"

"Done. I take it you've plans?"

"Maybe." Richard smiled.

Phone calls were made and everyone back in the UK, Victoria and Geoff included, happily believed that Richard was having to work hard in France, so hard that he'd not be able to get back until Saturday.

As the car took Richard back to his waiting lover, he contemplated his changing fortunes. In a matter of weeks he'd gone from bored, resentful loser to successful, if corrupt, executive, with a gorgeous lover and a significant amount of money available to him.

He went back up to their room where, as he'd hoped, Julie was waiting. He decided not to tell her about his fraud. No point in putting her in an awkward position. Well, outside of the bedroom anyway. Instead, he gave her the good news that by working hard today, he'd finished early and that they now had the rest of the week until Saturday morning all to themselves.

Julie, clearly pleased, said that she'd not call Lawrence yet. Better to call him on Friday and tell him there was some last minute delay. "He won't mind. Probably wouldn't even notice if I didn't come home until next week."

The next two days were spent in a whirlwind of visits to tourist traps; the Eiffel Tower, the Louvre and Notre Dame cathedral. Plus a wide range of food and drink, and, of course, a lot of time in the bedroom. They also acknowledged that they did have lives back in the UK and bought presents for their spouses and families.

Late Friday afternoon and they found themselves walking back from the Seine up towards Montmartre. It was a bit of a trek but there were plenty of attractions en-route. Walking up Rue St Denis, they looked in the windows of sex shops and then point-scored the prostitutes hanging around on the pavements. A large black woman in a fur coat smiled at them. Richard smiled back and she opened the coat to reveal that she was naked underneath.

"Monsieur? Madam?" She asked.

"Non, mais merci beaucoups," Richard replied, apologising but saying thank you in his schoolboy French.

"I'd give her eight out of ten," Julie said.

"I'd give her one," was Richard's reply.

"I bet you would," she said, squeezing his hand.

At Boulevard de Clichy the sex shops got bigger. They went in one where Richard made lewd suggestions about which of the toys Julie could, or couldn't manage to use, to which her response was, "Darling, believe me, I have the best sex toy available to me now. And it doesn't need batteries."

They took in a strip show on Pigalle and watched a succession of bored looking strippers, most of whom worked to the same formula of losing all but their underwear to a top 20 single, taking off the rest during a second song, and then spending the third going around the small stage putting a leg on a man's lap or ruffling his hair to try to get a tip.

The show wasn't particularly exciting, but Richard did enjoy Julie's whispered commentary, telling him which of the girls she fancied most.

A tall, thin, woman came on. Clearly a much better dancer than the others, and a plaintive piece of piano music came from the tinny speakers. "Eric Satie," Julie told the uncultivated Richard.

"Odd name for a girl," he joked.

Her movements were straight out of the ballet and Richard was captivated. Julie was quiet too. By the end of the second track, Richard was aroused and he pulled Julie's hand onto his crotch.

"She's having the same effect on me," Julie whispered. "I really would have a threesome with you and her. But I think you'd get a bit left out."

"That's okay. I'd watch," Richard replied.

More meals, more drinks, more sex and Richard and Julie were more and more happy.

A relaxed drive back on Saturday and some hours later, Richard found himself opening the passenger door for Julie to collect her car back at Heathrow.

She drove off with a wave back to Lawrence who, as expected, didn't seem in the least worried by her extended absence.

Richard drove back to Twyford and lugged his suitcase into an empty house. For a moment, he was worried that something had happened, or Victoria had found out what he'd been up to, but saw a note on the table. "Good trip? We've gone up to town with mummy. Back late. Food in fridge. Vx."

For no real reason, resentment welled up inside him. He'd had a busy week and she wasn't here to hear his carefully concocted stories?! The double standard didn't strike him immediately. Not until he was emptying the suitcase and found an empty Durex wrapper. 'Fuck. Good thing she didn't find this!' he thought, before carefully checking every other item of clothing as it went into the laundry basket for Victoria to wash at her convenience.

He sorted out a microwave pasta meal, put on Supertramp's *Crime of the Century* and settled down on the sofa to catch up with the newspapers. 'Not much of interest happening,' he thought as he drifted off to sleep.

The dream of a threesome with two ballet dancers was brought to an abrupt end when the women came back squealing and chattering. It was if he'd never been away. Virtually no questions about his week, just some minor excitement when he produced presents, all of which went down well. And, of course, no sex that night.

Monday morning back at work and he was still taking his coat off when Sarah knocked and walked into his office. "Hi Richard. Good trip?"

"Excellent thanks."

"The HPLC." She was straight onto the issue like a ferret down a rabbit hole.

"Yeah, I'll take a look, but I need to see Mr Bristow about

Cosion first."

"Okay boss. But let me know when you do look at it. I just wanted to point out the problems."

"Thanks Sarah. It might not be for a while; the French connection needs to take priority," Richard replied and took the opportunity to leave the room.

Geoff Bristow was easy compared to Sarah. Richard just went through his prepared story: Richard had been thorough in going over the Cosion paperwork and manufacturing methods. He (Richard) had spotted that the catalyst they were using was past its shelf life and that was why they'd had some poor quality products recently. Richard had introduced Cosion to a better catalyst manufacturer, who he happened to know, and he'd led the discussions between them. This had all taken a bit longer than a straightforward audit, but Richard was confident that the quality would improve (as a direct result of his intervention). Only minor issue was that the alternative catalyst was a lot more expensive and he could see Cosion having to increase their prices by a bit more than five percent, "but," he concluded, "it's a small part of the overall cost, and a small cost compared to what might have happened if we hadn't got involved."

The Chairman told Richard how delighted he was with his work. Increased costs weren't a problem. "And," he added, "I realise that you lost a day last weekend with the travel back. Take a workday off when it suits you to make up for it."

"Thanks Geoff."

Back in his office, Richard struggled to contain the grin on his face. Even the impending issue of the HPLC didn't spoil his mood. Money, sex and success. What more could a man want?

Again Sarah interrupted his reverie. This time with a minor headache to do with some QC results. The sort of thing she could usually deal with without Richard's help. He knew she was really more interested in gaining kudos, so said, "Sarah, thanks for the heads-up on the HPLC. You're right that there's something not right here. I'm not sure what it is yet so I'm going to send it back to the manufacturers, and ask them for a full report."

Sarah appeared satisfied with this and Richard knew that he'd bought himself some time. It would still need sorting, but based on recent events, he felt he couldn't fail.

The day off was taken the following Wednesday. This plus the excuse of evening classes gave the lovers a good twelve hours together. Their original plan had been to spend the day in Julie's house and then go out for the evening. Unfortunately, Lawrence went down with man-flu and decided to stay at home. A hasty phone call and they met up in an anonymous car park.

"Any ideas where to go?" Richard asked.

"Not a clue. Check-in at most places is two or three o'clock." Julie thought for a moment, "Go for a day out somewhere?"

"Well, we could." He replied. But it's raining. Nowhere much is open at this time of year. And the roads are crammed with Christmas shoppers. Which reminds me. Must get presents for Vic and the girls sometime. I hate shopping."

"Me too. But it would be tolerable if you were with me…"

Lost for anything better to do, they decided to share the chore of Christmas present shopping, after which they'd be able to get into a hotel room. Not willing to risk a shopping centre close to home, they ended up travelling an hour down the motorway to Swindon's Designer Outlet Mall, which contained rows of shops inside what was once one of the largest railway workshops in the country.

Richard found the preserved architecture and a lone steam loco interesting. But the shops… Richard avoided shopping at the best of times and was not into buying products according to their brand. If he wanted a jumper, he'd buy one that he liked, not one that cost four times as much but happened to have some silly logo on it. Julie disliked it even more. Her left-wing principles struggled within this cathedral of capitalism. But they ploughed on through and completed their shopping lists, with Julie suggesting female friendly gifts that Richard would never have considered.

Then it was back to the car and more pleasant prospects. A short drive found them in a gastropub out in the open countryside. A pub that just happened to have rooms available. They satisfied their needs in the restaurant with an excellent meal of local Wiltshire ham (although Richard thought tying the napkins up with pieces of straw a bit poncey), and a bottle of red wine. The pub was clearly a favourite of the horsey set. Ignoring Julie's muttered derision at the red corduroy trousered locals, Richard found himself engrossed in the photos that covered all of the walls – black and white newspaper-quality shots of racehorses in action, owners with trophies, jockeys spattered with mud. He found his attention wandering from the food, and even from Julie, as he worked out how some of the shots were taken. What lenses, what film and the like.

"Richard!" Julie managed to attract his attention. "I know that you like a young filly, but there's an old mare here which needs a stallion."

"More than happy to give you a ride."

A room was swiftly procured and he got himself back in the saddle.

Richard found his eyelids getting heavy and before the afternoon was over, he was snoring loudly. Julie also drifted off but woke with a start at the sound of a distant door closing. The room was in darkness. Turning on a bedside lamp, she looked at her watch.

"Shit! Richard! Wake up!"

"What...?"

"It's after ten!"

"Oh fuck."

No time for showers, they flung their clothes back on and he dropped the key back at reception, mumbling something about a family emergency they needed to get back to, and they got themselves back on the motorway.

'It'll be well after eleven,' Richard guessed. Julie would be alright; Lawrence didn't give a toss what time she came in, but Victoria was another matter.

Pushing his chances of being pulled over for speeding, they made up some of the time but it was still a good 45 minutes later than usual when Richard unlocked his front door and crept in. The lights were out. Hopefully, Victoria was already asleep.

He went into the kitchen and clicked on the light switch.

Victoria was sitting at the table.

"Bloody hell! You made me jump!" he blurted out. "What are you doing sitting here in the dark?"

"Just waiting for you," she said calmly, looking at her watch. "Bit late…"

"Yeah, sorry. Couple of us went over to The Jack of Both Sides for a drink."

"Uh huh."

"Yes. Sorry. I should have let you know…"

Calmly, Victoria picked up something from the table and without looking at him asked, "Who's Christine?"

"Sorry?"

"Who's Christine?"

"Umm, I'm not with you?"

Victoria looked at him and held out a business card. A card for a restaurant in Arromanches. "I found this."

Richard recognised it and knew only too well what it was. The telephone number from the holiday waitress. "Ummm."

"Let me help you," she said flatly. "I found it in your desk."

Richard stayed quiet, trying to think his way out.

"And while we're at it," her fingers idly toying with another piece of paper. "Want to tell me about wedbutlooking.com?"

"Sorry?" Richard really was confused by this reference.

"Okay. So you can't remember that you have a profile on a sex dating site or that you have a phone number of a woman in France who wants to see you, again?"

Richard realised that the second piece of paper was his log-in details to the website. He found himself feeling very calm.

He'd been caught and Victoria knew him well enough to spot a lie. At the same time, she hadn't said anything about Julie. No point in denying things he couldn't deny. But he might be able to limit the damage.

"Umm, okay. Yes. Well, there might be something."

"Might?…" "Something?!" she snapped. "Go on…"

"Well, yes. I did look at the website. But I never met anyone from it. I never did anything with anyone."

"I know. I read all your messages. But you would have done something if you'd had the chance. Wouldn't you?"

"I don't know. It's just that I was a bit pissed and wondered what it was all about," he pretended. "But yes, I was stupid. I didn't do anything with anyone though…"

"What about Christine?"

"What about Christine?" He stonewalled. Trickier one. Did she know anything? Surely not.

"So you didn't meet her in France when we were on holiday?"

'Oh fuck,' he thought, she does know…

"Well yes, she was the waitress in the restaurant. She must have liked me because she gave me her number. I meant to chuck it away, but must have forgotten."

"So why did she write 'encore'?"

"I don't know. Maybe she wanted us to come back to her restaurant."

"Crap!" Victoria snapped again. "I know you saw her."

"Eh?"

"It was the last night, wasn't it? When I came into the loos there. I thought I saw a girl come out of the one that you came out of later. I wasn't sure then. But I am sure now."

Richard could see that he'd have to admit something. "OK. Look I'm really sorry. She came on to me and I tried to say no. But Vicky love, on my life, we didn't have sex. I said no."

"Maybe you didn't have sex, but you did do something. I know you. I can tell…"

Richard wasn't good at lying. He knew not saying anything would be worse than trying to dig his way out and that if he told the truth, that she'd believe him. Whether he could get away with it was another matter, but he'd give it his best shot.

Putting on his most contrite face, he took a deep breath. "I'm sorry Vicky. Something did happen. But really, I didn't screw her. We just messed about a bit, that's all."

"Messed about? How exactly? You weren't playing cards…"

"She, well, I couldn't stop her. It was a blowjob."

"Blowjob," this was the first time he'd heard Victoria use the phrase, "you had oral sex?"

"Yes."

"And you couldn't stop her?! She just suggested sucking your dick and you just rolled over and said yes? Come on. I'm not stupid. Did you do anything to her? Or pay her?"

"No!"

"So out of the goodness of her heart, she just decided to give you a blowjob?"

"Well, yes, it is a bit like that. I don't know why. She must have mislaid her guide dog and thought I was attractive," he tried to joke, "and, I know I should've stopped her, but well, I just couldn't."

"Did you have sex with her?"

"NO!"

"How can I believe you?"

"Phone her." Richard knew there was no way Victoria would do this. "Or I'll phone her and you listen. She's got nothing to lose by confirming the truth."

Victoria looked up, tears in her eyes. "No. Richard, I don't know why, but that's about the only bit of this I do believe… I don't think you had sex… But you would have, given the chance."

"Vicky…"

"Okay…" she said, and then asked the harder question: "Why?"

Richard paused, thinking that honesty is sometimes the best policy. In a quiet voice he replied, "Because I have needs as well."

"And I don't meet them?" she asked quietly.

He knew his answer would cause hurt, but had to say it, "In most areas, of course you do. It's just in the bedroom where, just sometimes, I'd like a bit more."

"Okay," she said. "I need some time. Which one of us is in the spare room tonight?"

"I guess it's me," he answered, and they each went to their separate beds.

He didn't sleep much that night, not knowing what Victoria would do about Christine, and the website, but at the same time counting his blessings that she didn't know of his other secrets; Julie, fiddled invoices, voyeurism, fake identity.

In the morning he was surprised to find her cooking him breakfast.

"Don't think you're forgiven," she said, glaring at him, "You're not. But we need to work through this. We'll talk later."

The phrase "work through this" was music to Richard's ears. There was light at the end of the tunnel and it wasn't the 3:30pm express train hurtling towards him. More to the point, Victoria wasn't talking about doing anything which would jeopardise his rise to being the next Chairman of Maypharm.

*

They didn't talk about it that day, or for a while. Christmas got in the way. A second Christmas dealing with family infidelity.

It was a difficult period all round. For Victoria and Richard, there was the unspoken issue of Christine. For Richard and Julie, not being able to meet during this time of being with loved ones. For Lorna, being on her own for the first time. Then there was juggling meals with Richard's parents, Lorna, and Geoff and Dawn plus, for Richard, all of the usual mess of presents, cards, decorations and other disruptions to his usually ordered life.

Richard and Julie communicated by text over the festive season. Much as he wanted to get in the car and find somewhere to meet her, Victoria wasn't letting him out of her sight and was giving him numerous odd jobs to do. He couldn't find any plausible reason to be out of the house for half a day.

Geoff and Dawn came around on Christmas Day morning having already agreed with Victoria that they'd be away by midday. They brought with them overly generous presents for Victoria, Emma and Lucy. After they left, Lorna arrived (having previously phoned to check that the coast was clear of her bastard of a husband). She also proceeded to spoil the girls. The separated grandparents using their bank accounts to demonstrate how much better each was compared to the other. Boxing day with Richard's parents was a much quieter affair. With cheaper presents.

The period between Boxing Day and New Year is a busy mix of activities for some people. For Richard it was a combination of boredom, frustration and chores, all depending on what his wife and daughters were up to. He hated the lack of routine and freedom, but took every chance to text Julie describing fantasies that he was hoping they'd achieve in the New Year.

Richard was actually pleased that the holiday was over when he went back to work. Everything was more predictable there.

Wednesday evening came and Richard and Julie were, after too long apart, able to get back together. They went back to the hotel that they'd first gone to and had another good attempt at wrecking the bedding. Richard didn't risk leaving it too late getting home this time.

The following weekend Emma and Lucy had a sleepover at a classmate's. Richard didn't give it a second thought, the routine at home being back to normal, as far as he was concerned. Victoria ferried the girls around and picked up an Indian takeaway on the way back. As the two of them settled down to an extensive pile of naan breads, pickles, curries and rice, she looked down at her plate and pointedly said, "So."

"So?" Richard replied.

"So. Let's talk."

Richard's good mood dissipated. "Okay. Fire away."

"I need to know what you did and why," she said in a deliberate voice, still looking down at her food, picking at it.

"I told you what happened–" he started.

"Tell me again."

"Well, I was an idiot."

"I agree so far."

Richard collected his thoughts and continued. "I'd had a couple of drinks and, you know, the sun, sea and everything, and I'd been an idiot at the start of the week, and…" he trailed off.

"You mean that because I wouldn't do something, you thought it okay to break our marriage vows and do it with someone else?"

"That's a harsh way of putting it."

Victoria looked up, with tears in her eyes. "But it's the truth. Isn't it?"

"I wouldn't say that I deliberately ignored our vows. It was just that there was an opportunity and I didn't think it through."

"Hmm." Victoria went quiet and Richard wasn't going to drop himself in it by breaking the silence. They picked at the food. Once appetising. Now just a way of passing the time.

Eventually, Victoria looked up again. "Can I trust you not to do it again?"

"Of course!" He thought his response was too quick so waited and added, "Yes, you can."

She looked up again. "The thing is, I don't want to end up like mummy. On her own. If you do it again, then we're fucked."

"It's the lack of fucking that caused the problem," he quipped, immediately recognising that this was not a good joke. 'Prepare for an earful,' he thought.

Her reply came as a surprise, as in a quiet voice she said, "I know."

"Sorry?"

"I know that if I'd been more intimate, then you might not have gone with her. I do try you know."

Tentatively he said, "But if we both tried a bit harder…"

She looked up, gave a deep sigh and said in a resigned voice, "Yes, we should. You should try to keep your dick inside your pants. Look, I would be up for it a bit more but it's this house."

"Sorry? This house? What's that got to do with anything?"

"It's too crowded. The girls are up later now and I can't relax if they might hear us."

"What you're saying is that if they weren't here, then we'd have sex?"

"Or if we were in a bigger place, with more room, then maybe."

Richard thought. In for a penny…

"So the girls are away tonight…"

"If you think after all of this?!"

Richard might have thought, but he was wrong. No way was there going to be any conjugals that night. However, the next morning, Victoria initiated what he later thought of as probably the best bonk the two of them had ever had. She seemed to enjoy it for once, being remarkably responsive all the way through, rather than just lying there. They'd even changed from missionary to doggie halfway through. And that was at her suggestion.

Her tactics appeared to be working when later in the day Richard mentioned that he'd been looking at houses in the local paper and even showed her a couple that he liked the look of. She knew his sole motivation was the possibility of more sex 'but,' she mused, 'keep him busy enough on a larger house and he won't have the time or energy to get up to anything with anyone else'.

Richard's suggested houses were modest upgrades compared to what Victoria had in mind. She wanted a proper family home, like the one she'd been brought up in. Four bedrooms (three for the family and one for guests), en-suites throughout, good-sized kitchen and living room, maybe a study for Richard to hide in, double garage, large private garden (preferably south facing) and in a village location. Simple tastes really, she felt. There was a couple she quite liked the look of in the paper, so pointed them out.

"How much?!" Richard couldn't believe that Victoria was suggesting properties that were half a million quid.

"We can afford it."

"No we can't! We'd have to double the mortgage."

"No, we wouldn't." Victoria smiled, her surprise about to be unwrapped. "Mummy's going to sell some of her shares and we'll be getting some of the money."

"That's daft." Richard was disturbed. He knew that the Maypharm shares were giving Lorna a good income and security. She was a canny old bird and he couldn't see why she'd get rid of any.

Victoria had it all worked out, "No, it's a good idea. I've done the sums. She'll lend us the money and we put her on the deeds as part owner."

Richard could see that her money would get them a bigger house but still couldn't see the benefit to Lorna. The only way she'd get anything would be if they sold the house and paid her back along with any increase in value, and at her age, it would be unlikely that they'd move again before Lorna needed to move out of the large house she was currently in. He put this to Victoria.

Her reply alarmed him. "I know she won't get any immediate benefit. But we'd take her in when she couldn't stay at home. She'd come to live with us."

Victoria could see that her husband didn't like the idea. "Don't worry. It won't be for years. And by then, you'll be on the Board and money won't be a problem, so we could look at homes with granny flats, or she might be happy with an old people's home. She probably won't actually join us. It's just security for her and we get a better place."

Richard was mollified to some extent. Still uncertain, he tacitly agreed and left his wife to start the trawl of the estate agents.

*

Lying in bed with Julie the following Wednesday evening, his mind distracted by recent physical activities, he chattered away to her about the possibility of moving house. Julie was perturbed. She'd increasingly been thinking about a longer-term future with Richard, and here he was potentially investing heavily in a future for him and Victoria. Was he so thick skinned that he didn't realise that in an affair, you don't talk about the good times with your wife?

He was expressing his concern that his mother-in-law might one day move in when Julie interrupted. "So why are you doing it? What's wrong with staying in your present house."

Richard opened his mouth and inserted both feet, "Because Victoria's not comfortable about having sex if there's a possibility that the girls can hear."

"But you told me that you're not having sex…"

His stomach dropped as he realised what a hole he'd dug for himself.

"Well, no. We're not," he lied.

"But it could happen if you moved?"

"Well, technically yes, but I wouldn't do it if you and I were still together… Which we will be," he added rapidly.

Julie lay back. "I know we're having a fling. But I don't want it to end. And I don't want to be sharing you with another woman…"

"Well, to some extent you are sharing me. Like I'm sharing you with Lawrence."

"Okay." She seemed to accept what he was saying.

"Anyway, enough talking. My lips have other uses," and he started kissing her.

The conversation continued to rankle with Julie over the

next few days. She appreciated that they didn't have any claim on each other, but found herself jealous of Richard's wife. Julie didn't want Victoria's lifestyle – the kids, mother-in-law, job, or any of the rest of it – just Richard.

She pressed him on it the next week after suitably wearing him out. Again he said that he and Victoria were looking at moving up, that he didn't really want to move and their relationship was sexless.

"Just like mine," Julie said. "In an ideal world we'd be living together having a great time."

"Sounds idyllic," Richard agreed. "And I bet your husband and my wife would make a great couple as well. Both more interested in money and status than sex."

"So what's stopping us?" Julie heard the words slip out before she had a chance to think.

"Just the minor impediments of life my love. You know, jobs, marriages, kids, houses, to name but a few."

Julie noticed that Richard hadn't said anything about not wanting to be with her full time.

"We'll have to see what we can do then," she said quietly.

Julie found herself contemplating big changes in her life more and more. Richard might have done so as well, if he wasn't so focused on himself and wasn't so afraid of change.

Unfortunately though, just as Julie thought that their relationship could be moving into a new phase, fate stuck up two of its fickle fingers.

*

The first of Richard's problems hit on a Monday morning towards the end of January. Victoria came into the lab at work, not an unusual occurrence as she often said "Hi" to her husband if she was walking through that part of the site. But this time it was more of an official visit.

"Hi love," she started, "all okay? I've a quick one for you."

"I should be so lucky!" Richard joked, knowing that he'd get away with it here where a bit of banter was normal.

"Don't get your hopes up," she replied, although not in her usual bright voice. She lightened up, however, as she carried on, "No, it's an accounts query."

"That's fine. It'll save me having to buy any sleeping pills." Another vain attempt at humour from Richard, who was always reminding his wife that accountancy was generally regarded as the most boring job going.

"Ha ha. No, it's this invoice."

Victoria handed Richard a piece of paper that he recognised only too well. The invoice that he'd faked from Wesley Instruments when he'd got the HPLC refurbished, instead of buying a new one.

"What's the problem?"

"It's just that Sarah said you've a problem with the unit?"

'Bugger Sarah,' thought Richard, 'I tell her to leave it all to me and now she's flagged it up outside the lab.'

"Yes, just a minor technical thing," he said, "nowt to worry about. I don't really need the invoice. They've not asked for it."

"No, that's not the query," Victoria said. "It's just that I've just spotted an error on it."

"Error?"

"This invoice dates back to before we upgraded Sage accounts so it went through as a manual payment, so it's not surprising it was missed."

"What was missed?

"The serial number of the unit. Sarah gave me the number of the unit here, but it didn't match the one on the invoice. I'm sure that it's nothing, but can you look up the number of the new machine and let me know which one it is so that we can get the inventory right."

"I would, but it's back with Wesley's to be looked at." Richard hoped that this lie would not be challenged. The HPLC was actually being re-refurbished again, this time with anything old being replaced. The serial number plate though was not due to have anything done to it and he wondered what he could do.

"No probs. When it comes back, just let me know and we'll get it sorted. See you for lunch?"

"Yes, as usual," Richard replied, absent-mindedly debating how to solve this one.

*

The second problem came up a couple of days later. Richard had noticed that Victoria had been quiet but put it down to their recent problems, plus the general malaise of a dank and dark January. Emma and Lucy had just left for school and he was getting his shoes on ready to drive them both to work.

"Hang on for a minute?" she asked,

"We'll be late. Is it important?"

"Yes, it is actually. Come here a minute."

Victoria sat at the kitchen table and he joined her.

"What's up then, love?" Richard asked.

She took a breath, looked at him and simply said, "I'm late."

"Yes, so am I. But you wanted to ask me something?"

With a wan smile, she clarified her words. "No, I mean I'm late. As in my period."

Richard didn't know what to think or how to reply. Should he pretend to be overjoyed? Or should he be honest that another child was the last thing he wanted? He played it down the middle. "Bloody hell, I wasn't expecting that. What, I mean, how do you feel about it?"

"I don't know. It wasn't something I'd ever thought about. Having another. And I don't know how I'd cope with another one. But I can't get rid of it, can I?"

"God, I don't know love." He put his hands out to hold hers, a rare display of empathy. "How late?"

"It's only a few days, but well, there was that morning earlier this month…"

"How could I forget?" he replied honestly. "But what say we give it a few more days before adding another room onto our house search?"

She smiled back, "I thought you'd be the sensible one. I'm just a bit emotional. Being silly."

It wouldn't have been such an issue if Richard had kept his mouth shut.

The impending end of his world… The risk of being caught for the fake invoice and losing his job… The possibility of umpteen more years of having to be a good, and busier, dad… These thoughts got in the way of Richard's usual overly-rational thinking. Julie picked up on his distractedness on the Wednesday evening; firstly, when he accidentally used his real name when booking into their evening hotel and later, when she was giving him what she thought was an excellent blowjob, she noticed him looking at the ceiling without his usual expression of intense delight. She bit his cock gently, provoking an "ouch" and his return to the real world.

She stopped her oral gymnastics, provoking a look of dismay from him. "You're not with me are you?" she stated.

"I was enjoying that," he countered, "but sorry Julie." This was a rare event, he usually avoided using her name in case he got used to saying it and accidently used it when addressing his wife. "Sorry Julie, but my mind was elsewhere."

"I noticed. And I'm guessing it wasn't anywhere where I was?"

"Sorry no. Just problems at work and at home."

It was unlike Richard to open up like this. So Julie rearranged herself to lie next to him, put her hand around his erection and asked, "A problem shared is a problem halved?" while gently squeezing it.

He wasn't going to tell her, or anyone, about the invoice issue. Better to make something up, and the ongoing stimulation distracted him from thinking through his words.

"You're probably right, but I don't think you can help. Not unless you know how to analyse trace chloride levels in fluorocarbons."

"No, you've got me there. Home?"

"Victoria thinks she might be pregnant."

Julie froze. "Is she having an affair as well then?"

"No way! She'd never be brave enough." As the words left Richard's lips, he realised that he'd dropped himself well and truly in it.

Julie's next words confirmed it. "Well, it was Christmas wasn't it. And the Messiah's second coming is overdue. Was there a star in the east when the immaculate conception occurred?"

Richard flustered, "It was just the once."

Julie's hand was still on his cock and she deliberately started moving it up and down again, confusing him further. Was she accepting what had happened?

"She's your wife. Husbands and wives have sex. But you said you weren't."

"Sorry" – this was becoming a much used word – "I know you're upset."

"I don't know how I feel," Julie said. "I do want you and I do want you now…"

Richard started to move on top of her, but she retained her hold on him and added, "but hang on. Yes, you can fuck my brains out in a minute. But I'm not going to carry on like this if you and your wife are still having sex. I don't mind the thought of sharing you with another woman if we're having a threesome."

This was music to Richard's ears, she was still saying that she could be up for a threesome! "But…" and it all went downhill, "I can only accept you having another woman while I'm present. If you're going to fuck your wife in the marital bed, then you're not going to fuck me."

"That's easy," Richard replied. "I only want to have sex with you."

"When you say you only want to have sex with me, do you mean, and think about this very carefully Richard… The only woman you want to have sex with is me? Or, and this is very different, do you mean that you don't want any relationship with me, you only want me for sex?"

Richard was confused for a moment, but recognised how his answers might be received.

"I want you and you only," he answered carefully. "If I wasn't already married, and if you weren't" – a gentle reminder that she was in it just as much as he was – "then I would be looking for more than what we have now."

"That's good. We agree. And just for the record, if we were both single, I would have moved in with you by now. If you'd let me that is."

"I would."

Richard thought he'd pulled the situation from the fire, but he soon found his fingers getting scorched when Julie said, "So we both want each other and we want it long term. But Richard, for the moment I'm going to have to be hard on you. Until I can be absolutely certain that you and your wife are not doing anything, until then, this is the last time we will be in bed together."

Richard thought about making a quick remark that there were plenty of other places apart from bed, but saw that it would have been a dangerous and wasted line.

"Well, I know that I can be faithful to you," he said instead, "but how can I demonstrate that proof to you?"

"I'm sure you'll think of a way after a couple of weeks of celibacy," Julie grinned, "Now make the most of the little time you've got left this evening."

Richard did as he was told, whilst thinking – wrongly – that Julie wasn't serious in her ultimatum. He'd forgotten how a similar disagreement had killed her and Lawrence's sex life.

He got home freshly shagged and showered to find Victoria chatting with her mum and the girls. 'It won't be a problem if Lorna moves into the next house,' he thought, 'she just about lives with us permanently as it is.'

He said his 'hellos' and added that he was knackered after a busy day.

"You don't mind if I go on up do you?" he asked.

"Of course not," came the chorus. Victoria added, "By the way love, that little problem this morning? Don't worry. All sorted. The postman was just a bit late."

Richard went to bed kicking himself. No problem with Victoria and if he'd used his brain, there wouldn't have been a problem with Julie.

Next day, he texted Julie with the news. "That's gd 4 u," came the curt reply. "But what I said stands. If u want sex then I need to c that u r with me only." A couple of seconds later another text, "I want u, but u must be with me only."

"I can do that," he texted back. "My biggest problem is how to prove to you that I'm not doing anything with her. How can I do it? CCTV in the bedroom?"

"That would be perfect," came the reply.

Richard didn't have a solution, but he wasn't going to let that defeat him. Over the next weeks, they continued meeting up on a Wednesday evening, but went to pubs and restaurants.

"This is more like a conventional date," Richard commented once. There were long kisses and wandering hands which occasionally led to one or the other reaching a climax, but full sex was off the menu.

And Richard was getting hungry.

PART 3

TRANSACTIONS AND CONSEQUENCES

CHAPTER 12

HARD FI. "Stars of CCTV"

Spring 2000 and the Marsh's house went onto the market, and a full price offer was made within a week.

Victoria found the house she wanted. So what if 33 Acacia Avenue was a "bit" more expensive than their upper limit. They'd just have to cut back somewhere else for a while. The rooms were big. And the garden alone was worth the extra outlay. All that lawn for the girls to play on. And the estate agent reckoned that planning permission for a granny wing extension would be easy to get, which was good.

Richard didn't like it. Acacia Avenue was a lot more expensive than he wanted to pay and he didn't want to have to cut back on any of his lifestyle. The rooms needed decorating and at that size it was a lot of work. The same went for the garden, which certainly wasn't worth the extra money. It would really need a motorised mower and there'd be no money left for that. And the estate agent reckoned that planning permission for a granny wing extension would be easy to get, which was far from good.

He tried all of the rational arguments. None worked so instead he ignored the issue and hoped something better would come along.

Unfortunately for him, Victoria knew exactly how to defeat that one. She reminded him that their bedroom would be on the other side of the house compared to Emma's and Lucy's. And he'd seen how passionate she could get now, hadn't he? She could see him wavering, and when she started stroking his penis late one night, his resolve went out of the window. When Victoria next started talking about putting in an offer, he agreed and called the agent. The offer was rejected as was a slightly higher one. The seller would only take the full asking price. Never mind that the house had been on the market for months or that everyone said it was overpriced.

Richard was happy(ish) to pay the right price but not to be ripped off. That is until Victoria went back to her default plan to get him to agree to pay the higher price. A reminder of the possibility of more intimacy and a caress and he was putty in her hands (although part of him was not as soft as putty) and the full price was offered, and accepted.

The house move went like clockwork and before long the family was firmly ensconced in Acacia Avenue and Richard's evenings and weekends were spent covered in paint, dust, wallpaper paste or grass cuttings. Victoria was putting in plenty of work as well, not just with getting the house square, but with the usual round of kid's clubs, shopping and the like. At least, that was the reason she gave for being too tired for sex.

In a vain attempt to overcome the tiredness argument, Richard offered to pay for a cleaner. Victoria agreed. But if he had been hoping for an 18-year-old big-breasted blonde, then the reality couldn't have been more different. Victoria hired an elderly, grumpy woman who Richard (behind her back) nicknamed The Witch. Every Wednesday morning she came in and cleaned all flat surfaces, polished anything that wasn't matt and retuned every radio in the house to the local commercial station that Richard couldn't stand.

Victoria was still too tired for sex.

The streets around Acacia Avenue were also less conducive to Richard's voyeurism. It wasn't just that the bedrooms were harder to see into, due to high fences and hedges, but also because of Mr & Mrs Thwaites across the road. They used their positions as the local Neighbourhood Watch coordinators to justify their constant nosiness. Richard knew that any nocturnal strolls with a camera would be swiftly noticed, recorded and the details spread around the rest of the local busybodies. 'Not worth the risk,' he decided.

This, together with Victoria's continuing opposition to his going out, meant that he was not getting many opportunities to peer through the lace curtains of suburbia at the lace underwear of suburban housewives. He needed another way to satisfy his peeping Tom fetish.

During a routine visit to the dentist, he sat in the waiting room flicking through a well-thumbed copy of an old magazine when he spotted an article about the rise in covert surveillance devices, which were being used in schools to monitor pupils' behaviour.

'Never mind smoking round the back of the bike sheds,' he thought, as usual ignoring the basics of legality, 'what would you see if one of these devices was in the girls' showers?'

An hour later, back in the office, teeth gleaming and wallet emptied, he researched covert cameras online. There were a plethora of possibilities. Video cameras built into virtually anything that you could think of. There was also a lot of confusing detail about how to see what the camera was viewing. He understood the optical side of it; which ones were best for low light, the angle of view and effective focal length, but the connectivity was way out of his depth.

A phone call to one of the shops advertising the kit didn't help much. Still too much talk about Wi-Fi and frequencies. But a pharmaceutical conference in London gave him the chance to visit a specialist retail showroom.

"I'm after something to help me keep an eye on my office when I'm out," Richard said to the sales assistant.

They spent some time looking at cameras disguised as clocks, pens and desk ornaments, all of which offered scope for his desires. The assistant ("John," according to his name badge) asked pertinent questions about what Richard was aiming to achieve.

"Ideally," Richard replied, "I'd like something that I can just plonk down and then be able to see through it from somewhere else. No techy setting up. Something simple really."

"Well," said John, "I'd suggest our Optimus range. It's all

designed for ease of use. It's a modular system. Select any of the cameras. Any of the power sources, whether in-built or hard-wired. They all have a 900Mhz transmitter which can be picked up if you're within about 50 metres, subject to what walls, and so on, there are in the area, of course."

"And receivers?" Richard asked.

"Ah, well here's the other area where modularity can help," John continued. "A simple adapted hand-held TV is the easiest, but we also have DVD recorders, remote controllers, and all sorts more, so that you can watch and record up to eight cameras from a single monitor."

"Sounds good." But Richard could still see that the technical side would be an issue.

"And, of course," the salesman delivered the killer blow, "we would set them all up for you and give you a training session so that you can use them going forward."

"Sounds like you've got a deal."

They agreed on a selection of items, including recording equipment and a range of household items incorporating hidden cameras.

"For the wall clocks," the salesman said, "the camera lens is just here…" pointing to a small dot two or three millimetres across just below the number twelve. "It's not really noticeable as it is, but we can put a logo on the clock face to disguise it for a small amount extra. You can provide your own, or we have a selection already available." He produced a leaflet showing the same clock with various words and pictures added around the lens.

"That'll do nicely," said Richard indicating a picture of an owl – one beady eye able to see anything that was going on in front of it.

*

Over the same period, the issue of the dodgy invoice failed to go away. At the end of every month, Victoria's accounts team reviewed outstanding issues and this one soon became the one with the longest pedigree. He could probably have come up with a plausible argument acceptable to most of the team there (being the bosses son-in-law helped somewhat) but Victoria was more dogged and wouldn't let it slip. Richard found himself having to come up with new excuses as to why the report wasn't complete or the unit back. By the time three months had gone by the machine had been, according to Richard, sent to Japan for inspection by the original component manufacturers. He knew that he'd have make up something better eventually, but couldn't come up with a simple, believable answer yet and just had the vain hope that somehow it would be forgotten. If he really had to, he could buy a new unit with the Cosion money, but that again was something Richard didn't want to do if he could help it. Someone would probably still suss it.

The relationship with Julie had stayed firmly in the snog, chat and fondle arena. Richard was surprised to find that he could cope with this. He loved his time with Julie, even without full sexual contact. Deep down, he knew that he cared for her more than his wife, not that he was willing to do anything about it at the moment as the cost would be too high.

Instead, his warped logic put the blame for his sexual frustration on Victoria. Julie was doing exactly what she said she would and giving him some satisfaction whereas Victoria wasn't doing anything despite what she'd intimated, leaving him frustrated and resentful. The happily married couple (as far as the outside world was concerned) found themselves stressed and tired. Their repertoire of relationship management tools still did not include arguments or critical discussion, so instead, they coped with the occasional snipe at each other.

Things turned a corner towards the end of the summer. Victoria was round her mother's, Emma and Lucy, now teenagers, were away somewhere for the day and Richard had spent the afternoon pushing the lawnmower up and down the excessively long garden of the excessively expensive house that his wife had pushed him into buying through the simple expedient of implying he might actually be on the receiving end of some sort of sexual activity if he offered the seller the exorbitant asking price that they wanted. He'd spent the time making a mental list of things that he was unhappy with, intending to bring some of them up in discussion given the chance. At the same time, he knew that the right moment wouldn't occur.

Sweaty, grimy, sneezing from pollen and itching from the attentions of red ants, he was in dire need of a shower and a beer, and not necessarily in that order. The shower won and afterwards he found himself back downstairs, a crisp clean t-shirt and shorts replacing the workwear, still aching from the gardening but feeling a lot cleaner and enjoying the first sip of the beer. He heard the front door open and a cheery, "I'm home," and Victoria walked in.

"Is this how you've spent the day?" she asked joking. He didn't see the joke.

She started pottering around, not really doing anything but looking busy. He recognised this behaviour. She was avoiding starting the cooking, and instead looking otherwise engaged, knowing that sooner or later he'd get fed up and go and get fish and chips or a Chinese for them. Her lack of effort stoked his resentment over how she didn't seem to notice or care about all that he'd done. Even her good mood was getting on his nerves.

Eventually, he sighed and said, "Would you like me to go and get us some food?"

"That's a good idea."

"What do you want?"

"You choose," she replied, adding incongruously, "I don't really give a fuck."

He muttered under his breath, "Well, what do I have to do before you *will* give a fuck."

She wasn't meant to have heard, but she piped up unoffended, "Well, a new dishwasher would do it!"

He looked at her in astonishment and for once let his anger show. "Did I get that right? You won't let me fuck you as part of our marriage, but if I spend a couple of hundred quid, you'll open your legs?"

She thought that he was putting on the outraged voice and cheerily replied, "Sounds about right!"

He paused, simmering. "Get your shoes on," he ordered calmly.

"You're getting the grub, not me," she countered.

"Not talking about the food."

He calmed down as she duly got her shoes and followed him out the door and into the car. He drove them to the Comet electrical warehouse in a retail park on the edge of Reading, led her through to the white goods section and just said, "Which one?"

Victoria spent a happy quarter of an hour comparing dishwashers, asking her husband questions regarding which device he thought was better. Questions which he failed to answer. She eventually said to him, "It's between the Bosch and the Zanussi. What do you think?"

"Well… both will fit in the kitchen. They both have similar specs. The Bosch is 50 quid more, so it's just a question of whether you give me a fuck tonight or a fuck tonight and a handjob in the morning."

She stared at him.

"You started it," he said.

Again she smiled. "Well, you're getting a handjob in the morning."

The order was placed and they went home – via the takeaway – and Richard had missionary sex that night and a handjob in the morning.

Richard brought the subject up again at lunch on Monday. Talking quietly, in case their co-workers overheard, he asked, "Saturday. Where do we stand now?"

"?"

"You know, sex for favours."

She pushed her plate aside and looked at him. "I know I'm partly to blame."

"Partly to blame? For what? What do you mean?"

"For our arguments and for what you did with that French tart. I know that our sex drives don't match. There might have been times when I would have done more, but your behaviour stopped me."

"What did I do?"

"It's not what you did. It usually what you don't do."

"Sorry, I'm not with you?"

"You do bugger all around the house unless I ask you. And I have to ask several times. Virtually every room still needs redecorating. The car is always in a state. I agree that you did the lawn on Saturday, but the garden needs a load more done than that. You never put anything away. Does any of this ring any bells?"

"Okay, okay." He held up his hands. "I admit defeat. It's just that I don't feel like doing anything when you're holding back. I know I get grumpy, but…"

"I understand," she said softly. "We both need to try harder. You need to try harder around the house, and in return, I need to be more open to your… um… needs."

"One wall painted equals one handjob," he joked.

She looked at him, "Actually, that's about right."

He carried on. Not sure whether he was going too far. "Cutting the grass equals a Saturday night special?"

She nodded her head, "Go on."

"I don't know really," he said, "you tell me what you want and

I'll tell you what I want in return."

"Works for me," she replied, "and vice-versa, of course. You tell me what perverted little act you want me to perform and I'll tell you what you have to do to get it."

"It's a deal," he said.

"Deal," she agreed.

Both went quiet working out the possibilities.

"I quite fancy a new rug for the living room," Victoria speculated.

"Ikea or the shop in the high street?"

"Ikea, say two metres by three?"

"Sounds like doggy position to me," he replied.

"Missionary. Or two handjobs," she bargained

"One missionary it is. Tonight?"

"Get me the rug first."

The two of them dissolved into fits of giggles. It felt the early days before so many things went wrong. Victoria leant toward Richard and gave him a long kiss, oblivious to the glances of their co-workers. "I love you," she said.

"I love you too."

*

It turned into a game. A game that they both felt that they had won. Richard got a lot more sex and Victoria got a lot more support around the house. It actually seemed to be working. They soon found that the exchange rates were fluid. Richard would do more if he'd not had sex recently. Victoria would do more if she really wanted something. Outsiders may have considered what they were doing as odd, but they both recognised it as simply transactional.

Richard was the first to push it into new areas. He woke on Sunday morning fancying a quiet day; a drink down the pub with Geoff, then join Victoria, Lorna and the girls for dinner and a snooze on the sofa. But Victoria said she wanted him to help her with clearing out the spare room where a load of the boxes had sat since they moved in.

Richard thought carefully before saying in a falsely jolly voice, in case she took offence, "A blowjob would be good." She said nothing. "You don't have to swallow if you don't want to," he added graciously.

"How about a doggie style," she suggested.

"No. I really fancy a blowjob."

"We'll leave the spare room for another day then," she said, expecting him to concede.

"That's okay. We'll have a quiet day then."

She waited for him to give in, but he didn't. Eventually she broke the silence. "You might be able to get me to do that. But it's going to cost you a lot more."

"Such as?"

A long pause then, "Westlife. Tickets for Emma, Lucy and me, plus two of their friends to any of their concerts this year. You drive us, but you don't have to come into the gig if you don't want to."

Boy bands such as Westlife were anathema to him. But if he didn't have to go in... Plus he could stand outside watching teenage girls in boob tubes…

"You're on, but payment in advance."

"Okay, but what if you can't get the tickets?"

"I will."

"And I don't have to swallow it?"

"No."

"Okay. You'd better get those tickets though."

Richard just couldn't believe it.

He watched as Victoria approached his penis as if it was a dead rat that she'd just found behind the sofa. He was hard before she got there and then she hesitated.

"Don't worry, I'll get them," he urged, and gloried in the feel as her tongue touched it halfway up. "Go on," he urged again, "just put your mouth around."

And she did. She opened her mouth and closed her lips over his glans and he felt her tongue circulating the top.

"Now take more in," he instructed. Her mouth moved down, his cock disappearing into a warm, wet heaven. It was all he could do to hold back. "Now just move up and down. Careful with your teeth," he instructed, and he felt her change the position of her jaw. He moved his hand down her back towards her bum. She stopped, looked up and said, "I didn't say you could touch me," and he retracted his hand, laid back and looked down at her fellating him.

If this had been Julie the sensations would have been much more expert. She really knew what to do. But somehow the thought that this was Victoria's first ever time was way more erotic. He continued to watch her movements until he could take no more and felt his body go past the point of no return. He ejaculated uncontrollably, straight to the back of her throat at first and then continuing over his own belly as her mouth came away and she coughed and spat out his seed before disappearing to the bathroom to clean her teeth.

"Thank you," he felt he had to say.

"Hmm," she replied. "I think you got the better deal there."

"Are you kidding," he replied. "Westlife?!" before getting up to do his agreed chore.

*

As the game developed, so did the one and only rule.

Either could suggest something, and the other would suggest a price. They could bargain on price, but once an offer was made and price accepted, they couldn't go back. The deal was set in stone. Both parties had to do what they had agreed. No penalties for non-compliance.

Non-compliance wasn't an option.

*

They had their ups and downs. What couple doesn't. But their relationship was better than it had ever been. There were still hurdles, of course. The dodgy invoice once a month was one that got more and more serious. He couldn't keep the excuses going much longer. But all in all, Richard felt that he was having his cake and eating it. Wednesdays with Julie. No transactional relationship, more mutual love and uninhibited conversation. Life with Victoria, getting everything he wanted at prices which were, by definition, acceptable. Money in the bank and Chairmanship on the horizon.

Another Christmas and his stress levels again on max. Richard trying to find time for Julie; Victoria being queen bee of the household; noise, mess and chaos. But the biggest shock came on Christmas Day. Geoff and Dawn arrived and calmly mentioned that their wedding plans were underway as Geoff and Lorna's divorce was going through.

"Of course, we'd like the girls as bridesmaids," Geoff said, looking pointedly at Richard to remind him of their deal.

Victoria held it together until her dad and "his slut" had left, then burst into tears. All she wanted, she said, was to get Mummy and Daddy back together. Mummy would accept him if he dumped Dawn, or so she reckoned. And there was no way that she'd let him use her girls as bridesmaids.

Richard expressed platitudes while mulling over the problems this could bring.

Over the tedious days between Christmas and New Year – on the occasions that Victoria didn't have him decorating or pretending to enjoy meeting other people – he took the opportunity when he could to disappear off to his study to text Julie and look at pornography on his computer. He'd spent a very pleasant half hour combining both, texting Julie with vivid details of the scene he was watching; a petite white girl and a "BBC", or Big Black Cock, enjoying a variety of positions.

He was frustratedly re-running it in his mind later, lying

in the dark next to Victoria after she'd rejected his advances as normal.

"What's your ultimate fantasy?" she suddenly asked out of nowhere.

The effects of several days of Christmas bonhomie, plus several beers, wines and ports, not to mention the recent perusals of porn, had lowered his caution threshold to zero.

"My ultimate fantasy, Vicky? It's simple really; watching you with another man."

"Having sex I assume," she snorted.

"Of course." He smiled in the dark.

"And what would you be doing?"

"I'd be watching from some hiding place. He wouldn't know I was there."

"And what would I be expected to do with him?"

Richard thought back to the film. "You'd have a variety of positions. Lots of oral. You know, all the things I like."

Her silence prompted him to rabbit on, "After he's come you'd put on a bit of a show until he's ready for more. He'd wear a condom, of course. You'd be enjoying it. A couple of hours would be ideal. Sound enough of a fantasy?"

"Well it's not exactly a frolic in the bluebells is it?"

"No, but you did ask for my ultimate fantasy, and that's it."

"I did. You're right. And I'd hoped you'd ask for a Porsche!"

"Ha, I like it. Anyway, go on then," Richard said.

"What?"

"You know you want to. Tell me what I'd have to do to get you to do all of that."

Out of the darkness, Victoria spoke…

"Kill Dawn."

"You don't mean that?!"

"I do."

Victoria explained at length that the one thing she wanted more than anything was to go back to the days when Mummy and Daddy lived together, and the only way she could see that happening was if Dawn was no longer around. She couldn't see Dawn "the slut" giving up the golden goose voluntarily so it'd have to be something more drastic. Richard was sure that Geoff would never go back to Lorna. Even if Dawn was no longer around, he'd moved on. And anyway, Richard's fantasy was so far outside Victoria's comfort zone that he didn't have to worry about her trying to make a deal of it. Having said that, better to raise his price just to really emphasise how unfeasible it all was. Accordingly he said: "Well. I wouldn't commit murder just to watch you once with another guy. If you wanted me to do that, then I'd need more."

"Such as."

"Oh, I don't know, say go to wife swapping party or something like that."

In a light voice, she said, "I'll have to think about it."

Confident that that was the end of the matter, Richard went to sleep dreaming of Victoria being fucked by a BBC. But the dreams turned sour when he visualised himself strangling his soon-to-be stepmother-in-law.

*

Back at work, the end of the month came around far too quickly.

Victoria came into the lab. "Guess which outstanding bit of paper I've come about?"

"No need to guess," Richard replied before adding, "but we finally have progress on it all."

"Oh yes?"

"Yes, I've had a report back. Wesley used up some new-old-stock components in this unit. It was one of the last made before they went to a different model. They've agreed to change some of the bits free of charge and it'll be back with us shortly."

He didn't mention that, in fact, having laid out a further two thousand pounds of Cosion money, the re-refurbished unit had already come back with new lamp holder and various other components replaced. His problem was that it now had no serial number at all, let alone the "right one".

He had first tried to change the number on the original plate. No luck there, it was machine etched into the thin metal plate and all he'd achieved was to make it look like a three year old had had a go at using it for their first writing lesson.

Next he'd tried to remove the plate altogether so that he could have a replacement made and fitted. This had resulted in a mangled plate and a gouge on the housing. Dave Fletcher had sorted out the cosmetic damage, but there was still no serial number plate.

Lots of companies made identity plates and the like. He could get one made to his design (i.e. copying the Wesley one, except for the number) but Wesley plates had a hologram on them (to deter forgeries, of course) and he hadn't found a route to get anything similar. The hologram on the old one had been damaged beyond usability.

As usual, Richard had parked this problem hoping that it would go away. He now saw he'd have to do something.

Options:

If Victoria stopped bringing it up, he could tell Sarah that the unit had been traded in. She'd accept this, but he couldn't get his wife to drop the discrepancy without her getting suspicious.

He could buy a new HPLC. That would cost him virtually all of his slush fund. He'd also have to explain why it was a different unit, as it would come with yet another serial number.

Could he find a way to get Sarah to accept the refurbished unit back as being okay with a new plate but no hologram on it? Probably not: she was too much like him; analytical and tenacious.

Maybe he could bring back the refurbished unit and keep it from Sarah? Or sack her? High risk and high cost.

There wasn't an obvious solution and he parked the problem yet again, but he knew that by this time next month, he'd have to have an answer.

CHAPTER 13

THE BEATLES. "Please, Please Me"

"Evening classes" had resumed and Julie was his escape from the problems of day-to-day life. They went back to The Dewdrop Inn, scene of their previous al-fresco fun. Richard was hopeful of a repeat performance but Julie quashed that idea.

"I've said that I'd love to get back in the sack with you, maybe even share you with a girlfriend or let you spy on me with another man. But, until I can be sure you're not enjoying matrimonial pleasures, I'm afraid you'll have to make do with a lot less, and I'll have to make do with my little buzzing friend."

"I love the way you can sit in a pub and talk about threesomes, voyeurism and vibrators." Richard smiled and then kissed her on the cheek.

"Well, that's probably because I'd only talk about them with someone I'm in love with," she replied.

Without thinking, Richard let his natural reaction slip out, "I love you too, Julie."

He realised that this was the first time he'd said it aloud to her. Did he love her? Yes, he decided. Did he love her more than his wife? He didn't know. They were different parts of his life. It was just a pity that the home life was so full of niggles, whereas his few hours a week with Julie were filled with happiness. 'If only my wife could be like my lover,' he said to himself, as so many unfaithful husbands have done over the generations.

Richard's solution to this, and his growing list of other problems, was not typical of the behaviour of most unfaithful husbands.

*

Saturday. Emma and Lucy were off with friends to London. Richard wasn't going to ask for details. He simply enjoyed the peace he had when there was just him in the sprawling and oversized (as far as he was concerned) house. Victoria had driven the girls to the station and said she'd be popping in to see her mum on the way back. After all, it must be nearly 24 hours since they had last chatted.

Richard was sitting on the hall floor, paintbrush in hand, gently flowing white non-drip gloss up and down the bannisters, finding it oddly mesmerising. He was doing this now for two reasons. Firstly, because everyone was out and the paint should hopefully be dry before it was subjected to the unintentional vandalism of unthinking teenagers. Secondly, and more importantly, because he'd agreed to what he felt to be a very acceptable price with Victoria, and was looking forward to some bedroom entertainment later on.

The front door flew open and a clearly angry wife crossed the threshold with sufficient energy to power a small town for half a day. She slammed the door and stomped into the kitchen growling, "That fucking bitch! Why did she ever rise out of the sewer."

Richard thought to himself, 'Your mum's not that bad.'

He knew better than to say it out loud. Not unless he wanted the paint tin emptied over his head. Instead, he played it safe: "Not good news? You okay?"

Victoria stomped into the hall. "Daddy's slut. She just gets worse."

"What's she done now?"

"Where to start?! She's made him go for half of Mummy's house."

This wasn't a revelation to Richard, he'd been watching the divorce proceeding from afar, thankful that he wasn't going through anything similar. He'd expected Geoff to want what was his, with or without his new partner's input.

He risked saying something to this effect. "It's not that unusual is it? Most couples aim for a fifty-fifty split?"

Victoria didn't see it that way. "Why should mummy have to suffer because he couldn't keep his hands to himself?"

"I agree, but that's life, I'm afraid. We all get dumped upon for things that aren't our own fault sometimes."

His platitudes fell on deaf ears.

"What's mummy ever done to deserve this?" Victoria repeated. "Why should she have to move out? And we're nowhere near ready for her to move in yet!"

Richard hadn't thought about that not so welcome part of the equation.

"You're right, they should find a way for Lorna to stay there. Geoff's after a settlement. He wouldn't care whether it came from the house or her savings and shares. Can't she pay him off that way?"

"Nope. We went through the figures. Nowhere near what he's after."

Richard wondered if his own method of dealing with problems would work here. "Can't she just stonewall until he agrees a lower figure?" he suggested.

"You kidding? Daddy might accept summat. But queen bitch would still push for the lot. God I hate her."

"I'm sorry love. But bottom line it's their affair." Ouch he thought, wrong word there. "And there's not much we can do, is there?"

"Oh I know!" Victoria raged, then quieter. "I need a drink."

"I'll put the kettle on." 'I need a drink' meant beer to him, but he knew it meant tea to his wife.

"No, I need a drink drink. Have we got any white?"

"There's normally a couple in the fridge to keep your mum happy," Richard said, thinking: 'I could have put that better as well.' He went to the Smeg fridge (deal: Vicky on top for the first time) and opened a bottle of Picpoul de Pinet (Julie's favourite that he'd had to introduce to Victoria after she'd found a bottle in the car).

"Thanks love," she sighed as he gave her a large glass. "I know it's not our fight, but I just can't bear what's happening. You'd never do that to me. Would you?"

"Of course not," he replied, adding to himself, 'I know which side my bread's buttered,' before joining her at the table with a large glass of red.

An hour later, they were still at the table meditating on the unfairness of life, and both bottles well on their way to being emptied.

"We're not going to be able to pick the girls up you know," Richard remarked.

"Don't worry…" Victoria scrabbled around for her phone. "I'll ask mummy to do it."

Victoria called her mum who swiftly agreed to pick Emma and Lucy up from the station later on, and then volunteered to have them overnight at her house. Victoria agreed and gave Richard the good news that they'd got some time to themselves.

"That deserves another glass of vino," came his reply.

Bottles were emptied and fresh ones opened. The alcohol took it's toll. While Richard turned silly and chatty when tipsy, Victoria tended towards morose and angry. She soon started complaining about her parent's situation again, interspersed with long silences. After one of these she turned to her husband. "Your ultimate fantasy."

"Yep," he replied.

"Still the same?"

"Yep," he smiled, slurring his voice as he went on, "You and another guy with me hidden away."

"And a wife swap as well?"

"Who wouldn't?!" he grinned, looking into the middle-distance in his newt-like state..

"But you know that would only ever happen as part of that deal we said about." Her words were also slightly slurred.

"Yes, more's the pity." He joined her in a long silence then added, "I can just imagine us, putting the Renault keys into the dish, wondering who'd ever pick them from amongst the Mercs and Beamers." He didn't know why, but he found this really amusing.

"Or wondering who'd want you," she joked back.

"Oh, I don't know," he said, "Nice dark room and the lucky lady wouldn't believe her luck!" He chuckled, "And the blokes would be falling over themselves to be in a room with you."

"Yeah, in your dreams."

"Hmmm, yep, I can dream…" He paused again. "And then everybody would meet up for a group session… yep I can dream…"

"Well." Her suddenly hard voice startled him and he looked across at her. "Stop dreaming. It's going to happen. I accept the deal!"

When they'd sobered up, which was the next morning, as another couple of bottles had followed the first, both of them felt more than a little rough. Hangovers weren't common occurrences in the Marsh household, neither of them liking to drink sufficiently to lose control of their tightly controlled personalities. Victoria dealt with the situation in her typically efficient manner, calling her mother and asking if she would mind them not joining her for lunch, and could she keep the girls until the evening as she and Richard had things to talk about.

"Nothing wrong is there?" Lorna asked.

"No mummy, it's just that Richard has a killer of a problem to solve and I'm going to give him a hand."

Richard's call to Geoff was more succinct. "Sorry Geoff, I'll have to give the pub a miss today."

Two coffees and two ibuprofen each later, Richard asked, "Vicky, were you serious last night?"

She'd apparently been thinking about the same subject. "You mean the deal?"

"Yes."

"Yes."

"You mean you want to go ahead?"

"Yes."

"Okay."

Richard thought about it. He didn't consider murder acceptable. Who would? But at the same time, he saw that it would solve some of their problems. If not all. Without Dawn, Geoff could be persuaded to relent on the draconian divorce bill. He'd probably be too upset to run the company and Richard may get faster promotion than expected. Not only would Victoria have to agree to her side of the deal (which would be great), but as a co-conspirator, she'd have to stick by him, and he'd easily be able to get her to drop the invoice issue. Or as Chairman, he could simply tell her to drop it. The lab wouldn't know anything about the HPLC. He'd have more latitude to go off site and see Julie. In due course he could even end up with Julie properly. No, he didn't consider murder acceptable. But if it would solve his problems…

"Okay," he repeated. "I'll need your help though."

"How? It's your part of the deal, not mine."

"Oh, I don't know. I've never planned a murder before! I'll probably need to run ideas past you. And I'll need an alibi. God, I ain't got a clue."

"Nor have I." She actually smiled. "But I'll try to make sure you don't get caught."

"Thanks" he said dryly.

"And if you do, I'll come and see you in prison."

"Thanks again…"

Richard continued to ponder the situation – one big problem to replace all the smaller ones. 'That's better, I can focus better on just one,' he considered. He was contemplating a myriad of details when he felt Victoria's hand sliding down his body.

"A small down payment for you…" she said.

"I think the deposit will be in you…" he smiled back.

Afterwards, as ideas started to crystallise, his mind also started to stray into her part of the deal and he decided to get her on board now, before she could change her mind.

"So, this other guy," he started.

"I wondered how long it would take you to mention it. Later than expected, I have to say."

"Well, I was otherwise engaged."

"Glad you enjoyed it."

"But now the blood has returned to my brain… Vicky, I know you're not going to do this out of choice, but I do want you to enjoy it, or at least some of it, if at all possible."

"That's good of you." She still sounded in a good mood.

"Sex with someone else will be different. You don't know what to expect from sex with someone apart from me–"

"And you've experience elsewhere?" she interrupted.

"No!"

"Hmm, well, surprise you though this may, I don't see how being with someone new is going to give me any big surprises. Sex is sex."

"Yeah, I know what you're saying. I was just trying to think of it from your point of view."

"Okay, go on."

"But, if you're going to invite someone into our bedroom–"

"Spare room more likely," she interrupted again.

"What I was going to say is that I want you to at least like whoever you're with."

"It helps!"

"Which leads to the question; where are we going to find this person."

"Yep, it's totally insurmountable," she said sarcastically, "but knowing you, you'll find a way Richard."

"I'll take that as a compliment."

"But if you do find me Mr Right, there's another problem surely. How are you going to watch us? Stand in the corner of the room pretending to be a coat rack?"

"Well I'd probably have something sticking out well enough!"

"Don't I know it! But seriously? I don't mind you watching. Well, I do really, but I have to let you… But it's going to be hard enough–"

"It certainly is!" he couldn't help saying.

"You know what I mean. No, it's just that I'm not sure if I can cope with doing all this and having you watching me. It would probably put both him and me off so you'd not get the show you want…"

"Well." He stopped to think. He had ideas, but didn't want Victoria to realise how expert he was at being the unseen voyeur. "Just thinking off the cuff. I want to watch you in real-time, not via some recording that I could catch up with later. And, I want to be in the house so that I can rescue you if there's any problems."

"My hero," her sarcasm was plain to hear.

"So how about I rig up a camera or two. You know, like hidden CCTV that I can watch in another room. I think you can get cameras that look like clocks and things. Just need to hide the wiring and bob's your uncle."

"Sounds like you've got it all planned."

"No, not really, but it shouldn't be difficult. Either that or you leave the curtains open and I watch from outside."

"No way! I'm not risking the neighbours or some peeping pervert seeing me."

('Well you will have one; Me,' he thought to himself.)

"Anyway, let's say cameras are the way to do it." He kept talking so that she didn't have a chance to object. "What about the who? And I'm not talking the band here."

"Hmm?"

"Um, is there anyone that you'd like for this?"

"You must be joking! Unlike you, I don't spend my time fantasising about other men!"

"I don't spend my time fantasising about men either."

"You know what I mean. No, there's no one."

"Right then. So how about we use that dating site? You could have a profile on there and either look through the men until you find one you like, or you could put an ad on and see who applies. Either way you get to choose."

"Show me the site again."

They went through to the study and Richard found 'wedbutlooking.com' on the internet. He clicked on 'SEARCH'. Unlike his previous browsing, the criteria this time was based around straight males within 25 miles. There were pages of them. Victoria clicked on a few, noticeably the ones whose profiles didn't show them naked or consisted solely of a picture of an erection.

"I don't know. You can't tell anything from this," she said.

"Okay then." Richard already had a plan. "We'll put a vague

profile of you on here. Nothing to identify you, of course. And you can have an ad and see who replies. Treat it like a job interview."

Together they came up with a profile for "Innocent Lass, 38, Reading." Okay, so what if the age, location and most of the text wasn't quite accurate. Neither was anyone else's.

Innocent Lass's advert was a bit more specific, including a number of points that she'd insisted on: "Hi, I'm looking for a male to give me what my husband can't. You must be straight, not overweight, non-smoker, respectful, clean & discreet. Safe sex only. I'm looking for someone who can interest me intellectually, as well as in the bedroom, so let me know what your likes and dislikes are in life. Face picture essential. One line replies will be deleted."

Richard got Victoria to press the "Post Ad" button and then they went off to discuss ways of getting away with murder.

One of the advantages of working in a laboratory and reading scientific journals was that it had given Richard a basic understanding of forensic science. The lab also gave him access to a wide range of potential tools not easily available to most of the general public. He analysed what he had to do. In simple terms, the steps consisted of, get in, do what has to be done, get out, and throughout it all, not leave any trace of his temporary presence. He started to break this down.

Get in: i.e. get himself to where he could be certain Dawn would be alone. Think about who might see him. Whether there could be CCTV on the scene, around and about, or on his route. None of this could be sorted out until he had a better idea of where to do it. He would need to know Geoff and Dawn's routine. He couldn't exactly walk into his boss's office and ask when his wife would be alone. No, the most likely solution here would be to see what he could find out during a Sunday pub session.

Do the deed: How? Could he go for something violent, such as a knife, gun or strangulation. The problem was that these kind of methods usually generated a lot of forensic evidence. How about chemical means? It was less messy and potentially easier, but any trace would point straight back to him. But what about more widely available chemicals? Drugs? Say sleeping pills? They'd certainly do the job if used correctly. Even better, he had a ready source of the active ingredients at work. Yes, someone might realise that he had access to the drugs, but then, so did virtually anyone else. They were also so widely available.

Get out: well, that tied in with the getting in. Come back to that.

And how could he avoid leaving forensic traces of himself? This was a bit easier, he could get a Tyvek suit, hairnet, dust mask, nitryl gloves overshoes and other protective clothing from the lab. They used them all the time and as they were disposable, no one would notice any going missing.

Another question: should he leave the body where it was or try to hide it? His gut reaction to that one was that no matter how well hidden they were, bodies always seemed to turn up eventually. Plus how to move one? Best to leave it wherever he did the act.

Other factors: alibi. Victoria may be willing to lie for him, but a wife's evidence may be discounted. Was there any way else he could get an alibi?

Richard started a mental list of items and information needed. He didn't look up anything on the computer, having learnt his lesson some time back about what an investigator might be able to recover from a hard drive. He didn't want to write anything down for the same reason, but knowing how important the details could be, he decided to use one single notebook for the purpose and ensure that it was properly destroyed in due course. He found a suitable one in a drawer, with solid binding to minimise the risk of incriminating pages falling out anywhere, and he started to sketch out the bare bones of a plan with a shopping list of items needed. The Tyvek suit, gloves and so on went to the top of that list, all written in a basic code. Two of each, to be on the safe side.

Then he started to think about the sleeping pills. Maypharm made several types. Which would be best?

Their mainstay was based on diphenhydramine. It was a good routine-use sleeping pill, but it tended to take a bit of time to take effect and didn't always give a really deep sleep.

The lab had been working on a couple of new generics, but he couldn't risk them. They weren't fully developed and the contaminants might show up as unusual in the bloodstream, thus pointing back to Maypharm and him.

One of the benzodiazepines might be a better bet; stronger and more reliable. Some people disliked them due to the risk of dependency. But that wouldn't be a problem with this patient.

His musings were interrupted by the sound of the girls and

his mother-in-law returning. Richard carefully stowed away the notebook in a Kodak box and went to join them looking like any other law-abiding father would.

Richard and Victoria were careful to confine their time checking out 'wedbutlooking.com' to times when Emma and Lucy were not around. No opportunity on Monday, so it was early Tuesday evening (Girl Guides night) when they next logged on. There were 42 e-mails to 'Innocent Lass'. A quick first pass through them and about half were eliminated simply because their carefully thought out replies went along the lines of "You look fit", "I'm up for it" or several times "Check my profile and let me know what you think". A good proportion went because they'd omitted to include a face picture, or if they had sent one, it was conveniently obscured. Prose that basically said that the guy was the best lover in the world resulted in deletion, and by the end only a couple of replies remained. Victoria said that neither looked interesting to her but she agreed that they should keep them for the moment, just in case.

Several more sessions followed over the week. By the end of it, they'd deleted in excess of 200 e-mails from (according to the senders) the world's greatest lovers, talkers, thinkers and, in one case, drinker. There were about ten left on the shortlist, and they sat down to read them again.

"Tell you what," Richard said. "I'll go in the other room, you look through them and write down your number one and two, then I'll do the same."

They took it in turns and then read together the various claims of their choices.

Richard's first choice, Lee, was a muscular, six foot tall, thirty-something male nurse with a well-written e-mail that professed his desire to talk as much as make love. It was purely a coincidence (so Richard pretended) that he was black and said he was very well endowed.

Number two, Chris, was a very average looking man. In his forties, he admitted to being married but said his marriage was loveless. Richard couldn't put his finger on why he was a possibility, but he came over as honest and possibly a bit similar to Richard himself.

Victoria's preference went to another thirty-something; James, who had written half a page of prose describing everything in his life from home to work. There was no information about his physique or sexual likes or experiences.

Her number two was Chris, the same as Richard's.

They talked for some time but couldn't make a proper decision, although both agreed that the other's number one was a possibility. Richard felt slighted when she said that she'd ruled out the black guy because she thought Richard would feel threatened. An allegation that he was swift to dismiss.

"A suggestion love," Richard said, "why don't you e-mail each of these three and suggest that you meet for a drink to see what you think of them. Tell them upfront that you won't do anything with them that evening so that they know it's just a chat. Then you can decide."

"What? I'm supposed to meet three total strangers, all alone, and come back and tell you which one I'm okay going to bed with?"

"No! I wouldn't put that on you. No, I mean that it'll be a safe pub and I'll sit nearby, reading a book or something, and keep an eye on you."

She agreed and e-mailed all three. After some e-mail ping-pong, they managed (somehow) to arrange for Victoria to see all of them the next Friday evening, each an hour apart, at an anonymous pub on the A4. She told each of them that she'd be sitting on her own, wearing a maroon top and reading a paperback.

Richard and Victoria arrived early, so as to get a couple of adjacent tables where Richard could watch and listen but without appearing to do so. He'd kitted himself out with a couple of newspapers and a pen so that he could do the crosswords, looking like a business rep filling in time before going off to his lonely single room. Luckily, there wasn't another single woman in a maroon top in the bar, so Victoria should be obvious to her candidates.

Chris arrived first, dead on the dot of the agreed half-past six. They'd made him the first as he had openly said that he'd need to go by 7.30 in order to pass it off to his wife as a late evening in the office. He was a nice guy. A very nice guy. He came over as open, straight, honest and, as Victoria said later, just a bit boring. Despite her leading the conversation around to the reason for their meet several times, they still ended up talking about the weather and other non-controversial subjects. Chris was a "No."

James was a "NO" as soon as he opened his mouth and the halitosis hit.

Lee was a surprise, albeit for an unexpected reason. He walked into the bar, spotted Victoria's maroon top and paperback, walked over and said, "Hi?" in a slightly quizzical voice. Victoria took one look and said, "We've met. We have met haven't we?"

"You look familiar," he said. They sat down with drinks and Victoria and Lee nattered away trying to work out where their paths had crossed. They cracked it (eventually) when talking about work. Lee described some of the departments he'd worked in at the Royal Berkshire Hospital, none of which Victoria had ever attended, but then he asked what her work was.

Victoria's simple reply, "Accounts," led to him responding, "I did accountancy at college before going into nursing."

Victoria clicked. "Bloody hell, it's not Lee, it's Louis isn't it!"

"Uh, yes."

"But you were skinny?!"

"Amazing what a bit of exercise will do, isn't it?"

Lee and Victoria chatted away, while Richard earwigged from the adjacent table. He couldn't decide if he was happy that Victoria was getting on so well with the archetypal black sex god, or whether he was unhappy that Victoria was getting on so well with the archetypal black sex god…

They stayed until closing time and on parting, Lee very deliberately gave Victoria a kiss on the lips, instead of the more usual cheek.

"Will I see you again?" he asked.

"You might," she replied.

In the car Richard asked, "Well?"

She took her time replying. "Look, I don't want to do this. You know that. But if I have to, as part of the deal, then I'd rather do it with Louis than the rest of those players and losers."

E-mails and phone calls followed and the following Friday was set. Emma and Lucy would be away with friends overnight and supplies (drinks, nibbles, disguised cameras, and condoms) were procured.

The other part of Victoria's commitment, the wife-swap, could wait.

*

Richard assured Victoria that the plans for his part of the deal were progressing well. He showed her his "shopping list" and sketchily outlined his plan. It was deliberately simple involving going to the flat when Geoff was away, getting Dawn to drink a hefty dose of sleeping pills dissolved in wine, followed by him donning the Tyvek suit and associated kit before putting a plastic bag over her head. He wasn't worried about fingerprints in the flat; as Geoff's son-in-law it was not unexpected that he'd be there from time to time. He wasn't going to try to conceal or move the body, but had ruled out starting a fire as he didn't want to risk the occupants of the other flats.

He'd also decided, he told Victoria, that he and she would happen to be staying away in a Travelodge on the night. They'd make themselves very visible booking in and that he'd slip out of the window to go and do the deed. Victoria would say they'd been together all night. She felt this part of the plan was too weak and said she'd try to think of a better alibi.

The areas yet to be sorted he told her, were exactly when to do it and how to get in and out without being spotted. The in and out depended very much on the when, so his priority was learning Geoff's movements for the next few weeks so as to find a good window for his plan.

"Thank you, Richard." She squeezed his hand. "I'm still pinching myself that you'll do this for us. I'll always love you for this."

There was quite a lot more to Richard's plan, a lot that he wasn't willing to share with her. He knew she wouldn't like it.

CHAPTER 14

JETHRO TULL. "Watching Me, Watching You"

Friday arrived. Emma and Lucy were away as planned and Richard set to, transforming the spare bedroom into the set of a voyeur's paradise. He had several ways to watch, only some of which were known to his wife.

The first element was a spy camera built into a bedside clock. As far as Victoria was concerned, he'd just got it. In reality, it was just one of a portfolio of items dating back to his London shopping trip, topped up with more state-of-the-art covert surveillance equipment bought as soon as the deal was agreed.

Victoria had insisted that the camera clock was placed next to the top of the bed. From here, she hoped the angle of view wouldn't be too gynecological. Richard omitted to mention that other spying aids would enable him to see not only every inch of her body, but also in full colour and extreme close up. As well as a wall clock with a logo of an owl with particularly beady eyes, there was a camera in what appeared to be a standard burglar alarm wall sensor and, Richard's favourite, a full pan, tilt and zoom camera inside a mirrorball forming part of a table lamp. Placed near the foot of the bed, he was confident that this would gain images of professional porn film quality.

Connected wirelessly to the recorders, all he had to do was press a button or two, and the evening's fun would be recorded for posterity.

The other aspect of his observational plans was the one that had caused most debate between the two of them. Victoria had accepted the camera (not knowing about the others) but Richard wanted to be able to see what was going on. Not just on a screen, but as he put it, in 3D. He wanted a spy hole to look through. The epitome of voyeurism.

They'd ruled out a hole in the ceiling. It wouldn't give Richard the viewing angle he wanted, and Victoria wasn't having the risk of him coming crashing down on her from above. A keyhole in the bedroom door was also vetoed as Victoria said she'd always be on the alert for creaking floorboards.

However, the spare bedroom shared a wall with the main bedroom's en-suite. They eventually agreed that if Richard was willing to totally redecorate the affected areas (which he readily agreed to do) then Victoria would allow him to fit, for the evening only, a two-way mirror onto the bedroom wall with a very small portion of the plasterboard wall behind it removed. He could watch from inside the en-suite where, as Victoria so delicately put it, "You can wank away to your heart's content without disturbing anyone."

'Perfect,' Richard thought. As well as resolving his craving to be able to watch easily, the monitor and recording kit could be put in the main bedroom, all within his reach but out of sight of the copulating couple.

Over the day, Victoria endeavoured to keep her mind distracted from thoughts of what was to come. She vacuumed and dusted every part of the house despite it not being needed; the cleaner being more than capable. Richard worked away upstairs getting all his viewing aids in place. The two-way mirror had taken a bit of work when he'd cut away some of the plasterboard only to find wooden structural uprights, which had to be carefully remodelled before he could complete the job.

Dust and debris cleaned up, he moved on to setting up the cameras, watching out for obstructions, both current ones and ones that could be predicted; don't put a drinks coaster in front of a camera or someone would be bound to use it for its correct purpose and block the view. But having finished the work, he had a quick shower and was ready for the show to begin.

Victoria was actually shaking. He hoped it was from excitement rather than fear, but knew deep down that it was the latter. She spent an age making sure that snacks were in place, drinks were in the fridge and the room was tidy, and then spent considerably longer showering than Richard had.

The doorbell rang dead on the dot of seven. "I don't think I can do this! " Victoria squeaked.

"Vicky, I can see that you're not happy about it. If you want to back out, then I won't be upset," he lied, "but then I'd have to back out of my part of the deal as well."

"I'll get the door. You get yourself out of sight. If he sees you, then that's your fault, not mine."

Richard sped upstairs and Victoria let her one-evening-stand into the house. A well-groomed Louis came in, unexpectedly also looking nervous as he leant in to kiss her on the lips. They sat in the living room, the two of them on the one sofa, making inconsequential small talk and nibbling on cheese puffs. Eventually Victoria took a deep breath. "Shall we go upstairs?"

Louis stood, looked at her and held out a hand. "If it's okay with you?"

"Yes," she replied in a very quiet voice, allowing Louis to help her up off the sofa. From the en-suite, cameras were recording every detail of everything happening in the bedroom. Richard watched through his peephole. Victoria and Louis started to undress each other, the two of them fumbling with each other's buttons and zips until they were both down to underwear. Victoria flashed an anxious look at the mirror, which Louis didn't notice as he was busy removing his pants. He hadn't been joking, he was well-endowed. 'Go on love,' Richard said to himself as his wife reached out and put her hand around it. Louis hardened under her touch as he eased off her knickers. Richard stood there breathing heavily, watching the two of them playing with each other.

The couple dropped onto the bed. Louis starting to caress her breasts and suck her nipples before moving his head downwards. Richard watched, breathing heavily as Louis' lips reached her still wild pubes and she opened her legs for him without any asking or prompting. Her hands clenched as she relished the feel of him doing something that she'd never let any man do before. Her grip relaxed as she moved her hands onto the back of her temporary lover's head, pressing him into her until she climaxed. Eventually, he raised his face and smiled.

"OK?"

"Oh my God, yes!" she replied.

A move around found her bent over Louis as he lay back, cock level with her mouth. She hesitated and then tentatively put her lips over the end before moving her head to take in more. She started to move her head up and down, her right hand cupping his scrotum. Three or four, maybe five minutes of this and then he gently pulled away, reaching off the bed for his trousers. He pulled a packet of condoms from a pocket and sheathed his erection. Wordlessly she lay back, again glancing at the mirror, not knowing what her husband was doing and what he was making of the bedroom scene.

Richard was very happy on the other side of the mirror. Trousers and pants had been discarded some time ago and he stood there, masturbating, as he watched Louis move his large, hard cock between Victoria's legs. He entered her in a long, slow, fluid motion and Richard thrilled at the sight of Victoria's expression; a mixture of pain, excitement and desire. As Louis reached the point where he was in as deep as he could be, Richard came. As intense an orgasm as he could ever remember. Louis started to move in and out, speed increasing, thrusting hard.

Victoria was arching her body up to meet him, eyes shut, mouth open with small cries of joy coming from her. This wasn't what Richard had expected. It was so much better! Louis had staying power as well. Much more than Richard had ever managed, but soon he too reached that point. Richard savoured the sight of Victoria's face, clearly she knew that this man was coming inside her.

Louis lay on top of Victoria, their breathing heavy, before he slowly pulled out, still half hard, and lay back. For a while, recovering, there was silence. Each of them with a hand on the other's chest. Louis removed the condom and in a practiced movement tied a knot in it, dropping it into the bin.

They chatted about their sexual histories. Or rather Louis did, as he was the only one with much to report. A couple of girlfriends, then married since college years. Victoria expressing her surprise when she realised that she also knew Louis' wife from college days.

"What would I say if I saw her?!" she asked.

"Anything," replied Louis, "except anything about tonight. She'd kill me!"

The admission of infidelity did not to seem worry Victoria and as they chatted, she started to toy with his limp dick until it started to harden again. Another round followed. More caressing, more oral and more positions. Richard on the other side of the wall, controlling the moveable camera to get close ups, facial and genital, but more of the latter. Louis from behind, then Victoria on top. Movements fluid and then awkward. Real people, having real sex, not porn stars putting on a performance.

Eventually, they had both gone as far as they could and the two of them went back downstairs in a state of undress and worked their way through all of the food and a good deal of the drinks, rehydrating and recovering their energies.

Richard was frustrated upstairs. He could hear faint conversation and laughter, but not the words. He should have thought of this and put a camera down there as well. But not to worry, he'd had a great evening and could relive it all from the recordings over and over again.

He was sitting there, musing on it all, wondering how long they'd chatter before Louis went, when he realised that they were coming back up the stairs. To his absolute astonishment, he watched as Louis entered the bedroom followed by Victoria. The two of them again exploring each other's bodies, before yet another, this time longer and slower session of sexual fulfilment.

It was half past ten before Louis said something that Richard couldn't hear. Victoria gave him a long kiss and then Louis started to get dressed. Victoria just put on a tatty old dressing gown before the two of them left the room. A few minutes later and the front door closed and she came back upstairs alone. Richard came out to meet her, took her into his arms, hugged and kissed her.

"Not so bad then?" He asked.

"You were right," she replied. "I did enjoy it," then with an evil grin, "but don't take that to mean it's going to happen too often."

"But again?" he asked.

"I might be persuaded. If the price is right, of course."

Richard smiled. "You want me to tidy up while you take a shower?"

"I certainly need one," she replied. "That is, unless you want to go to bed with me smelling of another man?"

"Get in the shower," he replied. "Then you can go to bed with this very happy man."

She disappeared into the bathroom while Richard cleared up the en-suite, downstairs and the bedroom.

During his clean up, he put on a pair of blue nitryl laboratory gloves and carefully placed several items in a plastic bag before hiding them away in his study.

That night and again in the morning, they talked more about what had happened. There was also the milestone of Richard performing oral on his wife. And the first time in all their marriage that he helped her to reach orgasm. And there was no deal involved. They did it for pleasure.

*

Sunday and Richard phoned Geoff. "Royal Oak at twelve?"

"Of course!"

"It struck me," Richard said, "that we still don't know Dawn all that well. We've met a few times but, to be honest, in those busy family events, you never really get a chance to talk properly."

"Yes, she says the same."

"Why don't you bring her down the pub? It would be good to have a more relaxed chat."

"Good idea, hang on…" The phone went quiet until he came back saying, "She didn't need much persuading. Likes the odd G&T does my Dawn."

As he put down the receiver, Richard smiled at Victoria. "Sorted. She'll be there. Now all I need to do is get to know when she's going to be alone."

The lunchtime chat was relaxed and Richard found himself getting on better with Dawn than he had previously. As they gossiped away Richard started to appreciate what Geoff saw in the outwardly unremarkable woman. She had a keen intellect and an evil sense of humour (and an ability to put away more gin than Richard would have thought possible). Richard bore in mind the real reason for the conversation and he brought it around to what she did and when, learning that she'd quit Arcalside after moving in with, "Darling Geoff," but was now, "busier than ever I was before."

"What do you get up in the day then, if you're not working?" Richard enquired. "If that doesn't sound rude!"

"Horses. I enjoy riding."

Richard bit his tongue.

"You've got one?"

"Yes, he's a lovely 15 hand chestnut gelding."

"Sounds good," said Richard in total ignorance of what this all meant. Horses were not his thing. "And you ride every day?"

"Out to the paddock at Waltham St Lawrence every morning and afternoon. Give him a bit of a workout whenever I can."

"Sounds like it takes a lot of your time?"

"It can do. If it's a good day and we can get out for a trot, then

I can be there all morning. Then back at the end of the day to put him away for the night."

"And in between?"

"Oh, you know. This and that."

"Dawn's a lady who likes to lunch," Geoff added.

Richard didn't want to press too much and changed tack. "Anyway, following a train of thought, Victoria and I were thinking of trying to meet up with you two one evening. I don't know her diary at the moment, but generally speaking, when's a good time for you?"

"Most evenings really," Geoff replied. "For the next couple of weeks anyway. After that, I'll be out one evening a week. Can't remember which one at the mo though."

"Why's that?"

"Actually, I've taken a leaf out of your book. Evening classes."

"Really? What've you gone for?" Richard asked, desperately hoping that it wasn't French, otherwise he'd really be in it.

"Well, with retirement looming, I thought I'd finally get around to doing some painting."

"House or art?" joked a relieved Richard.

"I've had enough of decorating. No, it's oil painting, always wanted to do it."

"Sounds interesting. You'll have to let me know which evening it is so that we can get those diaries checked."

Richard reported this all back to Victoria later on. A window of opportunity was opening…

He was still contemplating the exact details of the "How." He had decided on a combination of sleeping pills and suffocation.

But maybe pills alone would suffice. Question was how to administer a fatal dose. Dawn wouldn't be overly receptive to him popping round and saying, "Hi, thought you might like to eat these capsule shaped sweeties." No, he'd have to disguise the drug.

Which one to use, and how much? Luckily, he didn't have to risk using the internet. His trusty work copy of the *European Pharmacopoeia* had all the drug data he could need. Of the benzodiazepines, the most toxic looked to be temazepam with an LD50 of 833 mg/kg in rats. 'Hang on, that can't be right, can it' he calculated. 'If she weighs 75kg, I'd have to feed her 62g of the drug to have a 50% chance of giving her a lethal dose?' he worked out. 'I think she'd notice tablespoons of the stuff.'

Reading on, the obvious additional factor was there: 'Alcohol increases the lethal nature of the drug, causing the victim to stop breathing,' he read. Hard data was scarce and there was no information about what ratio of alcohol to drug worked best. He'd just have to administer as high a dose as he could (of both drink and drug). Once Dawn was knocked out, he could either see if the cocktail did the job on its own or go to the original suffocation plan if not.

Reading on, there were some references to temazepam having a distinctive taste. 'No point in giving her laced drink if she spits it out,' he thought before his mind wandered to the thought of Victoria spitting something else out.

He went over to the locked drugs cabinet where reference samples of all the drugs used at Maypharm were kept. According to the register, there was 172g of temazepam. That would be plenty, but taking it would be noticed. There were also stocks on the shop floor, but these were keenly audited. How to get hold of sufficient active material without it being noticed? Sarah was tidying up some glassware and Richard watched as she emptied a couple of volumetric flasks into the hazardous waste container. Waste…

Checking the lab records, there had been a batch of raw temazepam quarantined some months back due to visible contamination. It was no good for inclusion in pharmacy drugs, but for this purpose it would be ideal. He could take a sufficient amount out of the quarantined stock, and as it was sub-standard, send the rest off for disposal to ensure there was no audit trail coming back to him.

The quarantine area was within the main stores. A highly controlled zone due to the dangers of the drugs and the risk of theft of tablets which could sell for big money on the streets. It was also a busy area so he needed to get in there when eyes were not watching. Tea break from quarter past to half past ten would be best. He checked his watch. Three quarters of an hour to wait. Plenty of time, so he put on his anonymous white lab coat, the most unobtrusive clothing you can wear in a pharmaceutical company, and pocketed a sample bottle, disposable gloves and a chemical scoop.

Arriving just as the warehouse team went off for their morning break, he signed in and entered the controlled area.

The raw materials shelves stretched for 100 metres or so, racked four pallets high, with the quarantine area at the far end and separated off by a metal grille. Anyone in there would be visible to anyone else in the stores area when they came back from their break so Richard didn't want to spend too long getting his sample.

Entering the compound, he found a mishmash of newish and old stock, some pristine, others with packs damaged, all bearing a telltale red "Quarantine – Do Not Use" sticker. This was the factory dumping area for anything not quite usable, and it was not particularly well organised as defective products, by their nature, were unexpected and difficult to plan for. He searched through the shelves of variously sized containers looking for the drug, eventually spotting some likely looking tubs towards the back of a shelf. Several plastic bottles at the front of the shelf were swiftly moved aside and he confirmed that the tubs, five of them, each the size of a bag of sugar, did indeed contain temezapam. Their seals were already broken from when they had been checked originally and it was an easy job to take a scoop from four of them and combine these in the jar. Placing the lid back on the last tub, he heard voices in the warehouse. Back from their break. Best be out quick.

Hurriedly replacing the bottles that he'd had to move, one caught the edge of the shelf. Richard swore under his breath as it fell onto the concrete floor. The lid popped off and a thick oil started leaking out. This was not good. Richard was well aware of the company rules for dealing with spillages. He was supposed to clear the area, get himself suited up in full protective gear, get other relevant specialists involved (including the fire brigade if necessary), deal with the spill and then the paperwork. All time-consuming and, more to the point, very high profile. 'Sod that for a game of marbles,' he thought before leaving the liquid to spread unimpeded while he left as unobtrusively as he could.

Back in his office Richard contemplated his actions. Okay, so he'd got the drug, but there was a five litre spill of an unknown chemical in the quarantine area. Should he do something about it? No; he'd be admitting that he'd been there. Should he just leave it for someone else to find? It wasn't very safe, but compared to the unsafe practices he was planning for Dawn, a bit of spilt liquid was nothing.

That evening he told Victoria that he'd got the drug. He told her for two reasons. Firstly, so that she remained as an active accomplice. Secondly, he needed her taste buds.

In the lab, he'd made a five milligram per litre solution of the temazepam and once again, breaking every established safety protocol in the book, put a few drops on his tongue. He thought that he could taste it at this very low strength, and if so, that could be a problem.

"Right my darling," he said that evening. "I'm just going to try poisoning you."

"What?!"

"No, it's alright really. I just want to know whether the drug's taste can be disguised."

"Why can't you taste it then?" she asked

"Because I'd know which sample was laced and that might affect how I perceive them. It's a very small amount and you only need have a sip."

"Okay…"

"So, I have three glasses of Picpoul here. Tell me if you can taste any difference."

Victoria took a sip from each.

"First two are the same, third a bit bitter maybe."

"Okay. Try this one…"

Eventually Richard had worked out roughly how much temazepam he could put in before Victoria could detect it. Of course, Dawn's taste threshold would be different, but at least he had a starting point.

"Next… Let's try it in G&T."

G&T was better; the quinine taste of the tonic effectively masking the temazepam.

"There is one other thing," he said. "In an ideal world, it would look like an accident or suicide, but if they find temazepam in her bloodstream and none in the flat, then they'll be looking for the source. That would put me and your dad in the frame. On the other hand, if Dawn has a ready stock of tablets, not Maypharm ones of course, then she might have committed suicide."

"Makes sense. But how would you arrange that?"

"That's where I need your help. If you were to go to see Dr Collins at the surgery and say you needed something to help you sleep, then he could prescribe them to you."

"Um, obvious problems. One, he might give me a different drug. Two, even if I get a prescription for temezy-wotsit, how do I get tablets that aren't Maypharm? Three, my name will be on the bottle."

"Good points deserve good answers. I thought about this. One. He knows where you work and that you've got access to more drug info than he'll ever understand. Say that the guys in the lab recommend temazepam is the best for your physiology and short-term problem."

"Okay. And avoiding Maypharm made tablets?"

"Go to the pharmacy in Woodley. They're part of a group that we don't sell to. They won't have our product."

And the name on the bottle?"

"Lab label printer. I can print a label with her name on it. We have the right bottles. Put the label on, pick away at the bottom of it like you do with sticky labels and I can get rid of the usual address bit so that no-one can check to see where she got them from. Okay, it might look odd, but it would never be traced back to us."

"Well, you have thought it out haven't you smarty-pants. Okay, I'll do it."

"Thanks love. Now fancy a proper glass of wine?"

"Yes, as long as it's not been fiddled with."

She slept well that night.

CHAPTER 15

THE POLICE. "Every Breath You Take"

The following Tuesday, Geoff started his evening class. And Richard started his spying on Dawn. Since agreeing the deal with Victoria, he'd used his considerable peeping-Tom experience in reconnoitring the area around the Bristow's flat. Being several floors up, the only way he'd be able to see into Dawn and Geoff's property would be if he could also get high up. The ideal candidate presented itself in the form of another flat, this one for rent in the block opposite. With his Roger Francis ID and a cheque book well bolstered by the Cosion commission payments, Richard rented number 46 The Paramount for the minimum period of six months thinking that not only would this give him the surveillance angle he needed, but if things went pear-shaped, he'd at least have somewhere to hide out.

Accordingly, several shopping trips later, the flat was well stocked with tinned food and drink that had a long shelf life.

6pm and the view from the flat was good. Very good in fact. From his vantage point he could see 15 properties; five floors with three flats on each, with a good mix of living rooms and bedrooms visible. About half had occupants getting on with their lives in full view. Nothing worthy of a camera yet, but it all showed promise. He'd worked out which was Geoff and Dawn's flat, but no one was in view and no lights were on. Still, plenty of other windows to watch…

By half past ten all he had to show for his evening was a couple of shots of a middle-aged woman in a towel as she closed her curtains. He was on the point of giving up for the evening when a light went on the Bristow's property. He watched as Dawn came into their main room, taking off an outdoor coat. And then she pulled their curtains.

He reported back to a disappointed Victoria that it looked like Dawn went out when Geoff was at evening class, and this might not be the opportunity they were looking for. But he'd have to see what developed next week.

*

"I'm coming down with something," Richard complained at breakfast on Friday. "Hot, sweaty, dizzy and my throat's giving me hell."

"Ergh, keep away from me then," was the sympathetic reply.

"Too late. If I've got it, then you have too."

"Thanks…"

"I don't think I'm up to work today. I'm taking a sickie. Tell the boss, will you?"

"Will do. Have a lie down." Victoria went off to work.

Richard was fit as a fiddle. Or, in his case, someone who enjoyed a good fiddle now and then. He wanted the day off and Victoria out of the way as he had an idea of how to get his relationship with Julie back on track.

Victoria was fine as a basic sexual release, but she wasn't Julie. Victoria would lie back and think of England and very occasionally get a bit excited, but it was all on her terms. She had to agree a deal and this would then set in stone what Richard could do, or more likely, couldn't do. There was no passion or spontaneity. It was so unlike sex with Julie, which was unconstrained, full of variety, passion and laughter.

While Victoria was out, he moved his essentials into the spare bedroom where he was to be found asleep when she came home from work. He stayed in the room for most of the weekend, making it look properly lived in, rather than just a bed that he happened to be occupying. Left alone on Monday ("Sorry love, still feeling like crap. Another day off should sort it though"), he picked up the phone and texted the object of his desires,

"Morning. How are you?" – their code for is the coast clear and can I call?

His phone rang in seconds and Julie's number came up on the screen (labelled as Pharmacy Supplies Ltd).

After the usual hellos, he moved on to say, "I've got something you might like here."

"Don't I know it! Go on."

"I want to show you that Vic and I are not having sex."

"Yes?"

"Yes. Why don't you come over? To Acacia Avenue that is."

"What! To your place? The fabled Land of Marsh where I've never been allowed before, in case a strand of my hair is left in view and your wife finds out? I thought there was a five-mile exclusion zone around it?!"

"Okay, I may have been a bit paranoid in the past."

"Bit?! When?"

"Now?"

"Give me half an hour. I need to get washed and dressed. A girl can't go out with a hair looking like this."

"I don't care how your hair looks, but I can save you some time dressing. Leave your knickers off…"

Phone call finished and Richard completed his preparations for the deception, collecting all his clothes from the main bedroom and moving them into the spare room wardrobe and drawers. Toothbrush, razor and toiletries were likewise transferred. A few more books, and possessions, and the room looked like his. And there was no trace of him in the marital bedroom.

It would all be put back later.

He was still extremely nervous about Julie coming to the house. She was right, he was worried that Victoria's sixth sense would register a foreign presence, or a neighbour would say something. If that did happen, he had his story worked out already; it would be a locum from the doctor's surgery on a home visit.

Julie arrived and they kissed. Indoors, of course. "

Okay then," she said, "show me around."

They did the full tour during which Richard derided his wife's choice of décor and explained how they were only really staying together because Richard would lose his job if they parted and they'd both be a lot worse off.

"So it's really just a marriage of convenience," he concluded, leading her into 'his' bedroom with, "And this is me."

She looked around , opening the wardrobe and drawers.

"Do I believe this?" she asked, pausing and teasing, then, "I'll put it this way. Fancy a fuck?"

"On my bed or Victoria's?"

They reminded themselves of the geography of each other's bodies for an hour – on Richard's bed – before he apologetically said that he needed to get back to work for the afternoon. A long snog and four wandering hands, and they agreed that Wednesdays would be back to full carnal delights. Julie drove off and Richard spent the rest of the day putting everything back as it had been and scouring the house for the least trace of a hair or other indication that Julie had been there. Emma and Lucy arrived home from school and ignored their father, being more interested in gossip about some boy they both knew. Victoria rolled in looking tired and after hearing that her husband would probably go back to work tomorrow said, "That's good. You can do dinner tonight."

"Doggy style?"

"Missionary."

"Deal."

That day Richard had his cake and ate it. A day off work and sex with two different women. Energetic and sensuous with his mistress and functional with his wife. Now, just the minor matter of a murder to carry out.

*

Tuesday evenings at Number 46, watching his father-in-law's flat slowly revealed a pattern. Geoff went off before seven and never came back earlier than ten. Dawn had stayed in every evening after the first week. She generally spent her time sitting in front of the TV – one so large that Richard could happily watch it from his remote location – or he might have if he had liked soaps and reality TV. Promisingly, there was always a glass of something on the go as well. Geoff would come home, curtains would be drawn, and Richard would drive home. In the course of learning all this, he also learnt several much more interesting facts, such as floor two, right-hand side, liked red underwear. Floor four, middle, was a guy with at least two girlfriends that he was having relationships with.

The Geoff and Dawn information was communicated back to Victoria. The rest stayed in Richard's head, and on his memory cards.

After several weeks of unaltered routine, they decided that the following Tuesday was to be the big day and plans were set in motion.

Richard moved all of his Kodak boxes to the rented flat

together with his covert camera equipment. He didn't want them in the house if there was a police search.

Victoria arranged for Emma and Lucy to have a night at Grandma's.

She also handed her bottle of prescription temezapam to Richard who, with gloves on, transferred them into a new bottle with Dawn's name just about visible at the top of the suitably distressed and untraceable label.

He found the strongest gin he could and prepared a concentrated solution of temazepam in Plymouth Navy Strength in the laboratory after the rest of the staff had left. The gin was transferred carefully to a hip flask; the equivalent of about 100 full strength sleeping pills in the hip flask of 57% alcohol.

Knowing that she'd say yes, he called Julie and surprised her with the offer of the Tuesday night away.

"Oh, and can you bring your vibrator?" he added at the end.

Roger Francis hired a car from one of the many busy companies at Heathrow Airport knowing that his face was just one in the thousands.

Gloves, overshoes, Tyvek full body suits, facemasks and safety glasses were placed in a disposable bag. Plus a couple of high strength plastic bags, heavy-duty tape, cable ties and anti-bac cleaning wipes.

Various other items were prepared and / or retrieved from hiding places and an e-mail was sent.

*

Tuesday evening arrived. After a day at work stressing about what was to come, Richard and Victoria were both edgy. They sat at the dinner table and he went over the basics of the plan that they'd agreed; a plan somewhat different from his original suggestion of a night away at a Travelodge.

"We walk to the Fisherman's Arms and both have a lot to drink, to the level that we'd both be incapable of driving. Or at least, that's what the barman will say when asked. We'll sit outside where the CCTV can catch us putting away the G&Ts. Except that I'll be having the Ts while you have the Gs. We stagger home. You stay home making it look like we've both been there all evening. You know, two dirty plates, empty glasses. Have loud conversations with me that anyone outside can hear – well, they can hear your part anyway."

He continued, "I've changed a couple of letters on the car registration plates with black tape and will drive to their flat. Then I'll park around the corner, wear jogging gear with the kit in my knapsack. About eight, I'll knock on Dawn's door and she'll invite me in. I'll just happen to have some of the tonics from the pub in my bag and get her onto the G&Ts, but with the gin from my flask added to hers. When she's out of it, I'll get togged up and do the deed. I'll be out and back well before the shit hits the fan."

"It just sounds a bit too simple…" Victoria said.

"The simplest plans are the best," he replied. "Now let's go to the pub."

At the bar, Richard ordered two double gins and two bottles of tonic.

"Just take the tops off and I'll pour them," he said. He also 'accidentally' knocked over the drink of another of their neighbours.

"Sorry John, let me get you another," he offered.

On the way back to his wife, he discreetly rearranged the drinks.

Over the next half hour, this was repeated three more times.

Victoria wasn't pretending to be drunk. She was well and truly plastered. The two of them made a very public exit from the pub and on reaching home, Richard helped a groggy Victoria to bed. So far so good.

He left the house, getting into their car and drove, not to Dawn's but instead 20 minutes to Shoppenhangers Hotel in Maidenhead to meet his true alibi for the night. He parked it directly in front of reception, 'accidentally' missing the fact that it was in a disabled bay and that cars not carrying a blue badge could be clamped.

He recognised Julie's car in the car park as he arrived and went to reception. "Hi, I think my other half has already booked in. Name's Francis?"

"Yes sir, room 27."

He knocked on the door. "Room Service" he called as she opened the door. They made love, still making up for the lost weeks, playing with each other and with the vibrator that Julie had bought along as requested (a request that he'd repeated ad nauseam during the lead up to the evening). Later, he reached into his bag.

"Rather than bothering the real room service, I thought I'd

bring a little something for us. You've got Victoria's man, so I thought a bottle of her wine might just finish it all off nicely."

He poured her a glass of Picpoul.

"You not having any?" she asked.

"I've got my own." He brought out a bottle of Merlot, pouring a large glass.

More sex. More wine. More sex. More wine.

Julie drifted off to sleep around midnight.

He gave it 10 minutes. "Julie love," he called quietly, then a bit louder. He gently nudged her. Out cold. Amazing the effect of a low, controlled, dose of temezapam in a measured amount of alcohol, on someone who usually wakes very easily...

His own wine hadn't been drunk. He needed a clear head for what was to follow.

Richard dressed rapidly and put the freshly wiped vibrator into an inside pocket of his jacket. The Merlot was emptied into the bathroom sink and the dregs washed away.

Room 27 had been specifically asked for by Richard.

"It's a special night for us, and it's my lucky number," he'd said on the phone.

He'd already checked it out a week earlier. It was ground floor, round the back, out of sight of cameras and with a concrete path outside, so there would be no muddy flowerbed to capture footprints. Opening the window he made a swift exit, ensuring that it was left slightly open with a small cardboard wedge in the hinge to stop it shutting while he was away. Following the path, he found his way onto Shoppenhangers Road where Roger Francis's hire car was conveniently waiting. 20 minutes later he was parked up, just around the corner from his own house.

Even though his DNA and fingerprints would naturally be all over the house, he put on the overshoes, Tyvek suit, gloves and face mask. He didn't want to take any risks.

No house lights. He found his way in by the streetlight, which also gave just enough light for him to find his way upstairs. Victoria was still in their bed. Exactly as he'd left her. He approached quietly, slowly. No obvious signs of breathing. But then, that was what he had hoped for.

After all, it had been easy to tip the gin out of her glass as he went from the inside of the pub into the garden. And just as easy to replace it with a concentrated solution of temazepam in Plymouth Navy Strength gin…

He got closer. Was she breathing? Yes, very lightly though. He raised her arm and let it go. It dropped.

"Vicky," he called quietly. Nothing. He felt the wrist. A very faint pulse.

He'd have to finish it himself. He'd hoped the drugs would be enough.

But first, there was some false evidence to plant…

With some difficulty he managed to strip off all of her clothes. These were thrown into the corner of the room as if discarded in the throes of passion. He turned her onto her back and put a condom onto the vibrator before pushing it into his unconscious wife's body. Post mortem traces of the lubricant would be found inside her, suggesting that she'd had sex that evening.

From a grippa bag came two used condoms, both distinctively

tied in a knot in the middle. One was placed in the bin as if it had been used earlier that evening. The other cut open with scissors and the contents dripped onto the bed and onto the fingers of Victoria's right hand. A smaller bag containing hairs that he'd picked from the spare room bed some weeks previously was shaken out onto the sheets. Then there was a wine glass. Fingerprints on it would match those of the owner of the DNA in the condom and on the sheets. If it was traced, then it would lead back to Louis. Louis who had been having an affair with Victoria, judging by the e-mails that had gone from Victoria's account. Louis who had come to the house this evening.

He'd claim that Victoria had invited him but say that the house had been silent and apparently empty when he arrived.

But then, a murderer would say that, wouldn't they.

Richard gently squeezed his wife's nostrils closed. Her mouth opened and the breath was faint and ragged. Richard's other hand went over her mouth. Despite her heavily sedated state some reflex of self-preservation kicked in and she weakly writhed under him. A couple of minutes and she stopped moving. He kept his hands there, counting to 300 in his head before taking them away. No pulse. He'd done it. He had killed his wife.

Richard was now a murderer. He felt no real guilt. If Victoria hadn't lied to him before they were married about their future sex lives, then he wouldn't have been forced down this route. Richard's reasoning was somehow that it was her fault. He conveniently ignored that it was morally and legally wrong, that he'd been happy enough to accept all the benefits of being married to the boss's daughter and that it had been his choice to have an affair and fiddle the company.

Carefully retracing his steps he got back to the hire car and removed all of the protective clothing. This was all stowed in a heavy-duty plastic bag, the one that already held the used condom from the vibrator and empty grippa bags. He drove back to the hotel. Not too fast. Not too slow. Wouldn't be good to be pulled for a routine roadside check now. There were still plenty of empty parking spaces in the road behind the hotel and he parked up. Taking the bag of evidence with him he walked quietly around the back of the hotel and climbed in through the window of room 27, removing the card wedge and closing it behind him. To the background of Julie's gentle breathing, he hid the evidence bag in the bottom of his suitcase before returning the vibrator to the bedside unit, removing his clothes and slipping into the bathroom.

Turning on the light he looked in the mirror checking for any telltale signs that he'd been out. The murderer that looked back at him appeared relaxed and no different from the face that looked at him every morning.

He used the toilet, washed his hands and face and turned off the bathroom light before climbing back in between the sheets. After waiting until his feet and hands had properly warmed up, he cuddled up to Julie and drifted off into an untroubled sleep.

*

The alarm went off at seven the next morning and Richard and Julie both awoke feeling tired and sore. Julie from their sexual athletics; Richard from other nocturnal activities. He toyed with the idea of staying in bed with Julie for a longer time, but appreciated that today of all days, he needed to go into work as if nothing had happened. Accordingly, they had a quick breakfast, during which Richard made a point of chatting to the waitress. Back to the room, he picked up his bag and the two lovers kissed.

"See you later," he called, leaving Julie in the hotel room. She would check out in a couple of hours, at her leisure.

Richard went out of the front door of the hotel to find a large sticker on his windscreen suggesting that he shouldn't park in a disabled space. After going to the receptionist to apologise, he spent some time scraping the sticker off before driving to work. He parked at the back of the factory and looked around. No one in sight, so he retrieved the bag of evidence from the bottom of the overnight bag. Feeling nervous that someone would see him, he went into the building through the workshop. Still no one around and the incriminating bag went into the incinerator. Reaching the lab, he put on a show of working as normal.

Even though he knew what had happened the night before, he still found himself looking out for Victoria. His nerves must have shown through as Sarah asked him if he was okay.

"Yes, sorry. All's fine."

At ten thirty everything stopped being all fine.

This week's temporary receptionist ('four out of ten for tits but eight for the short skirts' as judged by Richard,) rang to say that a couple of policeman were in reception and would like to speak with him.

"I'm a bit busy at the moment," he said. "Can it wait?"

"They say they need to talk to you now," came the reply.

Richard took his time walking to reception. A pair of the Thames Valley's finest plod stood there, both in street clothes. An efficient looking thin guy in his forties and a younger male who looked fresh out of school.

"Mr Marsh? D.I. Jenkins and D.C. Houghton," the older one said.

"Oh, good morning. Yes, I'm Richard Marsh. Can I help you?"

"Is there somewhere we could talk, sir?"

"Here?" said Richard, trying to give the impression that he had nothing to hide.

"If you don't mind sir, somewhere a bit quieter."

Richard couldn't remember the receptionist's name but didn't have to say it to attract her attention. She was all ears, keen to know what was going on. And no doubt keen to tell everyone else all about it, as soon as she could.

"Is there a meeting room free?" Richard asked.

"Number one is," came the reply.

They went through to the barely furnished room. Richard left the door open. Again, he had nothing to hide. Schoolboy policeman closed it.

"Mr Marsh, can you tell us where you've been over the last 24 hours?"

"Er, why? Is there a problem?"

"We'll come back to that, but can you tell me where you were yesterday evening and night?"

"Well, work to fiveish then home. We went out for a drink yesterday evening and then back to work today. But why do you need to know?"

"And can anybody confirm that?"

"Well yes, my wife can."

"Anyone else?"

"Well, I guess the staff at the pub. Why?"

The more senior policeman waited and then said, "I'm sorry Mr Marsh, but I am afraid I have some bad news for you."

Richard stayed silent.

"I'm sorry to tell you that your wife has been found dead."

Richard put on his best shocked face and made out that he was lost for words, just managing: "How? What?"

"Your cleaner, Mrs Morgan," (Richard realised he'd never heard the cleaner's name before) "found her this morning."

"What do you mean, found her?"

"When you cleaner arrived she found the, ur, your wife's body."

"Sorry, you're not making any sense here. What do you mean, body?"

"I'm sorry Mr Marsh, but there's no easy way to say this, but your wife was found dead in her bed this morning."

Richard sat there, doing his best to produce some tears, but none came.

"No, that can't be right. There's nothing wrong with her. She's... no, I don't understand. What happened?"

"We don't know yet Mr Marsh, but we are treating it as unexplained at this time." The policeman stopped, looking for any reaction.

Richard just looked bewildered. "This is a wind up, isn't it?"

"No sir, we are serious."

"No... my kids?"

"No, they weren't there. We understand that they are at school." A pause, "Mr Marsh, I appreciate that this has come as a shock to you and there are people you need to talk to, but we can take care of most of that. In the meantime though, can I ask you to just go through your movements since you and your wife finished work yesterday?"

Richard gave his first version of events. They'd gone home and then walked to the pub. He was sure someone there would confirm this. They'd had too much to drink, staggered home and gone to separate rooms to sleep as he was still getting over a bug. He'd got up this morning and driven to work, but hadn't checked how his wife was.

D.I. Jenkins thanked him for giving him this information and explained the sad but necessary logistics of the next few hours; Richard wouldn't be able to go back to the house until the police gave the all clear.

In the meantime, "Is there anyone who could be with you? And please don't discuss this with the press or anyone else."

"Of course," Richard replied, going along with everything that the police requested. After all, an innocent man would, wouldn't he?

Richard said that he and his daughters would go and stay

with his parents and gave D.I. Jenkins the address and his mobile number, confirming that he'd be available whenever needed.

They left the meeting room, watched by the desperately nosey receptionist whose curiosity was increased further when D.I. Jenkins asked to see Mr Bristow. Richard returned to his office ignoring the work-related questions from his staff. He picked up his jacket and case and walked out saying in a flat voice, "Sorry, I'm going to have to take a couple of days off."

He repeated this to the receptionist, ignoring her queries as the main door closed behind him.

In his car, he made a call. "Julie, it's me."

"You alright?" she replied, picking up on the tone of his voice.

"No, I'm not. Oh, and sorry I didn't text first, but I needed to talk to you."

"What's up?"

"Victoria's dead," he stated. Unemotional.

"What?!" a barrage of questions from Julie. The same questions that he'd been asked by the police. How? When?

"I don't know much at the moment. Just that the police are treating it as unexplained. The cleaner found her this morning."

More questions from Julie that Richard interrupted saying, "I'm sorry, I don't know anything really, but there's something I need to tell you."

A pause at the other end of the line.

"It's just that I may have to tell the police where I was last night."

"Yes. And?"

"And I might have to give them your name. I'd ask them to be discreet but…"

"Don't worry about me. I'm a big girl. If a handsome young copper turns up on my doorstep, I'll say that he can take down my particulars if he show's me his truncheon."

Richard found himself laughing. It didn't matter that it was inappropriate. The laughter took on a hysterical edge as the stress caught up with him, but he forced himself to stop.

"I'm sorry. I know I shouldn't. It's just…"

"Don't worry darling, it'll be okay" she replied.

"But what about your husband. If the police turn up and he finds out?"

"You know what?" she replied. "I don't care if he does find out. It's time he realised how he's neglected me. I don't need him. And anyway, you're free now."

"I am, aren't I…"

*

One loose end to tie up. There was a hire car that needed to be returned. Easy enough to do, but Richard hadn't factored in how he'd feel this morning. Everywhere he looked there were people looking at him. Or that's how it felt. No longer was he the one basking in anonymity spying on his subjects. Now, any one of these men and women could be plain clothes police, watching to see how their prime suspect acted. Sweating, he drove his car in the direction of home, checking the mirror to see if he was being followed. When he eventually felt safe, he changed course and made straight for Reading Station car park. He left the car there and bought a single ticket to Maidenhead desperately trying to avoid the CCTV cameras that recorded everyone going through the station.

Barely half an hour later, he was walking out into Maidenhead town centre. More CCTV. The walk to the car took another 30 minutes. A taxi would have been more comfortable, but there was no way he was going to risk a witness to his retrieval of an integral part of a murder. There was a moment of panic when he got to the car. Initially, he couldn't find the keys. But after going through his pockets again he found them and a sweating and stressed Richard drove back to the car hire depot.

It felt like an age later, but was probably only 20 minutes, when he handed the keys back and paid the excess charge for not having refilled the petrol tank (more CCTV on petrol station forecourts had put paid to that idea). Another rail journey. Back to Reading and he sat in his car reflecting that murder was easy. It was all the preparations and subsequent work that took the effort.

CHAPTER 16

ELVIS COSTELLO. "Watching The Detectives"

Richard briefly contemplated driving to Julie's place. He wanted to be with her, but now was not the time. Instead, he drove to his parents and told them the news. After their initial shock, middle-class stiff-upper-lip kicked in and Richard found himself being fed copious amounts of tea by his mother who believed that if one cup of Darjeeling would help, then ten cups would be ten times better.

Later, there was an emotional reunion with his daughters; the first time Richard genuinely shed a tear. Not for his wife, but for the distress of the girls. They all stayed the night and he fielded a couple calls from a reporter who had somehow tracked them down.

The next morning D.I. Jenkins called and asked him to drop

in to Reading police station, "Just to clear up a few points."

"Of course. I've just got a few things to do. I can be there at two?"

"I'd prefer it if you popped over now," was the worrying reply.

D.I. Jenkins and his assistant looked exactly as they had the day before, same ties, same impersonal expressions. The policeman enquired about Richard and his daughters. How were they doing? Had anyone called them? A few minutes of unimportant conversation and the Inspector moved on.

"Mr Marsh, there's a few points that I'm hoping that you can help me clear up."

"Of course."

"Would you like to go over your movements again."

Richard repeated his basic story that they'd gone out for a drink and then slept in separate rooms.

"The problem, Mr Marsh, is that your car wasn't in your driveway last night."

"Wasn't it?"

"No, Mr Marsh, we have several witnesses who confirm this."

"Ah. Okay. Look, there is a bit more, but well, it's not something that I wanted to mention."

"Yes?"

"Well, it involves somebody else."

"These things often do, sir."

"The thing is. Her husband doesn't know," Richard said, trying to put on a man-to-man voice.

"And I take it your wife was unaware as well?"

"Exactly."

Richard gave story number two. The one that he'd prepared a long time back. He explained that he'd been having an affair for some time and wanted to spend a night with his mistress. He'd booked a room at the Shoppenhangers Hotel in Maidenhead a week or so before and then spun Victoria a line about having to go into work that night as there was a lab test taking place that needed to be supervised throughout the night in case of a runaway reaction. He said that he'd pretended to Victoria that someone else would watch the reaction until eight o'clock when he would take over. Victoria had believed him and she had suggested that they go for a quick drink first. She had been drinking G&Ts at the pub and he'd stuck to tonic. This was the last he'd seen of his wife as he'd stayed the night at the hotel and gone straight to work the next day.

"And what time did you leave your home to go to the hotel?" the D.I. asked.

"Half seven, quarter to eight I think. The hotel can probably confirm when I got there."

"And you stayed there all night?"

"Yes."

"You didn't leave at any time?"

"No."

"And the name of the woman you were staying with?"

"Do I have to tell you?"

"Well, if you don't, we won't be able to confirm your version of events."

Richard gave the policeman Julie's name, address and telephone number.

"You will be discreet, won't you," he pleaded.

"We always are, sir." came the deadpan reply.

"What about my house?" Richard asked. "When can we go home?"

"Probably tomorrow Mr Marsh. We're still carrying out the investigation."

"Okay, so be it. I know you have to check everything properly," he sighed. "Can I go now?"

"If you don't mind, we just need you to give us the details again, get your statement written up, and then you can sign it."

Another hour and Richard was back with his parents and daughters for another day of stressed emotions. In the evening, he called Geoff Bristow's number. Dawn picked the phone up sounding tired.

"I'm sorry Richard, he doesn't want to talk to anyone. I'll tell him you called though."

Lorna Bristow on the other hand did want to talk. And cry. And talk. And scream in despair.

More than half an hour after calling her, Richard finished with the platitudes, non-explanations and meaningless commiserations, feeling more emotionally drained from this call than he had from any of the rest of his recent actions.

Thursday and another interview with the Detective Inspector and Constable.

After the same initial trivia, D.I. Jenkins said, "Mr Marsh, we have a few more questions."

"Of course, ask away."

"If you don't mind, we'll record the conversation if you'd like to come this way."

"Am I under arrest? Do I need a solicitor?"

"No, you are not under arrest and whether or not you want a solicitor is entirely your decision Mr Marsh. We've just a few loose ends to tie up and it's easier to have it all on record."

"Okay. Well, I've nothing to hide."

"That's good."

They went through to a small room with a basic table and chairs. The D.C. offered him a coffee, which Richard declined preferring to get it over and done with. They went through his account of the previous day, clarifying small points in the process.

"Mr Marsh, I am sure that you will not be surprised to hear that both the hotel and your girlfriend confirm your version of events," the Detective Inspector stated.

"But."

Richard had been expecting a 'but.'

"Can you just confirm again that you stayed all night?"

"I did, yes."

"And you didn't leave your room at all?"

"No. Didn't Julie confirm this?"

"She did. She said that even the smallest movement would have woken her, but with respect sir, we have to be cautious about the word of a girlfriend. No matter how honest she may be."

"Well, what about the hotel? Can't the receptionist tell you that I didn't leave until the morning."

"Well, they do say your car didn't move."

"There we are then. What's the problem?"

"No problem sir. We just have to check these points. And you don't have access to another car?"

"No."

"Okay. Moving on." D.I. Jenkins flicked through pages of his notebook as if checking a detail, although Richard was sure this was just for show.

The policeman continued, "You were having a relationship with Mrs White." He emphasised the 'Mrs'. "How would you describe your relationship with your wife?"

"Actually quite good," Richard replied. "We were more like brother and sister than husband and wife. Really good friends."

"Brothers and sisters can fall out," D.I. Jenkins said before continuing. "How would you describe your sexual relationship?"

"All but non-existent."

"When did you last have sex with your wife?"

"Months ago."

"Are you sure?"

"Yes," replied Richard, "it was usually Christmas and birthdays only… and even then only if the wind was in the right direction. But there was an odd occasion a couple of months ago when we'd both had a bit too much to drink. It sticks in my mind, not just because it was such an odd event, but because she thought she fell pregnant after it."

"And was she?"

"No, false alarm."

"And what form of contraception did you use?"

"She was on the pill."

"Even though your sex life was so occasional?"

"Um yes. I guess she hadn't stopped as it was routine."

"And you haven't had sex with her recently?"

"No."

"Not on the night of her death?"

No."

"And the two of you didn't use condoms?"

"No. Why on earth do you ask that?" Richard asked in mock outrage, knowing full well that this was leading just the way he had hoped.

"Just routine sir. Now, on another matter; can you tell me if the name Louis Clark means anything to you?"

"No, nothing. Sorry, was that Louis or Louise? I didn't quite catch you."

"Louis. Male. Your wife didn't mention a Louis did she?"

"Not that I remember. Who is he?"

"Well, I think that just about covers all my questions. For now."

Richard drove home feeling that maybe, just maybe, his plan was coming together.

CHAPTER 17

ABBA. "The Winner Takes It All"

Conversations with the police moved from subtle interrogation to practicalities. The house was finished with and Richard returned to find it in a state of disarray (despite being told everything had been put back as it was when the police were first called). His clothes rapidly developed a silver sheen as he brushed against surfaces still coated with fingerprint powder. Every drawer in the house seemed to have been gone through and mixed up. The computer was missing as were bedclothes, rubbish bins and, for no apparent reason, items such as the breadbin. He called in a professional cleaning company and they returned the house to a habitable, if somewhat sterile state.

He retrieved his Kodak boxes from the rented flat and returned them to the study shelves.

Another tearful evening followed with the girls coming home, Lorna coming by for an hour of further hysterics while his parents sat stoically unemotional in the background offering to make tea. Emma and Lucy found an inner strength that everyone else seemed to be missing. They made it very clear that they would take over running the house. Cooking and supporting their dad through the difficult days ahead, but could they have the cleaner in a few days a week? Of course.

Richard returned to work and the questions of his colleagues soon dwindled as he gave them the bare bones of the situation and made it clear nothing more was going to be forthcoming.

There was a difficult meeting with Geoff Bristow. Geoff was a broken man, not really interested in the company that was his life's work.

"You'd better get ready for my job," he told Richard in a depressed voice. "I'm going away. With Dawn. Don't know where. We just need to get away from all these memories. I'm just glad you're carrying on. Vicky would have wanted you to."

Richard spoke with Julie at least once every day. She was surprisingly upbeat, or at least, that was the impression that she gave Richard as she comforted him. Her marriage, she told him, was now definitely over. Lawrence's reaction when D.I. Jenkins and D.C. Houghton had turned up on the doorstep ("So much for discretion," Richard had said) had been the decider. Lawrence hadn't been worried about her infidelity. But a visit from the police! What would the neighbours say? And how would it go down at the golf club? Julie and Lawrence were now living separate lives in the house until it was sold. They'd agreed a 50:50 split of their assets and there was more than enough for both to live comfortably.

It was clear but unspoken that Richard and Julie would be living together when the dust had settled.

*

Three weeks passed with regular contact with the police, mainly over the phone. Usually this consisted of them asking how Richard was and whether there was anything to tell them. His standard reply was that he was okay, had nothing new to say and did they have anything to report to him? To which the answer was always, "The investigation is progressing."

This time D.I. Jenkins asked Richard to pop in.

"When do you want me?" Richard asked.

"Oh, any time before I go off shift. Before six please."

Richard was shown into a different room this time. A sofa rather than bare table and chairs. D.I. Jenkins walked in carrying two cups of coffee, although Richard hadn't asked for one.

"Thank you for coming in Mr Marsh." There were the usual pleasantries and then, "I'd like to give you an update on our investigations. Some of this will be in the public domain shortly, so it's better that you hear it from us first."

"Hear what from you first?"

"We've made an arrest relating to your wife's murder."

Whilst maintaining a serious and worried face, Richard listened with growing joy as the policeman outlined what they understood to have happened.

"I'm sorry to tell you this, but your wife was having an affair and the man she was meeting has been charged with her murder."

"You can't be serious? Victoria having an affair? But she hated sex."

"That may be, but I'm afraid it is the case."

"Okay. Look, yes, I'd rather hear it all from you than read about it in the papers. You'd better tell me what happened."

"As we understand it Mr Marsh, your late wife met him through a dating website."

"A dating website? No, she'd not do that. Who was he?"

"A Mr Clark, Louis Clark. They had known each other at college and then met again online and then the affair started."

"But has he admitted it? How do you know they were having an affair?"

"He's admitted meeting her once, and we have evidence to indicate later meetings, including on the night of the murder."

Richard knew that they had forensic evidence. He'd planted it. It had all come from the single time that Louis had come around. A drinks glass with Louis' fingerprints planted in the living room. A used condom in the bedside bin. Louis' DNA (from another condom) on the bottom sheet and Victoria's hand. A couple of Louis's hairs that Richard had found on the bed. And, of course, the traces of condom use that were left on Victoria when Richard abused her unconscious body with the vibrator.

There was also e-mail correspondence. After the one meet, Richard had changed the log-in details for Victoria's account on 'wedbutlooking.com', just in case she decided to access it. He'd also conveniently printed them on a piece of paper, deliberately badly hidden under the monitor stand so that the forensic team would find them. Since the meet, Richard (as Victoria) had sent a 'thank you' e-mail to Louis asking to see him again. Naturally he had replied positively and the two of them had, judging by the e-mails, started an uninhibited online conversation culminating in arrangements for him to visit on the Tuesday evening.

Richard knew Louis would have come over that evening, straight from work as arranged. The house would have been locked and quiet and Louis would eventually have gone back home frustrated. There was a good chance someone would have seen him, and he would have given his wife a false story, easily disprovable.

"But, how did she die? What did he do to her?"

"I'm sorry," D.I. Jenkins paused. "This isn't going to be easy for you to hear."

"I know, but tell me please."

"Okay. Well I regret to tell you that the drinks you had at the pub played a part."

"You mean it's my fault?"

"No, Mr Marsh. You didn't force her to take those drinks. That was her choice. No, I'm afraid to tell you that she also took a large number of sleeping tablets."

"But she didn't use sleeping tablets?"

"She did. Or at least, she had some that had been prescribed to her, and she took a large number on that evening. We don't know the exact sequence of events, but it looks like she passed out from the effects of the alcohol and drugs and then Mr Clark appears to have smothered her."

"Sorry, that doesn't make sense. Why would he smother her if she'd already taken an overdose."

"We don't know if Mr Clark realised that she'd taken an overdose. He could have smothered her thinking that she was asleep. I'm sorry, but we have evidence that Victoria wanted Mr Clark to leave his wife for her."

Again, this wasn't news to Richard. He'd written an e-mail, purportedly from Victoria, implying that she would tell Louis' wife about them if Louis didn't do what she wanted, and that they should discuss it after their next liaison. However, 'Victoria' had made a mistake in the e-mail address and it hadn't reached Louis. The police would have seen it in the sent folder and assumed that, even if their suspect hadn't received this e-mail, Victoria would have brought the subject up with Louis when he was there.

"Sorry, I'm confused here," Richard said, "Victoria was intending to leave me? What about our kids, the house and everything? It doesn't make sense."

"Relationships are strange things Mr Marsh. She clearly had a very different relationship with her lover compared to the one with you. We don't know what she said to him, but we can assume that he didn't want to leave his wife or for anyone to know about his affair. Maybe your wife took the tablets just to show him she was serious. She might have thought he'd get help. Maybe she really did want to take her life. However, unless Mr

Clark confesses we can never be sure."

Richard waited as if he was letting the news sink in, then replied.

"Thank you for telling me. I must admit I thought that you were trying to pin it on me."

The policeman smiled, his first smile as far as Richard could remember.

"Well, the husband is typically the most likely suspect in cases like this, but not this time."

"So what happens now?"

"Mr Clark has been charged with the murder of your wife and this information will become public very shortly. You can expect a significant amount of press interest, both now and when the case eventually comes to trial in a few months. We will, of course, be here to help during this time if you need us. I would suggest that you get your solicitor, if you have one, to appeal for privacy."

More, as far as Richard was concerned, minor details followed and then he drove home in a daze. 'Have I really got away with murder?' he wondered.

Over the next months the murder stopped being the first thing that they all thought about when they woke up. It didn't go away, but 'normal' life started to take over.

*

Richard knew that his relationship with Julie would become public knowledge at the inquest or trial so pre-empted the issue, telling his daughters that he had met someone new. They accepted it, the way that teenage kids do. Geoff accepted it, the way that another adulterer does. Richard's parents accepted it, the way that middle class emotionless people do. Lorna wasn't happy with the idea but knew there was nothing she could do to change things.

The murder charge against Louis Clark was the first element of closure for Geoff Bristow. Until then he'd not been able to understand anything about what had happened to his daughter. When the police updated him in the same way that they had Richard, Geoff believed it all. It made sense. Geoff knew only too well the emotions an affair can release. Now he could stop obsessing about why his daughter had been taken from him. He started to think about making the most of his own life with Dawn. Maypharm had become a means to an end. A paypacket at the end of every month. A pay packet that just increased their already more than sufficient savings. But what was the point of having money in the bank if you were in a coffin..

The Monday after the murder charges had been filed, Geoff called his son-in-law into his office.

"Richard," he told him after they'd each reiterated their grief for the umpteenth time. "I may not be your father, but you are like a son to me and you're the father of my grandchildren. I've lost Vicky but she lives on in you and them. And I'm not going to lose anyone else." He had rehearsed this speech earlier, but still found it difficult to get through, "I know you and she had problems, but I'm the last person to be judgmental about an affair. You're struggling to get over everything. Aren't we all. But you have Julie, like I have Dawn, and they'll help us get through it." A long pause, then he continued, "You and Julie have my blessing. I know you don't need it. I just wanted you to know."

"Thank you," Richard replied, "that really means a lot to me."

Geoff carried on, as if Richard hadn't said anything. There was a lot on his mind and he needed to get it all across.

"You know it's been my intention for some time that you should be the next Chairman when I retire."

"Yes."

"Well, all of this... this tragedy... has led me to see that I need to enjoy my time with Dawn while we can. I'm retiring now. That is, as soon as all the formalities can be sorted out."

Richard commiserated, saying how Geoff would be missed.

"That's as may be," the outgoing chairman continued, "but it's not as simple as just appointing you. You'd have no real control over the company without voting rights. I'm not in a position to give you all of my shares, and you certainly can't afford to buy them off me."

"I can see that could be an issue," Richard said. Something of an understatement.

"Dawn and I want to get married soon so I need my divorce to go through. Ironically, everything that has happened has brought Lorna and I closer together and we've been able to sort out the details. I'm not going to put her in a difficult position. It's not her fault that I'm with Dawn. But we've agreed a settlement which includes a fairly major reassignment of shares. We want you to be here for a long time and have designed a scheme that gives you the incentive needed."

Geoff paused and looked directly at Richard before continuing, "Of Maypharm's shares, there's 9.9% spread over several Directors of the company. The remaining 90.1% is going to be split between Lorna, me and you. Initially, it will be 40% with her, 40.1% with me and 10% for you, Richard. We will each give you a further 1% every year for as long as you are Chairman, and as long as we are alive. On our deaths, you get our shares. If you die or cease to be Chairman before you are 65, then all of your shares go to my granddaughters. There's some more minor details, but that's the headline facts."

Richard sat back and did the sums. With the share dividend from 10% alone, he and Julie would be very comfortable. Add in the annual increase in his shareholding and things could only get better. Voting rights would be slightly trickier. He needed to keep Geoff on his side for them to be in the majority initially. After a couple of years, he could manage with either of Geoff or Lorna on his side. And, after 20 years with 1% from each of them every year, he'd be the majority shareholder in his own right and not need to worry about keeping anyone else happy. "That's very generous Geoff. I don't know what to say."

"You don't need to say anything, Richard. Just run the company well and look after the girls."

The official announcement of Geoff Bristow's retirement and Richard Marsh's appointment followed a few hours later and a low-key transition took place over a matter of days.

In his new role, Richard easily quashed the problem invoice and closed off enquiries into other hassles like the spillage in the warehouse. His other fiddles; purchases from Roger Francis Ltd and the corrupt dealings with Cosion in France could continue in the background without any real risk of discovery.

He appointed Sarah to his old job, "You're in charge now," he'd told her. "I know you'll have your own ideas of how the lab should be run. Go with them. Let's start it all afresh. If you need new equipment, you've got it. Don't worry about anything from my time here, it's all in the past."

Sarah didn't notice that her new office happened to have a new wall clock. The clock had a modern design face and a fancy logo of an owl with beady eyes. Richard had decided that, just in case, it wouldn't be a bad idea to be able to see and hear anything that went on there.

The same clocks appeared in several other offices, as well as in the ladies changing room in which the factory shift changed into their workwear every day. In his ostensible bid to make the company more environmentally friendly he installed new cycle racks to encourage a greener commute. And showers in the ladies changing rooms so that cyclists could freshen up on arrival at work. The showers just happened to be directly across the room from another of the new owl-logo clocks.

Apart from these cosmetic changes, Maypharm plodded on. Their new Chairman didn't bring any major new ideas, but there was an increase in the number of busty female staff and an increase in the value of purchases from Cosion.

For Richard, in the space of just a few months, the very real risk of losing everything had been turned around into a very rosy future.

*

Richard and Julie talked for a long time about how they would live together. She was uncomfortable moving into his dead wife's house and they considered buying somewhere new, but doing so would have meant another upheaval for the still vulnerable girls. Julie started visiting during the weekends, getting to know Emma and Lucy before moving in full time. Julie had never been a mum. Mainly because Lawrence had been against the idea, but she fell into the role of stand-in mother like a duck to water and before long she had a better relationship with them than Richard did.

Not that that was very difficult.

CHAPTER 18

10CC. "Good Morning Judge"

A call from the police family liaison officer informed them of the date of Louis Clark's trial. They agreed that Richard, Lorna and Geoff would be in the public gallery and see the whole thing through. Geoff and Lorna wanted their daughter's murderer to see what he'd done to them. Richard wanted to make sure that nothing went wrong.

When Louis made his first appearance in the dock, Richard was shocked to see how much he'd changed. He no longer looked like the strong, confident, well-groomed African who starred in Richard's hidden CD recordings. Instead, he looked tired, untidy, shoulders drooping. Louis went through the basics of being sworn in and the murder charge was read out.

"How do you plead?" The judge asked.

"Not Guilty," he replied tonelessly, looking up at the gallery.

The prosecution laid out the outline of the case. Louis had met Victoria through an adult dating site. They had begun a relationship. They'd met on the evening of Tuesday June fifth for a pre-arranged liaison when the victim's husband was due to be out. A relationship had developed and the victim had put pressure on Louis to leave his wife. During one of their liaisons, the victim had taken a cocktail of drink and drugs, possibly as a cry for help, and when unconscious, Louis had committed murder. The prosecution would bring witnesses to prove that he had the motive, the means and the opportunity.

During this, Louis alternated between looking down at the floor, gently shaking his head, and looking up at the gallery. Richard followed his gaze to a trio that he guessed were Louis' family. An older couple, plump and proud in appearance, presumably mum and dad. There was also a woman of similar age to Louis. Attractive, intelligent looking and with a determined, hard expression on her face. Richard assumed that she couldn't be Louis' wife as she would not be allowed in the gallery if she was being called to give evidence. A sister maybe?

Richard had been so taken with looking at Louis' family, he hadn't noticed that there was someone new giving evidence. A distinguished looking man, in his 50s, with greying hair, suit and tie. The epitome of trustworthiness and believability. He recited his medical qualifications in a confident manner before going on to explain what he had found when carrying out the autopsy, the age, weight, general fitness of Victoria, and then the levels of alcohol and temazepam in her bloodstream.

"And what effect would this combination have had on Mrs Marsh?" he was asked.

"People do respond differently to drugs, but at these levels, she would have fallen asleep within 15 to 45 minutes of the drugs entering her body."

Richard noted the careful use of words, "the drugs entering her body." Not, "her taking the drugs." The doctor was being careful to leave all possibilities open, including her not having taken them voluntarily.

He continued, "and she would have lapsed into unconsciousness within a few more minutes."

"And would this combination have been fatal?" he was asked.

"At this level and without treatment, the likelihood is that it would have been fatal, yes."

"And what else did you find with regards to the cause of death?"

"There is evidence that the victim was suffocated while unconscious leading to her death."

Lorna started crying and Richard turned to comfort her, being the dutiful son-in-law that he wanted to appear, while the doctor went on in detail about marks around Victoria's mouth and nose.

The well-prepared questioning of the expert witness continued.

"What other evidence was there concerning the victim's activities that evening?"

The doctor carried on in a calm, measured manner.

"There was evidence of sexual intercourse. Traces of lubricant of the sort used on condoms was found on the pubis and one thigh, and semen on the right hand."

"And was this intercourse forced or violent in any way?"

"I found no evidence to indicate any force being used."

"So you would say that she had sex willingly?"

"It would appear so, yes."

The questioning continued until the defence lawyer, a podgy, small man, stood to ask a series of questions. Not really challenging the expert's testimony. More for appearance, Richard thought.

The court moved on to look at more of the forensic evidence. Another expert witness, this time a middle-aged woman confirmed herself as Dr Rose Billings. She was smart and soberly dressed with grey hair and very little makeup. Again, a look that the jury would subconsciously associate with her knowing what she was talking about.

The evidence was gone through in a good level of detail to show that Louis had had a relationship with Victoria and they'd had sex that evening.

Dr Billings started with computer data – proof of e-mails going back and forth over a few weeks. She detailed the timing of the e-mails and confirmed, when asked, that they could not have been fabricated at a later date. She couldn't know, and wasn't asked, who actually typed them.

The jury would now be sure that Louis and Victoria knew each other. The expert wasn't asked about the content of the e-mails. That would come up later.

Next, came the items found at the scene of the crime.

A drinks glass with four very clear fingerprints and a plate with a clear thumb print, both found in the living room. The foil envelope of a condom with a smudged thumb and forefinger print found under the bed. Several clear prints high on the bathroom wall tiles. All of them indisputably confirmed as belonging to Louis Clark.

The court wasn't to know that the fingerprint-bearing items had been collected by Richard after Louis' one and only visit. They'd been hidden away until being retrieved by Richard and planted by him in the house on the night he'd murdered his wife. The prints in the bathroom were pure luck. Richard didn't know that they would be there, believing that any left by Louis when he visited weeks before would have been cleaned away. The expert said the position of them indicated Louis had rested his hand high on the wall when going to the toilet.

Other items kept and planted in the same way would further damn Louis when Dr Billings moved on to the DNA evidence.

A condom had been found in the bin next to the bed. Neatly tied into a knot so that there was a good quantity of uncontaminated contents for testing. More traces of semen were found on the sheet towards the edge of the bed. The scientist speculated that this was consistent with a male sitting on the edge of the bed and his semen contaminated penis resting on the sheet. The same semen was found on the victim's right hand suggesting more intimate contact. None of this was news to Richard.

He had had some concerns that the forensic scientists may have been able to tell that the semen was weeks old, but if they had any way of telling this, it didn't come up in the cross-examination. 'Mind you, even if it had been mentioned', he theorised, 'it would still have indicated a long-term sexual relationship.'

Over the course of the next days the prosecution further developed the case. Louis' car had been seen driving onto the victim's driveway by Mrs Thwaites across the street. As local neighbourhood watch coordinator she'd written down the registration number and her vague description of the driver. She couldn't categorically identify the man in the dock as the evening visitor, but that didn't matter too much when taken as part of the bigger picture.

There were several days of this. The Bristow's and Richard occupying the same gallery seats every day, and the objects of Louis' occasional despairing glances at the other end of the viewing area. In between them was a varying selection of reporters, students and the plain curious.

Louis's wife was called. Richard could see that Josephine Clark could be a stunner – high cheekbones, ebony skin, a fantastic figure. But today she looked exhausted and tearful. She confirmed all of her details and was then asked about her and Louis' relationship. "It's good," she said, "no problems, we love each other."

Richard noted the present tense, "love," rather than past tense, "loved".

"I'm sorry, but I have to ask," the prosecution lawyer continued, "but how was your love life?"

Josephine prevaricated, but was pressed with a reminder

that she was under oath. She answered reluctantly.

"It used to be very good but not so much over the last year or two."

"And why was that?"

"Do I have to answer?"

"Yes, you do."

"There was an incident. He strayed. Just once."

"Thank you, Mrs Clark. You are confirming that he has been unfaithful in the past?… Mrs Clark?"

"Yes."

"And where was he on the night of Tuesday the fifth of June?"

Josephine Clark took a deep breath. Everyone in the courtroom could see that she didn't want to go on, but knew that she had to.

"He said he was doing a night shift."

"And was this normal behaviour?"

"He did work nights quite often. Yes."

"So you had no reason to be suspicious?"

"No. Not really."

"And he went off at the usual time?"

"A bit later than normal. But he said that he was doing a non-standard shift."

"And you believed him?"

"Yes."

"And what time did he come home?"

"I don't remember."

"Roughly?"

"I don't know."

"Was it daylight or still dark?"

"Just about day, I think."

The prosecutor turned to the judge. "My Lord. The prosecution will show that this must have been after 4.30 in the morning."

Then there were more routine questions and confirmations of previous answers. Josephine was finished for the moment.

The trial was adjourned for the weekend and the following Monday it was finally Louis's turn to give evidence. He confirmed who he was, where he lived, what he did for a living, all very routine.

"Mr Clark," he was asked. "Did you have a relationship with Victoria Marsh?"

"Not a relationship."

"Did you meet her?"

"We went to college together."

"And have you met her since?"

"Just once."

Louis answered questions about their one and only meeting. One and only as far as he was concerned. One and only as far as Richard was concerned too. First of several, the prosecution aimed to prove.

He accepted that they'd met through the website and that it had been purely for sex. Richard looked along the gallery. Louis' family weren't looking happy. Louis answered questions honestly. Yes, they'd had sex. Yes, it had been consensual. Yes, he'd used a condom. Yes, it was his habit to tie a knot in a condom as he took it off.

"No, I never saw her again," he answered to the next question.

"Did you arrange to meet on the night of Tuesday June fifth?"

"Yes."

"Did you then go there?"

"Yes."

Richard was delighted. Louis had not denied going to the house. He'd admitted that he'd had sex with Victoria previously. The key facts were established and the jury should be making up their prejudiced minds.

"Tell us what happened," he was instructed.

Louis started his version of the events. He said that after their first meeting, Victoria had asked to see him again.

"She said that she'd enjoyed it, and I thought she did as well," Louis said in all honesty, "and maybe I shouldn't have replied, but I did, saying that I'd be very happy to meet again."

He looked up at the gallery, apology written all over his face.

"We arranged to meet. I turned up, but the house was dark and there was no answer to the doorbell so I left."

"And how long did you wait before leaving?"

"I'm not sure."

"Roughly?"

"I don't really know."

"More than five minutes?"

"Yes."

"More than 30 minutes?"

"Probably."

"More than an hour?"

"No."

"So you admit that you were there at least half an hour. Did you see anyone else in this time? Or when you left?"

"No."

"So you confirm that you were there long enough to have sex?"

"I suppose so. But we didn't. I mean I didn't see her."

"And what happened after you left?"

"Nothing."

"I mean, did you go home?

"No."

"Where did you go?"

"I parked up in Maidenhead Thicket and slept."

"Was that because you couldn't go home without questions?"

"Yes."

"And did anybody see you parked up for the night?"

"I don't think so."

"Thank you Mr Clark, that will be all."

The defence team asked questions to show that Louis was honest. To show that he'd just sat in the car. To show that he'd only seen Victoria once. They didn't produce anyone to back up his story that he'd spent the night in the car. 'An unexpected bonus,' thought Richard.

They also emphasised discrepancies in the evidence. Why would Louis murder someone who'd already taken an overdose? This was also Richard's biggest worry. He knew that the prosecution had come up with an explanation, but to his analytical mind it was still an anomaly. Hopefully, the prosecution's evidence of motive, opportunity and means would be sufficient.

The jury eventually retired to debate their verdict.

By the end of the day no verdict had been reached.

At the end of the next day, they still hadn't reached a decision.

On the third day the Judge directed that he would accept a majority verdict and the Foreman indicated that by a vote of 11 to 1 they had reached their decision.

The jury returned to the courtroom. Richard sat fidgeting while the judge went through the formalities before asking them, "Ladies and gentleman of the jury, how do you find the defendant, Louis Clark, on the charge of murder?"

"Guilty."

Richard sat back, the rest of the judge and jury's words disappearing into the background. 'Bloody hell,' he thought. 'Guilty. Guilty! I've only got away with it.'

It was all he could do to hold in his emotions. The Bristows were crying. Louis's family were crying. Richard wanted to cry with joy.

Louis was sentenced to life in jail and to serve a minimum of 15 years before being considered for parole.

Richard left the court to go home to Julie and his daughters and to start their new life together.

Geoff Bristow drove back to Dawn. A long break, somewhere far away would be good, he decided.

Lorna sat in the foyer of the court, unsure of what to do with her life.

A black woman in her 30s who Lorna recognised as having also been in the gallery approached.

"Mrs Bristow?"

"Yes."

"You might not want to talk with me, but I hope you can. Even if just for a minute."

"Yes?"

"I'm Gloria Clark. Louis Clark's sister."

"Yes, I saw you in the court."

"I know this is difficult for you. And for us, I mean me. But, well, I know Louis was found guilty, but I don't think he did it."

"Go on?"

"I know my brother. He wouldn't hurt a fly. Yes, he'll chase any girl he can. But killing? That's just not him…"

The two women talked for a while, exchanging numbers before Lorna walked away, thinking.

Lorna had her doubts too. She'd not admitted them to anyone, but nobody had known Victoria as well as her mum did. The sleeping pills for example. Victoria never had a problem sleeping. And there was no way she would have got them to commit suicide. Victoria was too strong for that. And as for an affair? No way. Victoria had told her mum on many an occasion that she wasn't particularly interested in sex. And having an affair was just wrong, wasn't it? The way Victoria had reacted to her dad's infidelity alone showed this. Richard having one? Yes, Lorna found that easy to believe.

She'd believed the police case. The police were always right after all. But talking to Gloria…

If it wasn't Louis, then who? Richard was her immediate thought. The speed he'd hooked up with his new woman. His lack of emotion.

Lorna didn't know if Richard could have done it, but if he had, then she was determined to see justice done.

CHAPTER 19

IAN DURY. "Sex & Drugs & Rock & Roll"

A couple of days later, Lorna called by the Marsh household as she did most days, still trying to come to terms with what had happened, but now she had a plan.

Lorna said to Richard, "You look like you need a break. God knows we all do after the last few months."

Richard agreed saying that he was doing his best to keep everything together, but what with his new job, new responsibilities in the family, and new partner… Any one of these would have been stressful, but all altogether…

Lorna said, "I'd like to spend a bit more time with my granddaughters. You could do with some time off. Why don't you and Julie have a break and I'll look after the girls. Take a week off. Even a couple if you want."

Richard didn't see anything untoward in this.

"That's really good of you Lorna. Are you sure?"

"Of course. It'll do us all good."

The girl's loved being with Grandma and they were more than happy with the idea. Richard liked the idea of going away with Julie. It didn't matter where, just so long as there was a strong bed. Julie made the decision.

"How about Amsterdam?" she suggested. "Culture, sex and pot."

"I can probably tolerate the first. The second is a given. Not sure about the third," he replied.

"Don't worry. I'll look after you."

They elected to go by train. First Class, with champagne glasses in hand as they sped through the Channel Tunnel.

Unbeknownst to them, just as they were clinking glasses, Lorna was starting her search around Richard's house. She'd be there for the best part of a week looking after Emma and Lucy. If she couldn't find anything in that time, then she might, or might not accept the story that everyone else seemed to believe.

Richard and Julie booked into their luxury hotel in Amsterdam, typically overlooking a canal. A day's journey, plenty to eat and drink had left them replete but tired. For once, on getting into bed together, sleep was the top priority.

Richard may have been a youthful company Chairman, experienced voyeur, qualified scientist and a calculating murderer, but when it came to wider world he was naïve and ignorant. Julie was determined to change this and educate him in areas outside of his experience. Culture, arts, emotions, sex and drugs were all on the menu for this week.

A walk around the city centre started them off. Julie pointing out unique features of the city's architecture before they got on a tram taking them out to Museumplein. Richard was thinking back to his honeymoon, years before, and the French museum that had bored him witless. The Dutch museums were different, the Van Gogh museum in particular. He found himself staring at the swirling colours and brushwork of paintings that he'd seen so many times before on greetings cards and placemats. He couldn't put his finger on what it was that he liked, but in the flesh, like it he did, and unexpectedly, it was Julie who dragged him out of the museum several hours later, rather than him getting out fast. And he was up for more. But first Julie introduced him to the thick pea and ham soup, oude jenever, and other local staples that he would previously have ignored. More art was next and yet again he found himself just standing, staring, engrossed.

Julie was breaking him in gently. She left it until the next day to take him to a coffee shop. She'd told him many times that she'd enjoyed an occasional spliff in the past. This was way outside of Richard's comfort zone and he wasn't sure. He knew the theoretical effects of tetrahydrocannabinol or, "the good stuff," as Julie called it. He didn't like being out of control and wasn't sure about trying it, but she persuaded him. She selected 'Crystal Lady' from the long list of cannabis cigarettes as the one for him to try. He took a tentative drag of drug-laden smoke into his lungs. Then more. Not a lot happened. He thought. But slowly, he realised that the TV on the wall was showing a remarkably vivid and engrossing program of a brown bear roaming through a pine wooded wilderness. His mind drifted until he realised that Julie was laughing and asking, "You there?!"

Yes, THC was having an effect. A very enjoyable effect. He sat back with a big grin on his face.

They wandered. He didn't have a clue where. But it didn't matter. He was happy. And hungry. They found chips. The most delicious chips he'd ever had. They went back to the hotel. And slept.

Richard woke the next morning feeling more relaxed than he could ever remember. Julie was still sleeping, or she was until he cuddled up to her back, his erection pressed between the cheeks of her backside and his right hand cupping her breast, brushing her nipple. She moved up slightly, parted her legs and reached through to guide him in. A slow, gentle fuck.

About the same time, back in Berkshire, Lorna was entering Richard's study. She started by turning on his computer. 'Password' it prompted her. "Drat," she muttered, not knowing what the password might be. She moved on to the shelves and cupboards behind her.

Julie and Richard went down for breakfast, both with serious appetites that needed copious quantities of pale yellow scrambled eggs, bacon, toast and coffee.

Opening a cupboard, Lorna looked at the shelves of yellow boxes. 'Why,' she asked herself on seeing the 'Do Not Open' markings. 'Why would you keep unused photographic paper in a study. Why not with all of the other darkroom stuff?'

Julie gave Richard the excellent news that today would be

dedicated to naked bodies and sex.

Lorna ignored the label on a box and looked through a pile of photographs of naked bodies and couples having sex.

Julie and Lorna's views about sex couldn't have been more different, but they were both interested in Richard's attitude to it…

Lorna's look at the boxes was interrupted by the sound of the girls banging around the house. She didn't want the girls seeing the contents so closed the lid. They'd be at Guides this evening. She'd have a proper look when they were out.

Julie and Richard spent the morning in the hotel, just relaxing, and then walked towards the De Nieuwe Kerk, an imposing church near the city centre. As they approached, she pointed out the tall ground floor windows in the adjacent buildings. Red neon lights across the top of them. Some empty. Some curtained. Some with girls in bikinis sitting on bar stools. Julie commented on how much more honest this was than the Paris girls in their fur coats on the streets. Here you could see what you were getting and knew where you would be doing it. They looked into the windows, debating the attributes of the girls before plonking themselves down at a table outside a nearby bar, looking at the windows. A middle-aged guy walked along the street looking at each girl in turn. He stopped and they watched as the door-cum-window opened and he spoke to the prostitute within. A moment later and he was going in.

"Check your watch," Julie suggested.

Richard did as he was told. Eight minutes later and the man reappeared.

"You realise," Julie said, "in that eight minutes he's gone in. Paid money. Got undressed. Had sex. Got dressed again."

"I could have done it a lot quicker not that long ago," Richard replied.

They finished their drinks and walked on. Past a couple of large theatres advertising live sex shows before a tout persuaded them (with very little difficulty) that they'd love to go in and see what was happening in another one.

They were given a couple of drinks tokens each and walked through a curtained doorway. There was a small stage with bench seats around it and a bar area twice the size of the stage. A couple were just leaving and Richard and Julie took their front row seats. A bored looking waitress appeared and took their drinks orders and a couple of the tokens, before reappearing with a small lager and even smaller white wine.

Music started and a couple appeared on the stage. A mixed race guy, 40s maybe, skinny but not athletic. The woman was a similar age, heavily tattooed and with generous breasts. They went through a clearly well-rehearsed sequence of quasi dance moves before she removed his trousers and started to give him a blow job. Before long the two of them were going through a wide variety of sex positions. Him, thrusting into her in whatever configuration came next in the sequence. They looked bored and neither of them gave the slightest impression of having enjoyed any of it before going off to a smattering of applause.

Next up a mature woman with a big smile. She stripped off rapidly revealing an impressive pair of boobs and a pleasingly curved body. She lay on the stage and from somewhere out of sight produced a banana. This was quickly inserted into her pussy and she pushed it in and out several times. She removed it, stood up, and walked around, peering out at her audience asking for volunteers to come up on stage. No one moved. She became more proactive, pulling a Chinese tourist up and telling him to stand at the back, and did the same with a couple of more guys. She then latched on to Julie, giving her a smile which Julie returned. Theatrically she beckoned for Julie to come up. Julie pretended to be too shy before being persuaded to join the line of nervous guys. The stripper walked down the line, a hand on one guy's crotch a kiss to the next. She reached Julie and placed her hands on Julie's breasts, shaking them and then giving a thumbs up to her audience while Julie stood there grinning.

The stripper picked up the banana and peeled the end of it open before lying down and inserting the unpeeled end back inside herself. She beckoned the Chinese guy over. With sign language she instructed him to eat the end of the banana, much to the hilarity of the rest of his party. A similar instruction to the other guys and she was left with just a small amount of banana visible when she called over Julie. Julie licked her lips theatrically to the delight of the audience and moved between the woman's legs. As Julie moved in to bite the fruit, the woman put her hands on the back of Julie's head, thrust her hips forward and comically pressed the banana into Julie's face before releasing her back into Richard's care.

As Julie sat down, she turned to Richard saying, "I think I like banana's a lot more now."

A succession of acts followed. None as fun or interesting,

and Richard and Julie moved on.

They ended up at a small bar in the Jordaan. Drinking way too much and eating Oude Kaise. Delicious Old Cheese.

"Right then" Julie announced, looking at her watch. "Our next destination is now open. Time for a walk."

"Where to?"

"You'll see…"

They walked a mile or so before getting to one of the outmost canals. Shops and houses lined a wider road and Julie led them towards an anonymous looking door. She knocked. The door opened and a large bearded man asked, "Ya?"

"Club Erica?" Julie asked and the big guy opened the door to let them in.

Another pub Richard thought at first, seeing the round bar in the middle of the room. Except… Most of the people sitting there were only partially dressed. There was one couple wearing just underwear, and a bare chested guy wearing a kilt of all things. They ordered drinks and without any warning to Richard, Julie dropped her skirt and took off her blouse before sitting down again. She looked at Richard, standing there opened mouthed, and said, "Your turn."

He did as requested, feeling horribly self-conscious, despite the fact that everyone else there was in a similar state of undress.

"Ur, what do we do with these?" He indicated his clothes.

"The doorman will see to them," the barmaid replied as the bearded guy walked over with a large carrier bag. He took the excess clothes and they sat at the bar, Julie chatting to a slim blonde girl. In her 20s Richard guessed. Lovely eyes. Lovely other bits too. Richard wasn't really part of the conversation, but he enjoyed watching the women chat.

"Come on then," Julie said, her voice interrupted his reverie, and without a clue about what was going on, he followed her and the blonde, as they walked across the bar and then up a flight of stairs.

Meanwhile in Berkshire, Emma and Lucy were out, so Lorna started looking through the Kodak boxes in Richard's study.

The first floor in Amsterdam was furnished with wide mattresses and several strange constructions of wood and leather. Richard barely registered an intertwined group of naked people on one of the mattresses as Julie dragged him into a room, shutting and latching the door behind them and the blonde. Julie and the girl started to kiss. Richard watched as their hands moved over each other, the two women started making love in a brazen, explicit way that he'd only ever seen on a screen before. He watched as they went down on each other, each reaching orgasms in front of his earnest gaze.

Lorna looked at picture after picture of naked women, her hands shaking as she went from grainy nipple shot to glossy full frontals.

Julie lifted her head from between the other girls legs and said to Richard, "Your turn." He found himself in a blur of positions and feelings, snapshots in his mind; looking down his body as Julie held the base of his cock and the younger woman sucked it. Lying on his back, this stranger's pussy on his lips and Julie's mouth around his erection. His cock inside this girl while his tongue licked his partner's clit.

Lorna looked at snapshots of couples having sex. The participants oblivious to the camera's stare.

Richard lay back exhausted and spent, looking at the girl that he and Julie had met. Pert breasts and a pubic area shaved of all hair.

Lorna looked at a photo of a girl with pre-pubescent breasts and a pubic area still to grow its first hair.

Julie and Richard left their private room. A naked girl lay sleeping on a mattress outside.

Lorna looked at a picture of a topless girl in the back of a car. She looked unconscious. Or dead.

Julie led Richard into another room. It was dark inside with round holes in the walls at waist and head height. He looked through one to see another mattressed room with seven or eight naked bodies in a tangle of limbs in the middle. A male backside was moving up and down between a woman's legs. Richard grew hard again as he spied on the orgy. Julie pressed herself to his back, deliberately pushing him through the glory hole. He felt a tongue start to lick him. Then lips around his cock. He couldn't see who was doing it, but didn't care either as he climaxed into the warm moist space beyond.

Lorna looked at more photos that were clearly taken through gaps in fences or holes in walls. In one, a young woman, on her knees was performing fellatio. On the back of some of the photos there were cryptic notes. Lorna noted them all down. There were also some unlabelled CD-ROMs in one box, but she didn't have a way to see what was on them as Richard's PC was password protected and she didn't have one of her own.

Richard and Julie went back to the bar, smiling. Happy. Lorna went to bed. Frowning. Upset.

*

The rest of the break went by with a bit more of everything that Julie wanted Richard to experience. He didn't object to one minute of it and was overjoyed when Julie casually said, "Get used to it. This is what life with me is going to be like."

He knew that this was exactly how he wanted to spend the rest of his life.

*

Lorna knew that she didn't want to live the rest of her life with this uncertainty.

On a sheet of paper, she wrote the word 'Richard' and underlined it, and then put underneath:

'WHEN DID HE MEET JULIE?'

'AFFAIR?'

'PEEPING TOM'

'UNDERAGE GIRL PHOTOS'

'DEAD GIRL?'

'PHOTOS'

'CDS'

'MURDERER?'

Lorna was torn. She didn't know what to do. She'd seen enough in the pictures to know that some were probably illegal and that the photographer's actions could potentially put him behind bars, but what good would come of showing them to the police? Richard would get a slap on the wrist for taking mucky photos and Lorna's beloved granddaughters might lose their one remaining parent just when he was most needed.

Then there were the CD-ROMs that she couldn't do anything with. Presumably dodgy as well.

She sat there for another ten minutes. Her mind went back to the trial of her daughter's murderer, thinking about how the evidence had been exhibited and challenged. How Louis Clark had shaken his head as the fingerprint-laden glass was presented. How he'd looked up at the gallery…

"Talk to Gloria. Gloria Clark?" she said out loud as the idea hit her. Gloria would have access to a computer and be able to see what was on the CD-ROMs, and maybe have other ideas. Lorna dug out the number she'd been given back at the court. After five rings an answerphone kicked in.

"Hi. You've reached Gloria Clark. I'm travelling until Wednesday 14th. Please leave a message and I'll call you back on my return."

Lorna thought for a brief moment. Wednesday was five days away. Was that too long to leave it? No, it'd give her a chance to get her thoughts in order. She'd leave a message: "Hi it's Lorna Bristow here. You said you weren't sure that your brother murdered my daughter. Well, I have my doubts too and I have some things that I'd like you to look at. Can we meet when you're back? Can you give me a call? Thanks."

She put her phone down, tidied up her notes and left the study.

She didn't notice the wall clock behind her. The one with a modern design face and fancy logo of an owl. An owl with particularly beady eyes. The clock that had a motion sensor which activated a video and voice recorder that Richard would check within 24 hours of getting home tomorrow.

ABOUT THE AUTHOR

According to his family, David Wheeler is a balding, middle aged grump. He thinks of himself as a silver fox with a scintillating stock of stories from years of working in the chemical industry around the World. When not writing in his Wiltshire home, he spends his time building complex Lego models, drinking gin and travelling. He doesn't own a cat, dog or llama and hasn't murdered anyone. Yet.

To learn more about David and his books, please visit:

davidwheelerauthor.com

27208592R00218

Printed in Poland
by Amazon Fulfillment
Poland Sp. z o.o., Wrocław